Hugh walked to the door and raised the latch. He halted in astonishment when he saw the red-haired, green-eyed girl he had loved and been unable to forget, even after she had betrayed him. "Sara Dean!"

August Dale was alarmed. "Don't shoot him, Katie! He brought some soldiers with him!"

Hugh realized that Sara was holding a pistol, and that she was pointing it straight at him.

"Don't come any closer," she murmured.

Hugh laughed grimly, reached out, and caught hold of her wrist. She struggled, but was no match for him, and the pistol fell to the floor. He kicked it into a corner, drew a sword, and took his own pistol from his belt. "I've been waiting a long, long time for this reunion," he said.

Other titles in the Ace Hall of Fame series:

A
HALL
OF
FAME
Historical
Novel ™

Scoundrel's Brigade

CARTER VAUGHAN

ace books
A Division of Charter Communications Inc.
A GROSSET & DUNLAP COMPANY
360 Park Avenue South
New York, New York 10010

SCOUNDREL'S BRIGADE

An ACE Book

Produced by Lyle Engel

Published by arrangement with
Hall of Fame Romantic-Historical Novels, Inc.

2 4 6 8 0 9 7 5 3 1
Manufactured in the United States of America

To Bill

PAPER money was in those times [the years of the War of Independence] our universal currency. But, it being the instrument with which we combated our enemies, they resolved to deprive us of its use by depreciating it; and the most effectual means they could contrive was to counterfeit it.

Benjamin Franklin

1 / *April 1774*

ONLY the wealthy could afford to dine at the Sign of the Red Roan, one of London's most elegant taverns, and only the sophisticated felt at home there. But Hugh Spencer, who was neither worldly nor rich, was completely relaxed as he sipped a rum toddy in his private booth, and his broad grin was self-satisfied when he glanced at his reflection in a long, thin mirror set in an oak panel outside the cubicle. He could hear occasional snatches of the conversation of expensively dressed, heavy-set gentlemen in powdered wigs who had made their fortunes in the East India trade or in the American colonies, but the somber discussions of merchants meant nothing to a young man who was thinking about a girl.

"If the House of Lords had any courage," someone with a deep voice was saying, "the Earl of Chatham would be turned away at the door. Earl of Chatham, indeed. He was a damned radical when he was plain William Pitt, and he's still a radical. And a traitor, sir. He must know those inflammatory speeches he makes are reprinted in pamphlets and read in Boston and Philadelphia and New York. He actively encourages the Americans to revolt when he supports their cause! His conduct is disgraceful. He flirts with the colonies like a brazen wench who is trying to induce a man to propose marriage to her!"

Sara Dean, Hugh thought happily, flirted with him expertly but subtly, and she was a lady, not a wench. She was so charming and lovely that she undoubtedly received proposals of marriage regularly, and Hugh had good cause to believe that she was favoring his suit. In the past fortnight they had spent every evening together, and she had been pleased to be seen with him at theaters and taverns, she had held his arm in a proprietary manner when they had strolled together on the Mall, and their growing intimacy had not been marred when he had told her frankly that the estate he had inherited from his late parents amounted to less than three thousand pounds. She had made it obvious that she realized he planned to ask her mother for her hand, and knew he was anxious to meet Lady Dean when she returned from Bath, where, Sara had told him, she was enjoying a holiday as a member of the Prince of Wales's entourage.

The mother of an heiress had every right to investigate a man's background before she consented to a marriage, but Hugh was confident he could pass Lady Dean's scrutiny. The farmlands he owned in Cornwall provided him with a small but steady income, he had served with honor as a Lieutenant of Dragoons for four years, until his twenty-seventh birthday, and although he had lived in the colonies too long to have formed many close friendships in London, anyone who knew him would testify that he rarely drank to excess, that he avoided the gaming tables, and shunned the company of the cunning, attractive bawds who were the mistresses of most unattached young gentlemen.

He was prepared, too, to tell Lady Dean that he didn't care whether she settled a large dowry on her daughter. He realized that Sara's wardrobe was extensive and, although his knowledge of such matters was hazy, he assumed that she spent more money on her clothes than his limited income could tolerate. So he intended to tell Lady Dean that he would be willing to let Sara lavish her dowry on her person, but that he would support her. There were many gentlemen in London who married for money, and even though the practice was accepted, Hugh could not accept such a life for himself. Perhaps, he reflected, he had absorbed too much of the American spirit when he had been stationed in the colonies. In any case, he approved of the principle that the man of a family should be the head of his own house, and that his standing in the community should depend on the living he earned.

"Chatham," said a man with a rasping voice at a table outside the booth, "is no real danger. Luckily for England, his health won't permit him to form a new government. The devil who infuriates me is that pigheaded Edmund Burke."

"Did you hear his speech in the Commons last week, sir? I would have walked out of the gallery if my partners hadn't kept a tight hold on my sleeves. Burke is a revolutionary of the worst sort. He had the audacity, the unmitigated gall, sir, to suggest that elected representatives of the colonies be seated in the Commons. Can you imagine the type of legislation they'd favor—and what would happen to my profitable trade? Radicals like Burke apparently are incapable of understanding that colonies exist for the benefit and enrichment of the mother country!"

"I'm neither surprised nor shocked," the man with the rasping voice replied. "Our philosophers boast that this is an age of enlightenment, but I've yet to see real loyalty to England displayed by an Irishman."

Hugh, who cared nothing about the political and economic disputes that were causing strained relations between England and her North American colonies, reflected happily that some of Sara's ancestors undoubtedly had been Irish. Her copper-colored hair, fair skin and deep green eyes were as unusual as pretty, blue-eyed blondes were common in London, and Hugh was amused by the discovery that he resented the unseen stranger's slur. The man was not insulting Sara, however, so Hugh relaxed, sipped his drink again, and hoped that in the immediate future he would be entitled to act as her protector.

"I'm sorry I've kept you waiting," a soft, faintly husky voice said.

Hugh jumped to his feet quickly, surreptitiously straightening the lace frills on his shirt-front.

Sara smiled, accepting his admiration gracefully, and was not embarrassed when he stared at her. Like all great beauties, she accepted the tribute as her due. It was not accidental that her silk gown, which was looped in front to reveal an embroidered petticoat, matched her eyes, that its sash studded with brilliants emphasized her tiny, supple waist, and that a hint of the cleavage between her high breasts showed above the deep cut of her bodice. She looked daring and sophisticated, yet her smile was as disarming as it was warm, and her manner was so deceptively simple that even the diamond-shaped beauty patch of black velvet that she wore on her left cheekbone did not seem artificial.

"I enjoyed waiting for you," Hugh said honestly. "When we aren't together, I think about you."

A dimple appeared above the right corner of Sara's mouth when her smile deepened. She sat down opposite Hugh, smoothed her skirt, and made no attempt to withdraw when their feet touched under the table. "Obviously Mrs. Radway gave you my message."

"Reluctantly." Hugh had often thought it odd that the Dean family should employ a dour, taciturn woman as their housekeeper. Mrs. Radway never addressed him civilly, but as Sara seemed devoted to her, he carefully refrained from expressing his critical opinion too freely.

"They showed you to my usual booth."

"I would have been turned away at the door if I hadn't mentioned your name. But when I said I was meeting you, I was bowed in with great ceremony."

Sara shrugged her pretty shoulders to indicate that she attached little importance to the value of her patronage. "This is one of the few taverns in London where a respectable woman can spend an hour alone without being molested."

Hugh grinned at her. "They're so respectable I was afraid they'd throw me out because I'm not wearing a wig." He smoothed his dark brown hair and tugged at his queue, which was tied with a small strip of black ribbon. "The man who brought me up here glared at my head so hard I felt as though I'd been scalped by an Iroquois."

"That was Paul. He's very proper, but he's been very sweet to me ever since my father and my uncles started bringing me here years ago." Sara was carrying a beaded pouch on her left wrist, and loosened the strings enough to push them up to her elbow. "I do owe you an apology for causing you such inconvenience, Hugh, but I was called to our solicitor's office unexpectedly."

"I never find it inconvenient to meet you anyplace, at any time," he replied gallantly, hesitated, and asked, "There's no unpleasantness, I hope?"

Sara's green eyes became guarded. "Unpleasantness?"

"I served as a member of a court-martial board when I was stationed in New York, and I developed a strong dislike fo lawyers."

She laughed as she sat back against the padded partitio that separated the booth from the outer room. "Our solicito sends for me frequently to sign papers, but I have no hea for legal language or figures, so I simply do as I'm told."

They were interrupted by a middle-aged man in black wh looked more like a Pennsylvania parson than a Londo waiter. He was carrying a silver tray on which he balance a glass filled with a pink liquid, and bowed to the waist wit out spilling a drop before placing the glass on the table front of Sara.

"Thank you, Paul."

"It's always my pleasure to serve you, ma'am." The ma

bowed again gravely, glanced in obvious disapproval at Hugh's head, and backed out of the booth.

"I must be sure to buy a wig before I come here again," Hugh said.

"Paul has never liked any of my escorts."

"You've come here with a number of them, then?" Hugh couldn't control a surge of jealousy.

"No, very few," Sara replied demurely. "What's more, you're the first I've ever met without a chaperone. Mamma has always insisted on joining me, and I always wanted her. But I'm glad she isn't here now." An actress could simulate breathlessness, but the color that appeared in Sara's cheeks indicated that her feeling was genuine, and she raised her glass in a toast to hide her confusion.

Hugh felt a fierce glow of proud possession.

"This is a West Indian fruit punch," Sara said, changing the subject abruptly. "Paul lived in Nevis many years ago, and brought the recipe back with him. There are only a few drops of sack in it, to give it flavor, but it's a harmless concoction. There. Do you see how much I trust you, Hugh? I've never told anyone that secret. People who have seen me drinking the punch have always assumed that it has spirits in it."

Hugh started to reply, but someone appeared in the entrance to the booth and he looked up in irritation when he recognized the lugubrious Paul. "What do you want?"

"I thought you might want to order your dinner, sir," the man said, looking at Sara rather than Hugh.

"I'll ring for you when we're ready." Hugh touched a bell rope that was hanging only a few inches from his left hand.

"As you wish, sir." Paul continued to stare at Sara intently.

Apparently he was trying to convey a message of some sort to her. Sara seemed to understand it, and nodded almost imperceptibly.

"We require nothing more at present," Hugh said firmly, his annoyance mounting.

The man bowed and withdrew silently.

"Don't be offended," Sara said, and, reaching across the table, placed her hand lightly on Hugh's arm. "Paul was making certain that I was safe, that's all. A booth can be dangerous, and gentlemen sometimes forget their manners. He didn't realize I wanted to be alone with you, either."

"I suppose I should appreciate his loyalty to you," Hugh said grudgingly, and reached for her hand.

She withdrew it quickly, but smiled so he wouldn't think she was rebuking him. Then, suddenly, she became serious. "Hugh, could I ask a favor?"

"I'll do anything in my power to help you!" he replied eagerly.

She hesitated for an instant, and her eyebrows contracted. "You won't think I'm being silly or childish?"

"I shall always think you're the loveliest and most charming girl on earth!"

She returned his gaze without flinching. "I wish I could believe that," she said, and there was a wistful note in her voice that confused him.

Her comment was as challenging as it was enigmatic, and he was prepared to debate the matter, but she gave him no opportunity.

"My solicitor gave me some money," she said. "Actually, it's a rather large amount, as I must settle a number of accounts before Mamma comes home from Bath. Please don't laugh if I confess something to you. I don't usually carry more than a few shillings in my purse, and I'm afraid I'll be robbed before I can put the money in my strongbox."

"Forgive me if I boast," Hugh said soothingly, "but I was the best swordsman in His Majesty's Dragoons. Your funds will be safe, and so will you."

"I'm afraid a cutpurse might sneak up behind us without our knowledge," she persisted. "So I wonder if it would be an imposition to ask you to carry the money for me until you take me home."

"The favor is trifling." He enjoyed her display of feminine helplessness.

"Thank you," Sara said gratefully, and, opening her beaded handbag, removed a large number of folded notes, which she handed to him quickly.

Hugh riffled through the pack, saw that each bill was worth ten pounds and realized she had given him a considerable sum for safekeeping. "Shouldn't we count this before I put it away?"

"There's no need for that. It's either three hundred pounds or three hundred and fifty. It doesn't matter. I trust you, obviously."

Three hundred pounds was a small fortune, and her carelessness surprised him.

"You're very kind—and very understanding." Sara paused and glanced in the direction of the entrance. "I hope no one saw me give it to you. There are so many footpads masquerading as members of the gentry these days that you might be attacked when we leave the Red Roan."

Hugh laughed, removed a worn leather wallet from the inner pocket of his coat, and placed the money inside. "You can forget your funds until I see you to your door." He drank the last of his rum toddy.

"Would you like another drink before we eat?" Sara asked solicitously.

"One is my usual limit. Besides, you must be hungry."

"The veal pie here is excellent. Paul says that Dr. Johnson comes here frequently for it. He thinks it's tastier than the pies at the Cheshire Cheese."

There was a commotion outside as Hugh reached for the bell rope, and before he could pull it they heard angry male voices and heavy footsteps ascending the stairs from the taproom on the ground floor. The diners in the outer room stopped talking, and Sara looked at Hugh questioningly, but he smiled, even though he had no idea what was causing the disturbance.

A florid man wearing the blue, scarlet-trimmed uniform of a crown bailiff stood in the entrance to the booth; two deputies, armed with pistols and long staffs, crowded close behind him. "Your identity, sir!" the bailiff said in a loud voice.

If Sara had not been present, Hugh might have lost his temper, but he wanted to spare her embarrassment. "Hugh Spencer, Esquire, lately Lieutenant and Second Brigade Adjutant in the King's Light Dragoons."

The man turned for an instant and exchanged exaggerated, self-satisfied winks with his assistants. "You admit it, brazen and open as you please, eh?"

Hugh realized that a crowd was beginning to gather outside the booth, and could not curb his anger; it was outrageous to subject Sara to the bumbling investigation of a crown employee who had obviously made a mistake and was confusing him with someone else. "State your business and then take yourselves elsewhere," he said curtly.

"Now, then, you'll hold your tongue, sir, and show a bit of respect for them that wear the uniform of King George. It's my duty to enforce the law, and enforce it I will." The bailiff, speaking for the benefit of the throng of curious diners, was enjoying himself.

"You're a nuisance, and I'll have you hauled before a magistrate's court," Hugh said sharply.

"We'll see who does the hauling, and where he's hauled." The man's face became a deeper shade of red as he chuckled heartily. "We was told we'd find you at the Red Roan, Hugh Spencer, Esquire, and you've saved us the trouble of searching for you, so my helpers and I thank you. We'll go home to our suppers after a good day's work. There's no need for you to prove that you're Hugh Spencer if you admit in front of witnesses that you're him, eh? That saves me bother, too." Drawing a saber, the bailiff flourished it so clumsily that it became entangled in the velvet curtain that could be closed to ensure privacy in the booth. "In the name of King George III, I place you under arrest!"

"On what charge?" the astonished Hugh demanded.

The bailiff ignored his question. "Search him," he told his deputies brusquely.

Hugh reached for his sword, but changed his mind and let his hand fall to his side. Sara's mortification would be even worse if he became embroiled in a fight.

The deputies removed his belongings from his pockets and spread them out on the table: there were a small, initialed snuffbox of silver, a lace-edged handkerchief, and a heavy brass key to the small flat that Hugh shared with another former officer. His captors looked disappointed, but the bailiff drew in his breath when one of his assistants took the wallet from Hugh's inner pocket. "Ah, that's what we want!"

The smaller of the deputies removed the money and counted it carefully. There were thirty-five ten-pound notes, and several of smaller denomination, which belonged to Hugh himself. "You forgot my silver purse," he said scornfully, and, reaching into another pocket in the tail of his coat, he removed it and threw it onto the table. "A crown, two shillings, a sixpence and a few farthings," the deputy said after examining the contents.

"Make a list, Wiggins, make a proper list," his superior told him, and, taking one of the ten-pound notes, studied it carefully.

"Be careful with that money," Hugh said. "It belongs to the lady, not to me."

"What lady?"

Glancing across the table in bewilderment, Hugh saw that Sara had slipped away. He couldn't blame her for wanting to avoid the limelight of notoriety, and hoped the situation would be clarified quickly so he could find her and offer her his apologies. In the meantime, he had no intention of allowing her good name to become involved in the humiliating farce. "The lady is a friend," he said.

The bailiff laughed coarsely. "Met her in Newgate prison,

I'll venture," he said, and was pleased when several members of the crowd smiled appreciatively.

Hugh hoped that Sara was out of earshot. Had she been present he would have felt it necessary to vindicate her honor by trouncing the vulgar bailiff, even though the courts forced anyone who attacked a crown official to pay a heavy fine.

The more intelligent of the deputies finished making his list of the money he had taken, handed it to his superior, and gazed curiously at the bill that the bailiff was holding in his thick fingers. "Is it or ain't it?"

"I make the arrests, but I don't judge the evidence," was the crushing retort. "Do what you're told, don't try to rise above your station, and treat all who break the law without mercy. That's my motto, Wiggins, and if you hope to succeed me when I retire, you'll follow my example."

His assistant, unimpressed, continued to scrutinize the ten-pound note. "It looks real to me. Maybe Sir Harry made a mistake."

The bailiff's cheeks puffed indignantly. "Sir Harry has never been wrong in twenty years. He waits until he has all the information he needs to convict a criminal, and then he pounces, the way a cat leaps at a rat in the back streets of Wapping."

"No offense meant, I'm sure." Wiggins realized he had aroused his master's wrath, and tried to back away.

The bailiff reached out with his free hand, caught the lapel of the man's threadbare coat between his thumb and forefinger, and, still speaking for the benefit of the Red Roan's diners, thundered righteously. "There are experts who knows these things at a glance. They protect you, Wiggins, and hundreds of other innocents like you. Spencer and all the other scoundrels of his sort are caught sooner or later."

Hugh's patience was exhausted. "I suspect that someone hired you to play a prank on me, but I'm not amused by schoolboy tricks. Be good enough to return my property, and take your leave."

"The property we've confiscated is evidence," the bailiff replied ponderously, "and it can't be returned to you without an order signed by a crown magistrate. As for taking our leave, we'll go quick enough, but you're coming with us. Maybe you'll meet that lady at Newgate." He signaled to his assistants, who took hold of Hugh's arms.

"You can't arrest me without a warrant."

"Is that what you want, eh?" The bailiff reached into the pocket of his long, silver-buttoned coat and pulled out a sheet of paper which he unfolded triumphantly. "Here you are, then." He waved it for the tavern's guests to see. "An order for the arrest of Hugh Spencer, Esquire, signed personally by Sir Harry Gresham-Aston, royal prosecutor-general of the city of London."

Hugh insisted on looking at the document, and the official government seal, the blob of wax bearing the imprint of a lion and unicorn, and the scarlet ribbons hanging from the paper convinced him that the warrant was genuine. All that bothered him, however, was the knowledge that his pleasant dinner engagement with Sara had been interrupted. He had committed no crime, and felt certain that he was the innocent victim of a clerk's error, but he wanted to know why he had been arrested. "What is the charge that had been lodged against me?" he asked loftily.

"You are accused of high treason," the bailiff replied in a loud voice.

Hugh was shocked. "What am I supposed to have done?"

"You know right well, you rogue. Under the Revised Money Act of 1769, Parliament decreed that all makers of counterfeit notes are traitors. Take him, lads."

The deputies, holding Hugh's arms tightly, led him out of the booth, and the Red Roan's patrons stared at him in angry disgust.

"I hope," one of them said distinctly, "that they hang him!"

II / *May 1774*

NEWGATE prison was old, dilapidated, and crowded; its staff, underpaid and overworked, had become callous to human suffering, food was inadequate and unpalatable, and members of the House of Commons who urged that the prison be torn down called it "England's blight." The harassed warden, who was required to show members of Parliament through the place when they demanded the right, was careful to show them only the less revolting portions of his domain, and no reformer had ever seen the long row of stone-lined dungeons, where the more dangerous criminals were kept in solitary confinement.

Hugh, after spending ten days in a dark, cramped cubicle where he had seen no daylight, received no visitors, and had been forced to crouch on a filthy straw pallet for interminable hours, staring at the moisture gathering on stone walls, was as disgusted as he was angry. He would not have believed it possible for men to be subjected to such degradation by fellow human beings and, his clothes dirty and stiff, he followed a guard through long passages into the open, where he paused to breathe fresh air. A pistol was jammed into his ribs and, too weak to protest, he started forward again, wearily accompanying the guard to a building at the far end of a compound.

He was so tired that he paid no attention to the inmates wandering around the grounds who stared at him, and not until he entered the building and caught a glimpse of a man in a silk coat, powdered wig, and pale breeches did he feel ashamed of his own appearance.

He touched the thick stubble on his chin, gingerly raised a hand to his matted hair, and looked ruefully at his clothes. He hadn't washed, shaved, or bathed since his arrest, and had been alone for so long that his pride had almost been destroyed, but the sight of the nattily attired gentleman aroused him, and he straightened. The guard glanced at him and grinned.

"Quite a one, you was, when they brung you here. Now you look like all the rest." The man led the way into an anteroom, said a few words to a sentry stationed outside a heavy oak door, and then nudged Hugh with his pistol again. "Act respectful, now, or you'll be whipped. Sir Harry don't like it when prisoners put on airs."

A few moments later the door opened, and Hugh was shoved into a large, bright office. Sir Harry Gresham-Aston, the man in the silk coat and powdered wig, looked up from a desk and studied the filthy wretch who stood before him. There was neither compassion nor friendliness in the prosecutor's shrewd eyes, and he tapped a quill pen lightly against his cheek as he sat back in his chair, reached into a drawer of the desk, and raised a scented handkerchief to his nose.

Hugh forgot his weariness. "The odor," he said stridently, "is as offensive to me as it is to you. The slop they call food in this inferno is bad enough, but there's no excuse for refusing a man a bath."

Two sentries who stood inside the door were certain the prosecutor would become livid at the impertinence, but Sir Harry smiled. "Quite right," he said. "However, sanitation is the warden's concern, not mine. I spend only a few hours at Newgate each week—for obvious reasons." He picked up a sheaf of papers and began to scan them.

Hugh had been forced to endure vile living conditions too long to be diplomatic, and the prosecutor's sarcasm infuriated him. "Presumably," he replied in a cold, clipped voice, "you're concerned with British justice."

Sir Harry was startled, and raised his head.

"I've been held incommunicado for the better part of two weeks. I haven't been allowed to send word of my situation to anyone, and I've even been refused permission to engage a legal representative. The bailiff who arrested me and the guards who have brought me the garbage that's called food have hinted that I'm being held as a counterfeiter, but no charge has been lodged against me, at least to my knowledge. Neither you nor anyone else has the right to deprive an Englishman of his rights!"

One of the sentries started forward, a heavy club lifted, but Sir Harry waved him back to his post. "Your argument has a certain merit, Spencer, I must confess, and you argue nimbly. As it happens, however, the evidence in your case is so overwhelming that you've forfeited the privileges enjoyed by honest subjects of the crown. I can understand your inability to appreciate the hospitality of Newgate, but what else did you expect? You should have weighed the consequences before you embarked on a criminal career instead of waiting until you were caught!"

"I've done nothing wrong!" Hugh shouted hoarsely.

Sir Harry shuffled the papers and smiled. "How few have the courage and intelligence to admit their guilt. What a pity." His voice became hard. "I haven't been familiar with your case myself, as I've just returned to the city after attending the Prince of Wales at Bath. But the facts speak for themselves."

The realization that the prosecutor had seen Sara's mother frequently and that they might have discussed him filled Hugh with despair. He had continued to hope he would be exonerated, but the fear that Lady Dean would refuse to permit her daughter to see him again had tortured him during the long days and nights he had spent alone.

"In view of your record as a cavalry officer," Sir Harry said, "I'm prepared to recommend that the court treat you leniently, provided you'll give us information to help us round up others. Counterfeiters are the curse of England these days, and we'll do anything to be rid of the plague, including working with Beelzebub himself."

"I'm the innocent victim of a misunderstanding!"

"How I wish that were true. It would be a great help to use you as a decoy." The prosecutor looked at his papers, sighed, and shook his head.

"I don't care what sort of case has been developed, I'm not guilty." Hugh, encouraged by the official's silence, related his simple story and declared emphatically that Sara was innocent too. If the crown was searching for counterfeiters, he said, the hunt should begin at the office of the lawyer who had given Sara the money.

Sir Harry scratched his chin with the end of his quill pen. "What is the name of the solicitor?"

"I don't know, but I'm sure that Mistress Dean would be pleased to give you all the information you might want."

"Who is this Mistress Dean?"

It would be inappropriate to reply that she was the most desirable girl in England. "I'm sure you became acquainted with her mother, Lady Dean, in the Prince of Wales's entourage at Bath."

The prosecutor pondered for a moment, frowning. "I know all of the members of Prince George's party, but I met no one named Lady Dean. However, I can't afford to neglect any clues that might be helpful. I'll be frank with you, Spencer. You can help me, and I may be able to help you. I have political ambitions. I enjoy the friendship of the Prince of Wales, and if I can drive the counterfeiters out of England, I'll be in a position to demand and get a post in the cabinet." He turned abruptly to the guards. "See that this man is bathed and shaved, and give him some clean clothes."

Hugh was led away, and the sentry who had taken charge of him guided him to a one-story building where attendants scrubbed him, shaved the stubble from his face, and gave him a suit of bright blue velvet which, they said, had belonged to a murderer who had been executed the previous week. Sara would wince when she saw his attire, Hugh thought, but they would enjoy a hearty laugh together when the case against him was dropped. Refreshed, he was taken back to the prosecutor's office.

Sir Harry was waiting for him and took him to a carriage in which a pair of burly guards, both armed with pistols and clubs, were already sitting. "Where does this Mistress Dean live?"

"On Tottenham Court Road."

"A neighborhood favored by the nobility, I must admit," the prosecutor murmured, and after giving the necessary instructions to the driver, leaned back in his corner of the carriage.

The two guards kept close watch on Hugh, who ignored them as he enjoyed his first taste of relative freedom in many days. He stared eagerly out of his window at Londoners going about their daily business, and, seeing men and women walking and talking together, wandering where they pleased, he reflected that liberty was the most precious of all assets. The thought was not new to him, but it had become far more significant since he had been arrested, and for the first time he realized why the American colonists were annoyed by the restrictions and laws that hampered them.

"Here's the Tottenham Court Road," Sir Harry said suddenly. "Which is the house?"

"The small place on the left. The two-story gray stone building with the Greek columns on either side of the entrance." In spite of his unfortunate predicament, Hugh was excited at the prospect of seeing Sara again.

The carriage drew to a halt, the prosecutor jumped to the

ground, and the guards followed close behind Hugh when he descended. Sir Harry rapped the brass knocker smartly, and after a brief wait a sour-faced woman in black opened the door.

"I am Sir Harry Gresham-Aston," the prosecutor declared self-importantly.

The woman smoothed her gray hair and looked unimpressed.

"Good afternoon, Mrs. Radway," Hugh said politely.

She stared at him blankly.

"We've come to see Mistress Sara Dean," Sir Harry told her.

"There's no one here by that name," she replied curtly.

Hugh was bewildered. "This is serious crown business, Mrs. Radway. I can't blame her if she doesn't want to see me again, but I can explain everything to her satisfaction—"

"There's no Sara Dean here, and my name isn't Radway," the woman said in a dry, unpleasant voice. "This is the home of Captain Charles Wyler of the Royal Navy, and I am Mistress Wyler."

Sir Harry glanced at Hugh quizzically.

"Obviously you've come to the wrong house, so I'll bid you good day, gentlemen." The door slammed shut.

"It's plain," Hugh said heavily, "that she's been given orders not to receive me. Lady Dean has decided that I'm not fit company for her daughter, and—"

Sir Harry interrupted him by pointing to a small brass plate beside the knocker.

Staring at it, Hugh read the legend, "Captain Charles Wyler, Royal Navy," and blinked. The thought occurred to him that the plate was new, but he decided to keep quiet. The more he protested, the worse his situation became.

"If you're wasting my time, Spencer, you'll have ample reason to regret it." Sir Harry's anger was controlled.

"I swear I've been telling you the truth," Hugh said desperately.

"I might be more inclined to believe you if you can prove

this female, Sara Dean, isn't the product of your imagination. Some of your friends, men of repute and standing, can vouch for her existence?"

"I've spoken to several of them about her, but they haven't met her."

"How odd."

"Not at all. I met her a short time ago myself, and my interest in her was so great that I didn't want to share her time or company with anyone else."

"You're incriminating yourself with every word you speak, Spencer."

The shirt that the jailers had given Hugh was soaked with perspiration. "The principal waiter at the Sign of the Red Roan has known Mistress Dean since she was a child."

"Ah." Sir Harry waved the prisoner into the carriage, and they drove quickly to the tavern, which was located on a narrow street off the Strand.

If the proprietor was disturbed he was too urbane to show his feelings and, behaving as though he received visits from representatives of the crown every day, he ushered the group into a small office at the rear of the ground floor. Paul Bartley, he said, had been one of his most trusted employees for more than thirty years. Many members of the nobility who frequented the Sign of the Red Roan refused to permit anyone else to wait on them, and Prince Frederick, the Duke of York, the second son of King George III, had offered Paul the position of major-domo in his own household.

Hugh felt certain he would be vindicated, and, while waiting for Paul to arrive, stared out of a small window at the rear of the office. Soon he would be free again, but he realized that a formidable task awaited him. He couldn't blame Lady Dean for trying to protect her daughter from a man she believed to be a criminal, but Mrs. Radway's denial of her own identity had jarred him, and he realized he would have to exert extraordinary efforts to convince Sara's mother that he had broken no laws. It was probable that he would not be allowed to see Sara again until he established his innocence, and Lady Dean was wise to shield a lovely and innocent girl, but at the same time he wished Mrs. Radway hadn't gone to such lengths to pretend she didn't know him. She could have helped him to establish his innocence, but instead had complicated his position.

The proprietor returned, followed by Paul, who bowed to Sir Harry and smiled. "I've had the pleasure of serving you," he said. "You like your Channel sole grilled over hickory, you're fond of mutton and your favorite wine is a white Bordeaux."

"A remarkable memory!" Sir Harry exclaimed. "I haven't dined here in the better part of a year!"

Smiling faintly, Paul bowed again.

"Have you ever seen this man?" Sir Harry asked abruptly.

The waiter glanced disdainfully at Hugh. "Of course, sir."

"Will you tell me what you know about him?"

"Gladly, although my acquaintance with him is limited. I've only seen him once, Sir Harry, a little less than a fortnight ago. He sat in one of the private booths next to the main dining hall on the second floor, and he drank a rum toddy. I may have brought him a second, but I wouldn't like to take an oath on it one way or the other."

Hugh tried to interrupt, but the prosecutor glowered at him. "I'll conduct this interview, Spencer. Go on, Paul."

"There isn't much more to tell, Sir Harry. A bailiff arrived and arrested him as a counterfeiter. One of the deputies paid me for the rum he drank with some good coins of the realm taken from his purse. I dare say he would have tried to pass me one of his false ten-pound notes if he hadn't been caught, but I have no right to say that, I suppose. I'm merely guessing, and I should be fair." He gazed loftily at Hugh. "I know enough of the law to understand that even a common criminal shouldn't be punished for something he merely might have done."

"Was he alone in the booth?" Sir Harry asked.

"Yes, sir." The reply was flat and perfunctory.

Hugh gasped.

"There was no woman with him?"

"No, Sir Harry."

Hugh could not remain silent any longer. "Certainly you remember that a young lady joined me."

The waiter shrugged and shook his head.

"It was Mistress Sara Dean!"

"I don't know the lady, and I've never heard her name," Paul replied.

Frustrated and angry, Hugh started toward him, but the guards halted him. "You've known her since she was a child. Her father and her uncle were patrons of the Red Roan for many years."

"Sorry, but I can't oblige you. I don't know any of these persons."

"And you don't remember returning to the booth after serving her a West Indian punch? You don't remember wanting to make certain that she was safe and that I wasn't molesting her?"

Paul's smile was condescending. "I would make it my business to keep watch on the daughter of one of my regular patrons, you may be sure. But I know no family named—Dean, was it?—and I paid no such visit to the booth while you were here." The waiter turned to Sir Harry. "As to the West Indian punch he mentions, I'm not familiar with the concoction, sir."

The proprietor, a soberly dressed man in his late fifties, tugged gently at the gold watch fob that hung from a waistcoat pocket. "I can corroborate both of those statements, Sir Harry. I serve no drink here known as a West Indian punch. And I know all of my patrons, naturally. I'm sure you'll agree I'm not boasting when I say there's no finer tavern in London than the Sign of the Red Roan. The secret of my success is very simple. I cater to the same people year after year. The only Dean I know is Colonel Thurston Dean of Cornwall, who was a member of the Commons for several years after his retirement from the Light Infantry. I believe he's been afflicted with the gout for the past decade or more, however, and he hasn't made a trip to the city in years. He's a widower, incidentally, and has no children."

Hugh turned to the proprietor in astonishment. "You refused to give me a table when I arrived, but you changed your mind and showed me to the booth yourself when I mentioned the name of Sara Dean and said I was expecting to meet her here!"

The proprietor sighed. "I fear I can offer you no substantial proof that the scene this man has described is a figment of his own imagination, Sir Harry."

"Perhaps you'll be good enough to tell me what did happen," the prosecutor suggested.

"Of course. This fellow arrived at the afternoon dinner hour, introduced himself as Spencer, and said that he had a transaction of some importance to conclude. He intimated that his business was of a rather delicate nature, and although I would have refused him admittance under ordinary circumstances, Prince Frederick's equerry had arrived no more than a quarter of an hour earlier to inform me that His Royal Highness was indisposed and would be unable to use his booth. So, rather than allow the table to remain empty, I granted this Spencer person permission to use the booth. Needless to add, Sir Harry, it was a decision that I regret bitterly. A tavern's reputation is no better than the clients to whom it caters, and counterfeiters don't add to my prestige."

Hugh was so angry he was speechless.

"If you wish," the proprietor added, "you're at liberty to check on my story at Prince Frederick's household. He's in the city at present. In fact, he's dining in the booth at this very moment, as it happens. I feel reasonably sure you'll find his equerry at Whitehall."

"There is no need for me to embarrass any member of His

Highness's staff," Sir Harry said succinctly. "Your word is enough for me—and for any magistrate in the country."

Hugh recovered his temper sufficiently to regain his wits. "They're lying, Sir Harry, and I can prove it!"

Everyone in the office looked at him.

Realizing that his future depended on his ability to substantiate his claim, he spoke slowly and calmly. "When the bailiff and his deputies suddenly appeared at the booth upstairs, I wasn't alone. A young lady was sitting there with me. And I'm sure that a number of patrons must have seen her too." He paused, looked at the proprietor and Paul, then turned back to the prosecutor. "Question the men who arrested me. They'll tell you that Sara Dean is a real person!"

Sir Harry seemed a trifle less sure of himself. "Now that you mention it, Spencer, there was a brief mention of a young woman in the official report of the bailiff who took you into custody."

Hugh saw Paul exchange an uneasy, surreptitious look with his employer.

"It may be," the prosecutor continued vigorously, "that this female is a member of the counterfeiting gang we're trying to catch. Every clue is important, so we should make a thorough effort to learn all we can about her."

The proprietor held his ground. "I know nothing about any woman who is involved in this matter."

Paul shifted his weight from one foot to the other and wiped his hands on his apron. "I'm at fault, Sir Harry," he said lugubriously.

Hugh held his breath.

"I'm proud of my memory," the waiter continued, "but I'm not my own master, and there are occasions when I'm required to perform functions in which I can take no pride. So I prefer to forget them." He smiled self-deprecatingly. "This was such an occasion, I'm sorry to say, but the mystery is easily explained."

Hugh braced himself for another lie.

"Any tavern, even the Red Roan, must comply with the demands of its patrons," Paul said defensively.

"True," the proprietor added. "It isn't my place to criticize the tastes and personal habits of some of the nation's greatest men, but everyone is human, and an innkeeper knows, better than most, that men of stature and dignity sometimes like to forget their cares for a time."

"Our booths," Paul said, "are sometimes used by gentlemen for purposes other than dining." He cleared his throat and looked apologetically at the prosecutor. "I trust you understand what I mean, sir?"

Sir Harry nodded.

Paul seemed relieved. "Then I can speak more freely. This Spencer fellow asked me to supply him with a bawd. I find it distasteful to provide such services, but I have a family to support, and he promised to reward me liberally if the wench satisfied his fancy, so I agreed. No doubt he would have paid me with a counterfeit note if he hadn't been interrupted. Well, Sir Harry, I sent word to an establishment located nearby, and the woman who owns the place obliged by sending one of her young females across the street. The bailiffs arrived only a moment or two later, the wench disappeared at once, naturally, and the whole incident went out of my mind."

Sir Harry was disappointed. "Then you think it unlikely that the woman is a counterfeiter?"

"Babs has been in London for only two years, sir, and although I think she'd steal a wallet or make false money if she had the opportunity, she works for a woman who sees to it that her girls are kept busy at one trade."

Hugh thought he saw the opportunity to tear down the flimsy story. "Can you produce this wench to substantiate your claim?"

Paul glanced at the prosecutor before replying.

"The request is reasonable enough under the circumstances," Sir Harry said.

The proprietor pulled a bell rope, and a moment later a red-cheeked apprentice appeared in the entrance. "You rang, sir?"

Sir Harry took charge. "Are you familiar with a house of bawds in the neighborhood?"

"Not personally, I ain't. But I've gone there to fetch the trollops one time or another, if that's what you mean."

"Go there at once and bring a girl called Babs to us."

There was little conversation during the tense period of waiting that followed. Finally someone tapped at the door, and Hugh was so upset that he almost expected to see Sara. A girl with red hair came into the room, but she bore no other resemblance to Sara. Her lips and cheeks were heavily rouged, black antimony was smeared on her eyelids, and it was obvious that she was a trollop. Her stance was slack, one hip jutted forward as she sidled into the office, and although she was surprised to see so many men, she did not lose her composure. Halting, she put her hands on the hips of her sleazy satin skirt, wriggled one shoulder so the tiny sleeve of her blouse fell, and, smiling mechanically, demanded, "Which of you sent for me?"

"We'd like your help in an official crown investigation of a criminal case," Sir Harry told her.

"I didn't do anything wrong," she replied quickly in a harsh, high-pitched voice.

"All I want is your co-operation," the prosecutor said severely. "Tell me the truth, and no harm will come to you."

The girl lost her air of bravado, and, tugging at her fallen sleeve, she inched toward the nearest wall. "What do you want to know?"

"Have you ever seen this man?" Sir Harry pointed to Hugh.

She was silent for what seemed like a long time, and frowned as she studied Hugh carefully. Finally she shrugged and tried to laugh. "I meet a great many men in my work," she said apologetically.

"She has never seen me, nor have I seen her." Hugh thought it was absurd to prolong the farce.

Everyone ignored his interruption, and Paul, feigning sympathetic candor, moved closer to the girl. "He's the one who sent for you about a fortnight ago. You had just joined him upstairs when the king's bailiffs arrested him."

It was evident that the harlot had heard of the case, and she realized what was expected of her. "Oh, it's that one," she said, and smiled at the prosecutor. "I just had a glass of gin with him, I think it was, so it's no wonder I didn't recognize him."

"She hurried away as soon as the bailiffs arrived," Paul added glibly.

"A girl in my kind of work can't be too careful," the bawd said, "and I don't like bailiffs. Give one of them half a reason to put you under arrest and he'll stop you from earning a day's wages."

"There's nothing more to be settled here," Sir Harry announced grimly.

The guards caught hold of Hugh's arms, but before they could lead him away the young harlot, playing her role to the full, walked up to him, looking at him in mock sorrow, patted his cheek. "I thought you were a gentleman, but now I feel sorry for you. You'll end swinging from a gallows on Tyburn Hill, and that's a shame."

Hugh laughed unpleasantly, and the startled girl had no way of knowing that he had admitted the obvious to himself after trying to deny it. "Sara Dean," Paul, and "Mrs. Radway" were members of a gang of counterfeiters, and "Sara" had managed to avoid exposure and arrest by making him the custodian of the counterfeit money she had been carrying. "Sara," he reflected bitterly, was far worse than the girl who faced him now; the bawd, at least, didn't try to hide her identity.

"Remove the prisoner," Sir Harry said, and the guards dragged Hugh out to the waiting carriage.

III / *June 1774*

HUGH failed to appreciate the benefits of solitary confinement until he was given a cellmate. Benjy Flaherty, as he called himself, cheerfully confessed that he had spent most of his thirty-five years either making or passing counterfeit money, and although Hugh suspected for a time that Sir Harry had moved an informer into his cell, he finally changed his mind. Benjy, who talked incessantly about himself and his vocation, rarely bothered to listen to anyone else.

"This is the sixth time they've given me board and bed at Newgate," he boasted, "but I've never had a brand burned on my hands or back, and they've yet to find enough evidence against me to crop my ears."

Hugh, grieving because he had allowed himself to fall in love with a girl who had deceived him, was so worried about his own fate that he found it difficult to concentrate on Benjy's lurid descriptions of his past.

"Them that make the paper money are the ones who worry the crown," he said frequently. "The printers and engravers and the ones who know special ways to make notes, they cause the real trouble. But the coin men like me, we're little fish. They pull us into the net now and again, but they set us free again fast enough. Times aren't like they were ten years ago, when the copper lads nearly ruined England."

"Copper lads?" Hugh asked absently, wondering when he would be brought to trial and whether he could find any way to defend himself successfully.

"I learned my trade from one of the best of them," Benjy said proudly as he sat cross-legged on his pallet. "He'd have been a rich man today if he hadn't been too ambitious. It's greed that ruins an artist. The pennies and ha'pennies we made were masterpieces, and our farthings were so clean and sharp that sometimes we couldn't tell a genuine coin from one we'd made ourselves. But Roswell fell in love with a wench who fancied herself. She wasn't satisfied with satins from Southwark. She wanted the finest silks, and when Roswell gave her a ruby, she complained because it was too pale." Benjy sighed, and his thin, sensitive fingers explored a tiny crack in the stone floor.

Hugh was amused and interested in spite of his preoccupation with his own problems.

"Roswell worked day and night to satisfy her. He made copper coins that were gems, and he flooded the country with them. He kept pressing the rest of us to produce more and more, too, which was profitable for him, seeing we were using his molds. You may not believe this, but I swear it's true. At Roswell's trial I heard the magistrate say that at least three out of every five copper coins in England were counterfeits made from Roswell's molds. He set a record no one has ever equaled."

"What happened to him?"

"Oh, he swung from a rope on Tyburn. He couldn't destroy his molds soon enough the day the bailiffs came to arrest him. I had two in my cellar, a George II penny mold and a Duke of Marlborough farthing mold, but I was lucky. I heard those oafs who wear the crown's uniform crashing about upstairs, overturning furniture, and searching in the drawers of cabinets, so I had time to burn the molds. They found a few coins in my purse, but a magistrate won't send a man to Tyburn for that."

"You don't think they'll hang me, then?" Hugh found it impossible to dwell on anything other than his own predicament.

"They can't even crop your ears or sentence you to a beating," Benjy said scornfully. "All they can prove against you is that you were carrying a few hundred pounds in counterfeit paper. The law is helpless unless the bailiffs are bright enough to find your manufacturing equipment, and I've yet to see a bright bailiff." Lowering his voice, the slender man leaned closer to Hugh. "I burned my molds again when they came to arrest me the other day. It near broke my heart, I don't mind telling you. I had remembered everything Roswell had taught me, and I'd made a mold for a half crown that was perfect. It's ashes now, but I can't complain. They found my file and my clippers, but that isn't proof enough to cause me any serious trouble."

Hugh, knowing nothing about the techniques of counterfeiters, was bewildered.

Benjy rubbed one side of his short nose and blinked at his cellmate in surprise. "I've thought you've been fooling me all this time, but you don't know how to make counterfeit money, do you?"

"Until my arrest six weeks ago, I was accepted as a member of the gentry."

Benjy felt sorry for him. "They won't turn you free, not these days when politicians win votes by persecuting artists who know more about making money than the royal printer and the governor of the king's mint. So you'll need a trade after you've served your term. Would you like to learn the secret of coining?"

Hugh didn't want to hurt the man's feelings. "I'll be very grateful for your help," he said gravely.

"Roswell's system is the best. Cut two little blocks of cedarwood—"

"Why cedar?"

"Because it's hard enough, but not too hard. Press a genuine coin between the two blocks to get the general outlines, and scoop out little hollows in each. Then cover the coin with chalk and press it between your blocks again. The chalk will leave a print, front and back, and you can carve an exact reproduction of any coin that's minted, be it a silver crown or a copper farthing."

Hugh shook his head in wonder.

"If you decide to make silver your specialty—and you can earn a better living in it than in copper these days—start clipping every coin that passes through your hands. Spanish pieces of eight and Portuguese moidores are the softest, and they use a good quality of silver." Benjy paused and grinned amiably. "The rest is simple."

"Is it?"

Hugh's irony was lost on the counterfeiter. "I'm not suggesting that you make your own coins," he said seriously. "That's a real art. Take an English copper that's a bit smaller than the size of the silver piece you plan to make. Melt the silver you've clipped from the edges of the foreign coins, but don't let your crucible burn too hot. Then dust the insides of your mold with earth. Good, black loam is the best. Coat the copper coin with the molten silver, and let it cool inside your mold. Then all you'll have to do is file off the stem after your finished product is hard. Are you listening to what I'm telling you?"

"I'm remembering every word." Hugh stared at his cellmate thoughtfully. "Do you know how to make paper money, too?"

Benjy shifted uneasily on his pallet. "There are six or seven methods," he said evasively.

"Could you teach them to me?"

"I don't know all of them."

"But you are familiar with some of the ways?"

"I've seen paper money made." The counterfeiter's eyes had become guarded. "Why do you want to learn?"

"Because I'm in Newgate through no fault of my own except stupidity. I let a girl with a pretty face—no, a beautiful face—fool me. I want to find her and the people who work with her. I have a score to settle, and I believe that if I understand the techniques of counterfeiting paper money, I'll have a better chance of tracing her."

Benjy weighed his reply carefully. "You need presses and plates and special inks and paper for that kind of work," he muttered. "But if you still feel the same way when we get out of here, I suppose I could give you a few lessons."

"I can wait," Hugh said bitterly. "It would appear that I have no choice."

One morning late in June the guard who brought Hugh and Benjy the bread and watery stew that was always served as the prisoners' breakfast announced that the trial of more than fifty counterfeiters who had been taken into custody in recent weeks would be held at noon that same day. A short time later an assistant to the warden appeared and conducted the two inmates from their cell to a room on the ground floor, where they were given bowls of soft, yellow soap, metal dirt scrapers, and brushes. They were invited to help themselves to buckets of water, and Hugh scrubbed himself until his skin felt raw; and then he shaved himself under the watchful eye of a guard who kept a loaded pistol pointed at him. Several other prisoners were snatching clean clothes from a pile in a corner, and Hugh finally found a pair of breeches, an old linen shirt, and a coat that were not too disreputable.

The assistant warden, who had been glancing repeatedly at a huge pocket watch, finally called out an order, and each of the prisoners was subjected to the humiliation of standing meekly while heavy chains were attached to his ankles and wrists. Hugh felt a fierce surge of resentment, but his concept of justice had changed radically during the weeks he had spent at Newgate, and he knew that if he protested the members of the prison staff would either laugh at him or beat him. In theory, he thought savagely, an Englishman was considered innocent until he was proved guilty, but a miserable, half-starved creature in chains was not in a position to argue that principles were being ignored at Newgate.

Sentries armed with muskets prodded the prisoners, who shuffled in a long, straggling line across the compound to a two-story stone building. The room in which the trial was to be held was a large, bare chamber, and the prisoners were taken to several rows of benches that faced a podium on which there stood a large desk and several smaller tables. Clerks in powdered wigs were writing industriously in large, leather-bound journals, and there was no sound except the irregular scratching of their pens and the mournful clanking of the prisoners' chains. The windows had not been washed in many months, the hardwood floor was filthy, and the air was stale.

Most of the prisoners knew they would receive severe sentences and slumped dejectedly on the benches. Some of the hardened criminals, men who had been tried and convicted many times, were bored and conversed in undertones whenever the guards were not looking. Benjy Flaherty was nervous and fidgeted in his seat, but tried to hide his fears by winking and smiling broadly at anyone who glanced in his direction. Three boys in their teens glared at the attendants, contemptuously ignored the order to remain silent, and deliberately provoked the guards by whispering. Finally, after one of them laughed aloud, the assistant warden separated them and placed the ringleader beside an old man with white hair who was staring vacantly into space.

Hugh discovered that it was almost impossible to maintain his equilibrium; the despair of the men who surrounded him was so intense that he felt crushed, too, even though he knew he was innocent. It was unlikely that the magistrate would give him an opportunity to establish the true facts, and as he didn't know the real identity of "Sara Dean" he couldn't prove that he was the victim of a conspiracy. At best, he thought dully, he would have to reconcile himself to three or four years of imprisonment; he was afraid to hope that the court would deal with him leniently.

A guard pounded on the floor with the heavy butt of his musket, the clerks rose to their feet, and the sentries who were near the prisoners ordered their charges to stand too. Chains rattled, and a moment later a man in a high, powdered wig and long black robe swept into the chamber.

"Make way for His Excellency, Lord Barsbury," a bailiff shouted.

The magistrate sat down behind the desk, arranged his robes carefully, and took a pinch of snuff. The clerks remained standing, and everyone watched the entrance; there was a wait of some moments and at last Sir Harry Gresham-Aston walked briskly into the room, followed by several aides. The prosecutor bowed to Lord Barsbury, who accepted a thick sheaf of papers from him.

"Accept my congratulations, Sir Harry. You've harvested a splendid crop." The magistrate's voice was cold and impersonal.

"We disposed of the more important felons yesterday, milord. Most of these fellows are the scum who were brought to the surface when we agitated the waters."

"They look like a sorry lot, but no matter. The newspapers will be pleased, and praise won't hurt your career or mine." Lord Barsbury paused and glanced dubiously at the papers. "I trust all of your documents are in order. I have a dinner appointment with a minister of state and don't want to keep him waiting."

"There will be no delays, milord. My day is crowded too." Sir Harry grasped the lapels of his scarlet robe, faced the prisoners, and, scarcely bothering to raise his voice, addressed them briefly. "His Majesty's government has been plagued by the manufacture of counterfeit money for years, and the Parliament has therefore passed an act which increases the penalties imposed on those who make or pass false money. All who engage in such criminal endeavors are now classified as traitors, and will be dealt with as such by this court. As guilt has been established in every case, it would be a mockery of justice and a waste of His Lordship's valuable time to grant you the luxury of legal representation. We will dispose of your cases in an orderly fashion. Step forward as your name is called."

A clerk called a name, chains rattled, and a prisoner shuffled toward the podium, but Hugh didn't bother to look up. His worst fears had been realized, and he knew there was no chance he could obtain a fair hearing. He listened lethargically as the magistrate pronounced sentence in one case after another. A man who had been caught with plates for five-guinea notes on his person made no protest when he learned that his ears would be cropped and that he would spend the next five years in prison. The brash, talkative youth was silent when he received a sentence of forty lashes and three years in prison, and the old man moaned but said nothing when he heard that he would be given ten lashes each day for ten days. Without exception the prisoners accepted the verdicts and made no attempt to defend themselves.

"Hugh Spencer!" the clerk called.

Hugh stood, and although his chains were heavy he held himself erect as he walked to the front of the chamber.

Lord Barsbury glanced quickly through a document. "Hugh Spencer, you have been found guilty of possessing three hundred and fifty pounds in counterfeit money. Do you have anything to say before sentence is passed?" The question was rhetorical.

However, Hugh had no intention of submitting meekly. "I do, milord!" he said firmly.

The magistrate looked surprised.

"I am not guilty, milord!"

Sir Harry stepped forward, frowning. "If it pleases the court, a full report of this fellow's claims has been prepared."

"It pleases the court to ask the crown prosecutor for a summary of them." Lord Barsbury stifled a yawn.

"They're false, milord. I spent several hours investigating his story. His powers of imagination are excellent, but I found no truth in his inventions."

Hugh realized he had nothing to gain by protesting, but he decided, recklessly, that there was nothing to lose by remaining silent. "The waiter at the Sign of the Red Roan lied to you, Sir Harry! And so did Mrs. Radway! If you'll give me a chance, I can prove—"

"Quiet!" Lord Barsbury declared sharply. "This is a crown court, and any person who violates its dignity will be made to suffer the consequences." He glared at Hugh, then turned back to the prosecutor. "Why did you engage in a personal investigation of this man's case, Sir Harry? Isn't that an unusual procedure for you?"

"It is, milord. However, he held a position of some standing in society, he was formerly an officer in the Dragoons and it was my hope that he might lead me to more important persons, specifically, the men who made the money he was carrying. But I gained no information of value, and I suggest that if your lordship intends to keep that appointment with a minister of state, no further consideration be given the case."

"This court always appreciates the advice of Sir Harry Gresham-Aston." Lord Barsbury glanced again at the paper he was holding. "You stand convicted of treason, Spencer, and in the name of His Majesty, George III, I fine you the sum of six thousand pounds."

Hugh clenched his fists. "My total estate is worth slightly less than four thousand, milord." The disgrace, he thought, was far worse than financial ruin.

Lord Barsbury chuckled dryly. "Your arithmetic tallies with the figures that have been prepared for the edification of this court. Therefore you owe the crown a sum in excess of two thousand pounds, Spencer."

"I'll try to raise that amount, milord," Hugh said forlornly, realizing that none of his acquaintances could advance him a small fortune.

"Do you suppose that this court is insensitive to the security of the English people?" the magistrate asked angrily. "Do you suppose this court would permit a convicted traitor to wander freely about the land, preying on the innocent and gullible? No, Spencer, you will not try to raise the sum. The crown prosecution is in agreement with this decision?"

"Full agreement, milord," Sir Harry said promptly.

"Your education, your physical appearance, and your former military experience make you a property of some value, Spencer." Lord Barsbury gazed reflectively at Hugh for a moment. "You will be sent to the North American colonies and sold to anyone who is willing to pay the necessary two thousand pounds for your services as an indentured servant."

The sentence was appalling, and Hugh gasped. "Milord, you're condemning me to spend the rest of my life as a slave!"

"Remove the prisoner," the magistrate said coldly. "Sentence has been passed, and the clerk of the court is ordered to make the appropriate notation in his records. The bailiff will call the next case."

Two guards dragged Hugh out of the chamber, and he was so enraged by the unfair sentence that he fought them, blindly and savagely, until they beat him with the butts of their pistols. But he continued to struggle, lashing out with his chains, shouting, and cursing; reinforcements were called, and at last he was subdued, but even though he was bleeding and dizzy when he was shoved into his cell, his anger remained unabated.

IV / *August 1774*

TWENTY-THREE convicts who were being sent off to spend terms of seven years or longer as indentured servants in the New World were crowded into the forward hold of the little brig *Lilian Rose*. Benjy Flaherty, who had received a sentence more severe than he had anticipated, was delighted that he and Hugh would make the voyage together, and spoke enthusiastically of the bright future that awaited them. But Hugh could not share his optimism, and spared the counterfeiter's feelings by refraining from explaining that, while Benjy had always led a precarious life on the outer fringe of respectable society, he himself had been stripped of his privileges and ruined.

When he had been stationed in the colonies as an officer, he had been a frequent guest of the leading families of New York, but he was returning as a penniless criminal outcast. He had seen indentured servants in the homes of some of the wealthy merchants, and had been shocked by the callous brutality and indifference that supposedly civilized people had displayed toward them. Bonded servants were no better than African slaves in the opinion of their masters, and although they theoretically earned their freedom in time, Hugh was convinced he would spend the rest of his days in bondage.

Even if he were granted a credit of fifty pounds per year in return for his services, he would be forced to work for more than forty years before he could pay off the exorbitant price of more than two thousand pounds that the crown was asking from prospective bondholders.

His ever-present feeling of frustration contributed to his gloom too, and the knowledge that he was being forced to endure hardship because of the criminal activities of others continued to infuriate him. It was difficult for him to believe that the lovely girl who had called herself Sara Dean would have wanted him to suffer so ignominiously, but he could find no excuse for her shameless trickery, and although his last hope of finding her died when he was rowed out to the *Lilian Rose*, which rode at anchor in the Thames, he still dreamed about Sara. It was futile to imagine that he confronted her, forced her to confess her duplicity, and won complete vindication at her expense, but his dream was always the same, and his sense of despair was all-encompassing when he awoke, heard the creaking of the brig's lines, and, turning over on his pallet in the hold, realized that he would be denied the satisfaction of obtaining justice.

After the first few days at sea, however, Hugh's outlook began to improve. He was young, his health had not been impaired by his imprisonment, and the salt air unexpectedly sharpened his appetite. The crown bailiffs who were in charge of the prisoners had learned through experience that they obtained a higher price for indentured servants who looked strong, so the felons were given ample quantities of bread and beef, salted fish and pickled pork. They were allowed to spend part of each day in the open on a portion of the aft deck so they could acquire sun tans, and Hugh, more cheerful in spite of his bleak predicament, began to take a greater interest in Benjy's cheerful conversation.

"I've always wanted to go to America," the counterfeiter said eagerly. "After my indenture ends, I'll be rich."

He could look forward to a short period of servitude, as

the small price of one hundred and seventy-five pounds had been set on his head by the court, but his assumption that he would earn a fortune was puzzling. "Don't believe the stories you've heard about the colonies," Hugh told him, amused. "You won't catch beaver in the streets of Boston and New York, and you won't find diamonds and rubies in farmers' fields."

Benjy chuckled and looked out at the rolling sea. "There's gold and silver in America, and I'll be satisfied to stuff my pockets with either. I'm not interested in beaver pelts, and I don't plan to waste my time looking for gems."

"You won't find gold and silver, I'm afraid," Hugh said. "I hate to discourage you, Benjy, but I've traveled through all of the colonies except Georgia and the Carolinas, and I've seen no more silver and gold there than you'd find in London."

The little man ran a hand through his sparse hair and, still looking out at the waves, laughed slyly "Your trouble, Hugh, is that you didn't know where to searcl You were raised as a gentleman, you see, so you didn't bother to get down on your hands and knees. But the wealth is there, waiting to be taken, all the same." Several other prisoners were standing a few feet away at the rail, so he lowered his voice. "I've seen samples of the ore, so to speak."

Hugh thought he had lost his reason.

"Don't stare at me that way. I'm talking about money. Every last one of the colonies prints its own currency, and I've never seen more miserable, clumsy, slipshod work in my life."

"I think I'm beginning to understand," Hugh said slowly.

"Amateur counterfeiters make so much in America they can retire after a few years, I'm told. And professional men, like me, who really know what we're doing, can live in luxury for the rest of our lives. The easiest bills to copy," he added, "are the Rhode Island one-pound notes and the Connecticut ten-shilling notes. The New Jersey and New York money is a bit more complicated, and the paper is a better grade, but there aren't any real problems copying their currency. As to coins, I can't wait to make some molds. They're all very crude and inferior."

In the days that followed he talked frequently about the techniques he intended to employ, and Hugh, with nothing else to occupy his mind, listened and learned. Amateurs, Benjy told him scornfully, made the mistake of trying to pass coins they had just manufactured without aging them, and therefore risked being caught. He never made such a stupid error himself, he declared. Some of his colleagues liked to boil their coins in concentrated coffee, but only a few who possessed a special sense of timing could manage the trick successfully. All too frequently, he said, the outer silver shell fell away after several minutes of immersion in boiling liquid. He preferred to fry his coins lightly in bacon grease and then let them dry in the open air for a day or two. When a little dirt was then rubbed on them to remove the last traces of grease, they looked as though they had been passed from hand to hand and wallet to wallet for years.

There were several types of counterfeiters, Hugh discovered, and the men who were considered the best by their colleagues were the printers, forgers, and silversmiths. They were creative artists, Benjy said, and relied on their own skills, shunned trickery, and tried to make perfect copies of bills and coins. There were only a few specialists who belonged in that exalted category, and to the best of his knowledge none of them had migrated to the colonies. The majority lived in London, there were a few in Paris, and a handful in Amsterdam. All of them, he declared, engraved plates, and made coins imitating the money of the American colonies, and all were highly successful because they had reduced risks to a minimum. If caught by the English, French, or Dutch authorities, they could not be imprisoned because they were not making local counterfeit money; they passed no bills or coins themselves, and all of them employed representatives in the New World who bought their products for a set fee, usually one quarter of the face value of a bill or coin.

These middlemen were sometimes captured and punished in the colonies, but the men who actually made the money were safe. However, Benjy said, their profits were relatively small, and he had long wished he could set up his own plant in America. He intended to dispense with the services of operatives, and would reap the entire profit himself. Perhaps, he suggested, Hugh might want to join him after his term of indenture ended. Realizing that his friend was complimenting him by offering him a partnership, Hugh refrained from saying that he wasn't interested in a life of crime, and instead thanked Benjy warmly.

Counterfeiting was forgotten when, after five weeks at sea, the *Lilian Rose* reached Philadelphia. Hugh knew the city but had no chance to see it, for the prisoners were marched off under a strong guard to a barracks near the markets behind High Street Hill. More than two hundred and fifty convicts who had been sent from England were gathered there, the majority of them criminals with long records. There were thirty or forty women who were being housed in a separate building, and Hugh hoped that "Sara Dean" was among them, but when he saw the group taking an airing on the morning after his arrival he was disappointed. Almost without exception the women were husky young slatterns.

The sale of crown prisoners was always an important event in the colonies, and citizens who were willing to risk taking convicted felons into their homes or businesses paid much less than those who dealt with private traders. Owners of plantations, textile mills, and large farms came from all of the thirteen colonies to Philadelphia for the widely advertised semiannual sale, which was held on the last three days of August, and as the time drew nearer, every inn in the city was filled to capacity.

In the meantime the prisoners were fed large quantities of potatoes, rice, and inexpensive cuts of meat, were forced to exercise daily, and were examined regularly by physicians who had come to the New World from London in order to help obtain the highest possible price for the convicts. A half battalion of British light infantry was stationed at the compound behind High Street Hill, and red-coated sentries armed with muskets and bayonets stood watch twenty-four hours a day to make certain that no one escaped. Indentured servants had become an important source of royal revenue.

Hundreds of buyers came to the compound on the morning that the sale opened, and after scanning lists that extolled the virtues of the men and women they planned to buy, they wandered from one barracks to another, studying the prisoners and questioning them. Hugh, dressed in a clean white shirt and snug woolen breeches, stood beside his pallet, as he had been instructed, and stared into space as men examined him, circled around him, and discussed him as though he were inanimate. His humiliation was even greater than it had been during the weeks he had been held at Newgate, and even though he realized that the men who scrutinized him were not responsible for the vicious system that transformed free human beings into slaves, he hated them for their greedy willingness to take advantage of the helpless misery of others.

His anger became greater through the long hours of the morning, and the expression in his eyes made some of the clients uneasy. "He's a surly brute," one said. "Anyone who takes him is buying trouble."

The guard who was in charge of the barracks overheard the remark, and when there was a brief lull he came to Hugh. "You, there," he said sharply, "if you don't want a beating, stop scaring off the buyers."

Hugh made no reply, and when another group came into the barracks he continued to gaze stonily into space, ignoring them.

Benjy apparently felt no shame at being placed on exhibit, however, and happily spoke to anyone who came near him. His friendliness was rewarded late in the morning when a

Philadelphia printer named Richardson agreed to buy his
bond after receiving earnest assurances that Benjy was familiar with the printing trade. Even Hugh forgot his own mortification and smiled when he heard his friend say, "Mr.
Richardson, I know more about inks and presses and paper
than any man in the colonies!"

Benjy's new master allowed him to say good-by to his former cellmate before taking him away, and Hugh shook hands
with the only person on earth who cared whether he lived or
died. "Take care of yourself, Benjy—and be careful not to
break any laws."

The little counterfeiter grinned. "I'll manage, never you
fear. And someday we'll meet again, Hugh. I'm sure we will."

Hugh felt completely alone in the world when Benjy's
shackles were removed and he followed Richardson out of the
building.

Few of the buyers stopped to interrogate Hugh during the
afternoon, and it was almost dusk when a thick-chested man
in his forties came into the building, accompanied by one of
the principal bailiffs. "Is that the fellow?"

"Yes, Mr. Fleming."

Hugh paid no attention to the man, who inspected him
carefully.

"He looks like a healthy specimen." Fleming spoke in a
high, nasal drawl.

"There's none healthier in the lot."

"Then he must be a weakling."

"Test him yourself, Mr. Fleming."

"I will. You! Take off your shirt!"

Hugh wanted to punch the arrogant buyer, but controlled
his temper and slowly, reluctantly, peeled off his shirt.

Fleming felt his muscles, poked a finger into his back, and
pinched the flesh around his waist, treating him as though he
were an animal. "You're right. He seems strong enough."
Fleming paused and peered suspiciously at Hugh, his heavy

eyelids narrowing. "I haven't seen better all day. Why hasn't someone bought him earlier?"

"His price is high, Mr. Fleming. The crown wants two thousand, three hundred and seventeen pounds for him."

"He isn't selling cheap, I'll grant you. But anyone who takes him will have his services for the rest of his life, and some of the best African slaves in their prime cost almost that much. How old are you?" he demanded, thrusting his face close to Hugh.

"Twenty-seven."

"Call me 'sir' when you speak to me!"

Hugh swallowed hard. "Twenty-seven, sir."

"That's a bit better." Fleming turned back to the bailiff. "The price isn't the only reason you still have him on your hands. What's the rest of the story?"

"People seem to be afraid of him, from what I've heard," the bailiff said reluctantly.

"Oh?" Fleming stared hard at Hugh and fingered the butt of a pistol he carried in his belt. "Is he a brawler? Did he cause trouble on the voyage?"

"No, Mr. Fleming. It's his attitude that scares them."

"Is he a murderer?"

"We don't sell murderers into indenture any more, Mr. Fleming. Not since that riot in Massachusetts eight years ago. Spencer has never been violent. He's a counterfeiter."

"I can handle him." Fleming's laugh was unpleasant. "Your list says he knows something about horses."

"I'd hate you to be dissatisfied, Mr. Fleming. You're too good a customer. So I suggest you talk to him yourself."

"You! As you aren't deaf, you've heard what we've been saying. Tell me about yourself."

"I know horses," Hugh said curtly, and when Fleming glared at him, he remembered to add, "Sir."

"Were you a farmer?"

"No, sir. I was in the Dragoons."

A gleam of excitement appeared in the buyer's eyes. "I intend to check your records, so don't lie to me."

"I'm not lying, sir." Hugh wondered how much longer he could curb his desire to drive a fist into the red, leering face.

"You were a groom, I suppose?"

"No, sir." Hugh stared at the far wall.

"He was an officer, Mr. Fleming."

"Then he's worth every penny of the two thousand pounds! Most of my grooms are clumsy louts or ignorant savages who should be working in the tobacco fields. This fellow should be able to take charge of my stables after I've broken him to my ways."

"He should, Mr. Fleming," the bailiff agreed.

"You! Look at me when I speak to you. I'm going to buy you. Do you know what that means?"

Hugh made a supreme effort to speak calmly. "I believe I understand the principles of indenture, sir."

Fleming laughed again, more loudly. "In the first place, you'll forget that you were once a gentleman. You're my property, and I can do with you as I please. If you disobey me, you'll carry the stripes on your back for the rest of your days. When I give you an order, you'll jump to obey it. If I tell you to lick the dust off my boots, you'll do it, and then you'll thank me for the honor."

Color rose in Hugh's face, but he made no reply.

Fleming chuckled as he turned to the bailiff. "I'll take him. I've tamed worse, you know. I've never yet seen a slave who felt very brave after tasting that ox whip of mine."

v / *April 1775*

OSBERT FLEMING'S plantation in southwestern Virginia was the largest property in Bedford County. The great house, with mock Grecian columns supporting a white portico, stood high on a bluff overlooking the James River and, like Fleming himself, dominated the area. The tobacco fields stretched out toward the Blue Ridge Mountains, which rose in the west, and the servants' quarters, a collection of one-story frame houses and huts, were clustered in a hollow near the river about three quarters of a mile upstream from Fleming's imposing red brick mansion.

The African slaves, virtually all of them field hands, lived in the huts, and Fleming, the most prosperous planter in the county, was believed to own more than three hundred of them. The fifty indentured servants, who theoretically enjoyed a somewhat higher status, slept in the unpainted frame buildings, but they enjoyed few luxuries and privileges. All of the skilled laborers on the estate, the stonemasons, carpenters, tailors, and supervisors who dried the tobacco in long, low sheds, slept on straw pallets, cooked their own meals, and were fed the same monotonous diet of potatoes, rice, and salt pork on which the Africans subsisted.

The overseers, bondsmen who had been in Fleming's employ for many years, were housed in two large buildings that stood near the water's edge, and were permitted various comforts that were denied the others. They slept on real beds with feather mattresses, they wore sturdy leather boots, heavy linen shirts, and stout breeches, and they were allowed to draw on the commissary of the great house for such delicacies as beef, ground corn, and melons. All carried pistols in their belts and, depending on whether they worked in the fields or curing sheds, were allowed to arm themselves with heavy-handled whips or knives. Most important of all, only Fleming himself was allowed to reprimand them, give them orders, or punish them for misdemeanors.

Hugh's rise in the hierarchy of the plantation was rapid, somewhat to his surprise, and a few months after his arrival he was made an overseer and placed in charge of the stables. He realized that his knowledge of horses was partly responsible for his promotion, but he knew, too, that luck had played a part in his progress. Fleming, congratulating himself on the acquisition of a chief groom who meekly submitted to higher authority, still didn't understand why Hugh had not created a scene on the day they had first arrived at the estate, and as that incident had been the most significant since the start of Hugh's indenture, it was in his interest to make certain that Fleming remained ignorant.

Hugh had been forced to walk behind Fleming's horse from Philadelphia, still wearing his shackles, and consequently had been exhausted when they had finally reached the plantation. Fleming, following his usual custom, had then beaten his new servant with a whip "to teach him his proper place," and had been pleased when Hugh had accepted the assault without a murmur. Only the plantation's physician, an elderly Scotsman who had been working out his indenture for more than twenty-five years, had known that Hugh had been too weary to fight, protest, or curse.

"You're lucky, lad," Dr. Campbell had murmured as he had applied salve to the welts on Hugh's back. "If your bones hadn't been so weary, you'd have no bones unbroken now. I saw your eyes, which Fleming didn't, and your luck was with you again. I know what's in your mind, but don't do it. If you raise your hand against him after you've recovered your strength, he'll beat you as he's beaten others, so you'll never stand straight again. Wait—and your time will come."

Hugh didn't understand the physician's cryptic reference to the future until he was made an overseer, and as the two houses were crowded, Dr. Campbell offered to share his room with the newcomer. "There are forces at work in this land that are going to bring changes for the better, violent changes, although you'd never know it from Fleming or his son or his daughter. Have you heard of Patrick Henry, lad?"

They were sitting alone at dusk on the small porch of the house overlooking the James River, and Hugh noted that the physician glanced around cautiously before he mentioned Henry's name. "I'm afraid I must plead ignorance. Does he live in Bedford village?"

"No, he's a lawyer in the eastern part of the colony, and he's a patriot if ever one lived!"

"There was a time," Hugh replied bitterly, "when I was a supporter of the crown too. But after all that's happened to me, I can't believe in King George any more than I can in royal justice."

"Patrick Henry," Campbell said softly, running a hand through his thick white hair, "is an American patriot."

Hugh remembered that a few students from King's College, Harvard, and other schools had spoken of independence for the colonies at dinner parties he had attended when he had been an officer in the Dragoons, but he hadn't paid much attention to the youths' fiery speeches. "You don't really believe that the colonies will rebel—or that they could succeed if they tried?"

"I never wore a red coat, as you did, lad, so I'm not awed by the might of the king's arms, as you seem to be. Patrick Henry is going to be one of our delegates to a congress from all thirteen of the colonies, and they'll talk of independence, mark my words. There's freedom for America in the air. You can smell it, you can almost feel it. Fleming is the only planter in Bedford County who stays loyal to the crown, and you'll find the same situation in scores of counties all over the land. Why, I've even heard it said that men like Colonel Washington, the most respected landowner in Virginia, favor independence!"

Hugh stared silently at the river.

"Have I misjudged you, lad? Have I spoken too freely when I should have held my tongue?"

"No, I was thinking of what it would mean to be free." Hugh turned to the old man, his eyes glowing. "When the time comes to act, you can count on me."

It was difficult to remain enthusiastic over the possibility of America's becoming an independent nation, for little news of the outside world reached the plantation, and Hugh worked long hours at the stables, supervising a staff of three indentured servants and twenty African slaves. Fleming, who was proud of his wealth, kept five carriages and insisted that they be maintained in good condition. He entertained lavishly, and there were usually at least half a dozen guests at the great house, almost all of them "Yankee-hating Tories," according to Dr. Campbell. The master of the plantation enjoyed showing his friends his extensive holdings, and as they invariably rode around the property on horseback, it was necessary to have all of the thirty-four mounts in the stables ready to be saddled at a moment's notice. Fleming never rode the same horse twice in succession, and if he thought an animal looked unkempt, Hugh received a tongue-lashing and one of the unfortunate grooms was sentenced to a whipping.

However, Fleming respected ability, and when he saw that his stables were being operated with military precision, he gave Hugh a comparatively free hand. Hugh, taking Dr. Campbell's advice, avoided the master whenever possible, spoke to him only when Fleming addressed him, and on the rare occasions when he was given an order that could not be obeyed, he tactfully remained silent. Fortunately Fleming's memory was poor, and as he took it for granted that his staff heeded all of his commands, Hugh avoided trouble with him.

Fleming's children complicated his life, however, and Dr. Campbell said they had become increasingly imperious and callous each year since their mother had died. Edmund Fleming attended school in New York, so Hugh luckily was forced to endure the boy's domineering attitude for no more than a brief period, a four-week holiday at the end of the year. It was fortunate that Edmund returned to his studies, for Hugh was uncertain whether he was patient enough to tolerate the youth's mistreatment of the horses for more than a short time. At fourteen Edmund was developing all of his father's worst qualities.

Jordy Fleming, Dr. Campbell said, was more like her mother, and as he had brought her into the world twenty years earlier, he was prejudiced in her favor. Hugh had to admit that she was beautiful, and he could understand why suitors from all over the colony were attracted by her lithe figure, long blue-black hair, and violet eyes, but he saw how carelessly she dug her spurs into a horse's flanks when she started off on her daily ride, he was disturbed by her frequent use of her pearl-handled riding crop, and, not allowing himself to forget that she was a Fleming, he treated her with courteous, impersonal respect whenever she spoke to him, but he made it a rule to avoid her, and usually retired to his small office beside the hayloft on the upper story of the main stable in midmorning, at the hour she normally appeared for her ride.

It did not occur to Hugh that Jordy, spoiled by the admiration of many men, would be piqued by his indifference, and he was surprised one morning in April, when she appeared unexpectedly in his office. He had been writing on a long sheet of paper, but when he saw her he dropped his quill, pushed back his chair, and bowed.

Jordy leaned against one side of the doorframe and tapped her riding breeches with the tip of her crop. "I didn't know you were a scholar," she said, a hint of amusement in her eyes.

Hugh carefully refrained from looking at her shirt, which was buttoned carelessly, revealing the swelling of her breasts. He hadn't taken a woman in a long time, and instinct warned him that Jordy was baiting him. "I've been making a list of some items I need from the general store in Bedford, Miss Jordy. Horseshoes and axle bits and carriage paint." He glanced down at the paper and smiled faintly. "I wouldn't say I've been engaging in a scholarly pursuit."

"You're a strange man." She continued to study him.

"I hope," Hugh said carefully, "that I haven't been negligent in my duties."

"There have been all sorts of rumors about you. And just last week, when Grace Timberly rode over from Winchester to visit me, she said she thought you were the most handsome man she had ever seen."

Certain now that she was badgering him, he inclined his head slightly.

"Does that mean you share her opinion?"

"No man in my position can think very highly of himself," Hugh replied, speaking more curtly than he had intended.

Jordy laughed huskily. "I suspected you had a temper. I'm delighted to discover I was right."

He refused to allow a personal discussion to develop. "You're riding Mimsi again today, Miss Jordy? Shall I see if the boys have saddled her for you?"

"My ride can wait," she replied flatly. "You haven't yet admitted that you have a temper."

"Bond servants must learn to control their emotions."

"Yet they have feelings." She took a step into the room and deliberately struck a provocative pose.

Hugh's throat was dry, but his face was impassive and he spoke calmly. "All human beings have feelings, Miss Jordy."

"Are you trying to argue that an African field slave is as sensitive as the owner of an estate?"

Hugh realized it was wrong to let himself be drawn into a controversy, but he couldn't resist saying, "Both will bleed if they're hit with a whip."

"Precisely my point. The chances are rather strong that a field slave will be beaten, but it's unlikely that a landowner will be whipped." Her tone was mischievous, and there was a curious expression in her eyes.

This was no light conversation between social equals, and Hugh withdrew, shrugging and bowing woodenly.

"I've been informed that you wore the king's uniform, so you're in an unusual position. You can see the problem from both sides."

Either she had learned something of his background from her father or had persuaded Dr. Campbell to talk too freely.

"Well?" She tapped her crop more rapidly. "Were you really a king's officer, or did you invent a romantic story to make yourself more attractive to the girls?"

Hugh smiled wryly. "Indentured servants have no personal lives, so I have no reason to attract young ladies."

"I find you extremely attractive," Jordy said boldly.

Startled, he reached for her involuntarily, but let his arms fall to his sides again.

"Are you afraid of me, Spencer?" she asked tauntingly.

"Not of you, Miss Jordy."

"Spoken like a true officer."

"Permit me to remind you—and myself—that I'm your father's stable overseer." A cool breeze was blowing in through the open window of the little office from the mountains to the west, but Hugh began to perspire.

"I'm glad you've made it unnecessary for me to remind you of your place. It's good you haven't forgotten my name is Fleming."

He wished there were some way to blot out the knowledge that she was his master's daughter.

"You're obliged to obey my orders," Jordy said, and took another step toward him.

"I'll obey any reasonable order," Hugh replied, losing his temper. Certainly she realized, as he did, that they might be interrupted at any moment by one of a score or more of her father's employees. And he had no doubt that she knew the law: an indentured servant who was discovered making love to the wife or daughter of his owner, or who confessed to such an act, was condemned to death by hanging. And Osbert Fleming would need no urging to obey such a law.

Jordy, enjoying herself, looked up into Hugh's face, her violet eyes soft. "Suppose I order you to kiss me."

"I hope that you won't."

"Why, Spencer? Would you consider it less than reasonable for a man and woman who are attracted to each other to demonstrate their feelings? You've admitted you have feelings, remember, and it's plain that you don't think I'm ugly."

"If I were a free man," Hugh said in a low voice, "our situation would be different. As it is, I'm shackled."

"Not by me."

His desire was mounting, and he discovered that his control was slipping.

"I've given you an order," Jordy whispered. "Are you going to obey it, or must I report you for insubordination?"

He knew she was torturing him, and, casting aside all caution, he swept her into his arms. Jordy pressed against him, and when Hugh bent his head, she opened her mouth to receive his kiss. The intensity of her passion startled him, and he forgot that only a board floor separated them from her father's indentured servants and slaves. Unable to curb his appetite, he began to fondle her, and Jordy moaned softly; Hugh slipped a hand inside her shirt, and she responded violently to his caress, digging her long fingernails into the back of his neck.

"Has anyone seen my daughter? I was told she was walking down this way. Don't stand there like a pack of dumb animals. Answer me, one of you!"

Hugh and Jordy sprang apart at the sound of Fleming's voice below, and for an instant they stared at each other wildly. Then the girl, displaying a surprising presence of mind, buttoned her shirt and quickly straightened her hair. "I'm here, Papa," she called, and, picking up her riding crop, started toward the ladder that led to the stable below. "Follow me," she murmured.

A few moments later Hugh, still breathing hard, was facing an irate and suspicious Fleming. "What was my daughter doing in the loft?" he demanded.

"Miss Jordy was in my office, sir, not in the loft." Hugh had never been a convincing liar and felt trapped.

Jordy coolly came to his rescue. "I was complaining about the feeding of my mares, Papa. Spencer has been giving them too much bran mash, and they've become sluggish. I like a horse with spirit."

Fleming chuckled, but his mood changed when he turned back to Hugh. "Two years ago," he said, "a bondsman tried to become familiar with my daughter. His unmarked grave is located somewhere on the property."

A slave had finished saddling Jordy's horse and led the animal toward the front of the stable. She mounted with graceful ease and smiled down at her father. "You needn't worry about Spencer trying to become unpleasant, Papa. I won't let him forget his place." She glanced at Hugh briefly. "Remember what I told you, Spencer, and the next time I give you an order, do what you're told without wasting so much of my time."

The riding crop whistled as it cut through the air, and Hugh felt a sharp pain shoot through his left shoulder. Not until later did he realize that Jordy had slashed through the fabric of his shirt and raised a nasty welt on his body. She might try to persuade him that she had struck him in order to allay her father's suspicions, but he knew better. She had enjoyed lashing him, and her pleasure had been all the more intense because she had been conscious of his helplessness and had taken advantage of it.

His shoulder throbbing, Hugh watched her as she raked her mare's sides with her spurs and cantered across the open fields. His desire for her was unappeased, but he knew that taking possession of her would not be enough to satisfy him. He wanted to repay her for taunting him until he had lost his self-control and then striking him deliberately when he had been unable to protect himself.

Each day, it seemed, his need to obtain vengeance, to redeem the honor that the Flemings had taken from him, grew more compelling.

VI / *December 1775*

VIOLENT incidents, seemingly unrelated, began to form a pattern, and the thirteen American colonies gradually became aware of their destiny. The most significant took place in Massachusetts on April 19, 1775, and it did not matter that some men thought of the affair as a battle, while others referred to it as an unfortunate brawl. General Thomas Gage, military governor of the colony, had learned that a group of rebels led by Samuel Adams, the hotheaded editor who was preaching the doctrine of independence, were collecting arms and munitions in the village of Concord, northwest of Boston. Gage sent a detachment to seize the muskets, but a company of local militia blocked the advance of the troops on the village green at Lexington, a few miles from Concord.

No one knew whether a nervous soldier or an untrained militiaman fired the first shot, but the fact remained that British troops and American provincials became engaged in open hostilities. Gage's detachment dispersed the rebels and proceeded to Concord, as ordered, but that was the beginning of the incident, not the end; when the soldiers started their march back to Boston, militiamen hiding behind trees and boulders fired at them, then vanished in the dark, and the supposedly invincible red-coated troops were badly beaten.

On May 10 the Continental Congress convened to discuss ways to obtain redress for legitimate grievances, but it was too late for the colonies and England to reconcile their differences. On the same day that the Congress sat down to deliberate, forces led by Benedict Arnold of New York and Ethan Allen of Vermont captured Ticonderoga, a strong British fort in New York. In mid-June the New Englanders tried to force the British to evacuate Boston, but Gage defeated them, at great cost to himself, at what came to be known as the Battle of Bunker Hill. The news spread quickly through the colonies that raw militiamen had repulsed Gage's regulars twice, and had been forced to abandon the field only when they had run out of ammunition.

By autumn even moderate men were saying that independence was the only solution to America's problem. George Washington of Virginia, the most respected soldier in the New World, had accepted a congressional appointment as commander-in-chief of its army, and recruits flocked to his banner from every colony. An American force succeeded in capturing Montreal, Arnold assaulted Quebec in spite of great odds against him and his untrained troops, and General Gage, who had made war inevitable in the opinion of his superiors in London, was supplanted by General William Howe.

Life at the plantation near Bedford remained almost unchanged, however, in spite of the ferment everywhere. Osbert Fleming and his friends toasted King George every night and, refusing to allow rebel agitators to set foot on their land, swore they would remain loyal to the crown. The militia sent recruiting teams into every county, but only free men were being accepted by the army, so Hugh and the other indentured servants who were Fleming's bondsmen were not eligible for service.

Hugh, increasingly restless as news of the developments from the outside world reached the plantation, saw a chance to improve his own lot, and expressed his mind freely to Dr. Campbell. "Freedom for America can mean freedom for me," he said vehemently. "Why shouldn't I just disappear some night and join the militia?"

"You'd be returned in chains, lad," the physician replied flatly. "Liberty doesn't mean license to run wild. I have no way of guessing whether the colonies will take up arms formally or whether Lord North and his ministers will have the good sense to make peace while they can. But I do know that no matter how hard they curse the colonial leaders at the great house, General Washington is no radical. Neither is John Adams of Massachusetts, and gentlemen like Robert Morris believe in maintaining law and order."

"But if America is fighting for her independence—"

"There's been talk of independence, but the Continental Congress is still trying to negotiate a settlement with the king's ministers. The colonies aren't so desperate that they'll accept runaway bondsmen in their army. They might be tempted, I'll grant you, because they're suffering from a shortage of trained officers, but we're still living under the jurisdiction of the king's courts, and Fleming would be within his rights to hang you."

Hugh was silent, and a stubborn expression appeared in his eyes.

"Promise me you'll do nothing rash."

"I can't, Doctor. I've been patient long enough."

Campbell sighed. "If you'd spent a quarter of a century in bondage, as I have, you'd have a right to speak of patience. But the young are always eager." He put his hand on Hugh's shoulder. "If you won't give me your promise, do one thing for yourself, lad. Wait until you're sure the wind is strong before you send your kite aloft."

The plantation was unusually quiet during the Christmas season. The tobacco planters of Bedford County, sympathizing with the American cause, saved themselves embarrassment and avoided the red brick house on the bluff overlooking the James River. Osbert Fleming, aware that he and his family were being ostracized, retaliated by becoming active in a league of conservative men opposed to the rebellion. Plans were made to form a regiment of loyalist troops, and Fleming went off to Richmond to attend a series of meetings and pledge his financial support to the crown.

The indentured servants and slaves were given a holiday on Christmas Day, but Hugh, thoroughly dissatisfied with himself and his drab life, wandered down from his little house to the deserted stables. The horses had been fed shortly after dawn, and most of them were quiet, but a two-year-old gray stallion, Toby, was restless. Hugh understood how he felt and decided to exercise the beast. Toby permitted no one else to ride him, much to Osbert Fleming's annoyance, so Hugh felt closer to the animal than he did to any of the other horses, and, saddling the stallion quickly, started up the trail that ran parallel to the river.

There was a hint of frost in the air, although the sun was warm, and after he had ridden past the tobacco fields, the pastures, and the land where the slaves grew potatoes, beans, and corn, he increased his pace. Toby responded eagerly to his touch, and only when they reached a stand of hemlocks did Hugh realize that he had gone beyond the boundary of Fleming's property. Not even overseers were permitted to leave the grounds without first receiving specific permission, but Hugh didn't care, and galloped on toward the Blue Ridge Mountains, whose pine-covered peaks had become a symbol to him of the personal liberty he had lost.

Realizing he could reach the mountains in a quarter of an hour, he urged Toby up a slope, and the stallion, sensing his excitement, pounded recklessly across rocky ground. Hugh was staring so intently at the sky line that he paid little attention to his immediate surroundings, and was startled when three men appeared unexpectedly from behind a large boulder some distance in front of him. Two wore buckskins, the third was dressed in somber, homespun linsey-woolsey, and all were armed with rifles, which they raised threateningly.

Reacting instinctively, Hugh reached into his belt for a pistol, remembered that he was unarmed, and, as chagrined as he was annoyed, drew Toby to a halt. One of the men in buckskin, who seemed to be the leader of the group, approached the horse and rider slowly, a guarded expression in his pale blue eyes. "Are you in a hurry to get somewhere, mister?" he asked, still aiming his long rifle at the stranger.

Hugh bristled. "I was minding my own business," he replied curtly.

The man motioned to his companions, who moved forward cautiously, one on the left and the other on the right. "There's no call to be so testy, mister," the leader said calmly. "Hereabouts we claim that anybody's business is our business. Who are you?"

"My name is Spencer."

"That don't mean a thing to us," the short man in linsey-woolsey retorted. "Where you from?"

"Fleming's."

The younger of the pair in buckskins, a youth of about twenty, laughed grimly. "It's like I said right off. He's a Tory spy."

Hugh was bewildered and indignant. "I'm neither a Tory nor a spy." He refrained from adding that he couldn't imagine what an espionage agent could learn in this uninhabited wilderness.

"You sound English," the leader declared.

"I am. Or I was, rather. Is that a crime?"

"Anybody who sounds like an Englishman and who is visiting Fleming is sure to be a Tory!"

In spite of his anger Hugh was amused. "I'm not considered a guest there," he said dryly. "I'm one of Fleming's bondsmen."

The trio relaxed slightly, and the man in linsey-woolsey looked aggrieved. "Why didn't you say so in the first place?"

"Why didn't you ask me?" Hugh countered.

"You got a sharp tongue, that's sure," the youth said. "Maybe you're what you claim, and maybe you're not."

"There's one way to find out," the leader said mildly. "We know how Fleming treats his people. Strip to the waist."

Hugh was in no position to argue, and after glancing at the muzzles of each of the rifles, he peeled off his old coat and shirt.

The leader walked to a position behind Toby and studied Hugh's back. "He's marked, all right," he announced. "Who beat you—Fleming himself?"

"Yes." Hugh was surprised to detect a sympathetic note in the man's voice, but nevertheless he resented being treated in such a peremptory fashion. "Now that you're satisfied, I'd like to dress again."

"Sure." The leader moved forward and lowered his rifle. "Folks can't be too careful these days. You've been testy, and I reckon maybe we haven't been friendly. But we don't love Fleming any more than you do." He gestured to his companions, who lowered their weapons. "Now we can all be more sociable, and maybe you'll be more agreeable to telling us what you're doing up in these hills."

"I wanted to breathe some free air, that's all."

The leader and the man in linsey-woolsey exchanged long, significant glances.

"You didn't have anything special in mind?" the youth demanded, still a trifle suspicious.

"I don't know what you're talking about," Hugh replied flatly.

"If you satisfy us, we'll explain all you need to know," the leader said. "What's your opinion of the things that have been happening in the colonies since last spring?"

"I'm in favor of independence! I was a loyal subject of the king all of my life, but I've learned that crown justice is incompetent and that crown officials pay lip service to principles in order to further their own ends." Hugh was warming to his subject. "I can't say that I'm familiar with all of America's grievances, but I know how you feel, and I stand with you."

"How far on our side of the line do you stand?" the leader asked quietly.

"If I could, I'd join your militia right now!"

"What's to stop you?" The youth continued to regard him with reserve.

The older man replied before Hugh could speak. "You know blamed well that he can't, Ned. There's royal bailiffs in every county, and we've had orders not to interfere with civil law until we become a free country. Then we'll ship every last bailiff back to England and make our own laws."

Hugh, certain they were not highwaymen who intended to steal his horse, felt it was his turn to indulge in a gesture of good will. "Do you mind if I stretch my legs?" he asked, dismounting.

The leader understood and grinned at him. "You're all right, Spencer," he said, shaking hands. "Seeing you're bound to Fleming, it will be healthier for you if we don't tell you our names. But it might be helpful if we pass along some advice. It doesn't pay for strangers to wander into the Blue Ridge foothills these days. Some of the boys who are going off to join the army in the spring are training hereabouts—never mind exactly where—and they get to feeling annoyed when Tories come snooping around."

"I see, and thank you for your confidence." Hugh stood erect and inhaled deeply. "The day that America becomes independent and I can't be returned to Fleming as a runaway, I'm going to enlist."

"If you know how to shoot," the youth declared, "Dan Morgan could sure find a place for you in his rifles."

"Any colonel could use a man who rides the way he does," the man in linsey-woolsey said.

The prospect of freedom was exhilarating. "If you wish," Hugh said, "I'll gladly sign a paper right now promising to enlist."

The leader shook his head. "A man who has any sense doesn't stick his neck into a noose and then wait for somebody to jerk it tight."

Hugh wanted to explain that he was trying to reassure himself.

"Papers," the leader continued, "have an odd way of turning up where they're not wanted. I'll take your word, Spencer, and I hope I'll be on hand to welcome you."

"How soon," Hugh asked, "will the colonies declare themselves independent?"

The man in linsey-woolsey shrugged. "If it was up to us, we'd be a free country right now. But there aren't many in the Congress like Tom Jefferson of Albermarle County and Patrick Henry."

"The Continental Congress," the youth added contemptuously, "is a pack of old women, all of them scared of finding a redcoat under their beds."

"The members of Congress," the leader told his subordinates firmly, "have their own problems trying to prepare the country for political independence. Your job is to help them in the field when they need you."

The young man fondled his rifle. "I'm ready right now."

The leader turned back to Hugh. "I can't answer your question, and I don't think it likely that anybody meeting up in Philadelphia knows, either. There are some who still think a compromise can be arranged, but they're wrong, as time will prove."

"The lads who are up in New England fighting redcoats don't talk about compromise," the man in linsey-woolsey declared vehemently.

His superior silenced him with a frown. "The best advice I can give you, Spencer, is not to be too hasty. If they delay too long in Philadelphia, Virginia isn't going to wait forever, and from what I hear, neither is Massachusetts. But all you need to worry about is Virginia. When you hear that we've formally renounced our allegiance to King George, ride up this way. If I'm not in these parts myself, I'll leave word that somebody is to keep watch for you. In the meantime, you haven't seen anybody and you haven't talked to anybody."

"It's in my own interests to keep my mouth shut," Hugh assured him, and, after shaking hands with each of the trio, mounted Toby and started back downhill.

For the first time since he had been imprisoned in the dungeons at Newgate he had real reason to hope that his freedom would be restored. His personal future depended on the cause of the American rebels, and although the thought of taking up arms against his former comrades would have appalled him before he had been treated unjustly, he welcomed the prospect eagerly. He rode rapidly back to the estate and smiled quietly as he dismounted, opened the stable door, and led his stallion inside. He could tolerate his bondage because it would end soon, and he was undismayed by the knowledge that the court had stripped him of his possessions. He would be penniless, but he had learned that liberty was man's most precious asset.

"You look very pleased with yourself," someone standing in the shadows of the stable said.

Hugh, instantly alert, saw Jordy Fleming in a dark corner. She was wearing a low-cut gown of pale silk and looked completely out of place. In spite of his surprise, he took care to bow respectfully to her.

"You haven't answered me." Her tone was mocking, but her face was hidden and he couldn't see her expression.

"If I had known you wanted to ride today, ma'am, I would have made certain that some members of the staff were here," Hugh replied carefully.

"Do I look as though I intend to go riding?" Deliberately raising her skirt, she lifted a high-heeled satin slipper. "I came down here looking for you, and when I saw you riding toward the stable, I slipped inside to wait for you."

She was slurring her words, Hugh realized, and he realized she had probably drunk too much.

"It was terribly dull at the house," Jordy complained. "I'd have brought you some of the brandy punch, but I didn't know how to carry it." She gestured vaguely and giggled.

Familiarity with Jordy could ruin Hugh's hopes, and he became wary. He had avoided her since the day she had teased him into making love to her, and he had no intention of becoming involved with her now. "They must miss you at the great house," he said.

"My aunts, all three of them," she replied scornfully, "are sitting near the fire, drinking as much punch as they can hold and pretending they're conversing like sober ladies. My father's cousin and her husband ate so much at dinner they had to be excused, and will probably sleep until morning. And my brother is composing another of his violent letters offering his services to General Howe. You're the only person within fifty miles who can save me from suffering the most boring Christmas I've ever known."

"There must be scores of young men in the area who would leap at the chance to spend an hour or two in your company," he said carefully.

Jordy's laugh was harsh. "The Flemings aren't popular in Bedford County these days. We've been denounced because we won't become traitors, but Papa will take care of our enemies. They'll start singing 'God Save the King' instead of that stupid 'Yankee Doodle' soon enough."

It was impossible for Hugh to pretend he was disinterested.

Jordy laughed again, more softly, and moved closer to him. "I've made you curious, haven't I? Admit it."

Hugh's face became blank. "If you'll pardon me, ma'am, I'll see to the horse." He unsaddled Toby and led the stallion to his stall.

Jordy was waiting for him when he dropped the bolt of the stall door in place. "I'll trade information with you," she said, standing so near to him that he could see the teasing light in her eyes.

He was afraid he had been seen talking to the militiamen

in the hills, but was determined to reveal nothing about the encounter. "I can't imagine anything in my life that would be worth your attention, Miss Jordy," he said, hoping he sounded calm.

"You're mistaken. And I don't intend to discuss the subject with you here. We'll go up to your office." Not waiting for a reply, she walked to the ladder, and, climbing it, drew her skirt higher than necessary, revealing a silk petticoat edged with lace and a pair of pale stockings so sheer they could have been made only in Paris.

Hugh searched desperately for an excuse to avoid following her, but his fear was too great. Jordy could become dangerous if she knew of his meeting, so it would be wise to humor her, within reason. Trying not to look at her legs, he wished she were less attractive; it would be far easier to deal with a plain woman.

Jordy perched on the edge of the desk in the small office, smoothed her skirt, and smiled brightly. "You'll tell me first, naturally."

"What would you like to know?" He remained near the entrance that led to the hayloft outside.

"Oh, many things, but I won't be greedy. I understand you better than you know, Hugh. I've watched you when you haven't realized I was looking at you. I've seen you so angry at Papa that you've wanted to kill him. Don't bother to deny it."

Under the circumstances he thought it best to say nothing. If she was trying to trick him into revealing information, silence was his best weapon.

"You've been so annoyed with me that you've been tempted to strike me, too. But far more often you've wanted me."

Her candor startled him.

"You want me right now. That's why you won't look at me." Jordy clasped her hands around her legs. "I do wish you'd stop looking so embarrassed. Surely you must realize that I'm flattered by your attention."

"I'm at a disadvantage. I'm cautious, not embarrassed. I haven't forgotten that your father has forbidden me to admire you."

She flirted with him boldly. "Papa is at the other side of the colony, a two-day journey from home."

Hugh shifted uncomfortably and stared at the mounds of hay piled in the loft.

"In all the months you've been here, I've never seen you look really happy—until today," Jordy said. "You've had little enough cause to be pleased with your life, I'm sure, but today you were changed. The light I saw in your eyes as you rode across the grounds to the stable intrigues me." She leaned forward and stared at him intently. "Well?"

Apparently she knew nothing about his meeting with the militiamen, and Hugh relaxed. "I suppose," he said, "I was enjoying my first holiday in a year and a half."

"You were with a girl," Jordy retorted. "You took one of the slave women to your house." Apparently it didn't cross her mind that she had no right to become jealous of him, and that the scraps of a private life that he could piece together were his own business.

Hugh shook his head. "I've spent no time at my house or elsewhere with a slave girl or any other woman, as Dr. Campbell can tell you." He saw that his reply left her unsatisfied, and decided to elaborate. "A man who has been free most of his life can never become accustomed to bondage. I had no duties to perform today, so I must have been enjoying my comparative freedom. And that," he added firmly, "is the only answer I can give you."

Her slow, cynical smile indicated that she felt certain he was being evasive. "You can't convince me that you weren't spending the day with some wench."

She had given him a better excuse than any he could have created himself, and the secret of his meeting with the militiamen was safe. "If you won't believe me, there's nothing more I can say, is there?" he asked lightly.

Jordy accepted the challenge, and her attitude changed subtly; she feigned languorous amusement, but there was an air of feline watchfulness beneath her façade of indifference. "Was she attractive?"

"Beauty," Hugh replied vaguely, "is always a matter of personal opinion."

"Do you think I'm beautiful?" It was not accidental that the tiny left shoulder cap of her bodice slid down her arm.

It was obvious that she wanted lavish compliments, but he didn't dare let himself look at her too closely, and he was afraid that too intimate a conversation would lead to dangerous complications. "You know what I think of you," he said curtly.

Slightly mollified, she laughed, and the left side of her bodice slid a little lower. "Am I as attractive as the wench you visited today?"

Hugh was caught in a trap of his own making. "I've never known anyone like you," he said recklessly. "You're incomparable." Now, perhaps, she would stop tormenting him.

Jordy slid to her feet, her eyes shining, and moved toward him. Her vanity was insatiable, and she demanded more than a verbal tribute.

Common sense told Hugh that he should remind her of the difference in their stations and insist that they return to the stable below. But he felt powerless when she stood close to him, and his desire robbed him of reason. Cursing himself for being weak and stupid, he reached for her.

Jordy pressed against him for an instant as he took her in his arms, but she averted her face when he bent to kiss her. "I haven't kept my part of the bargain yet," she murmured.

He was too aroused to know what she meant, and pulled her closer.

"I said I'd exchange information with you."

The faint odor of spice brandy punch on her breath mingled with the heavy scent she wore, and Hugh scarcely heard what she was saying.

"Papa is sending me away."

He continued to hold her firmly, but realized that she might be telling him something of importance.

"He's afraid the rebellion may spread, so he's sending me to New York for a few months. He has reason to believe that the Admiralty will send a fleet to teach the rebels their place, and if necessary the army will be strengthened, too. He says I'll be safer in New York, where people haven't forgotten they're subjects of the king. Now you know why I came to see you today. I wanted to say good-by to you." There was an expression of mock innocence in her eyes as she gazed up at him.

It was clear that she was inviting him to have an affair with her before she left, and he could not control his desire any longer. He kissed her, and Jordy responded with an urgency and fervor that matched Hugh's. They stood locked in a tight embrace, swaying slightly as they strained against each other. Suddenly they moved apart, stared at each other hungrily for a moment, and reached an immediate understanding. Jordy turned and walked out of the tiny office, Hugh followed her into the loft, and there was no need for words as they embraced again.

Hugh's caresses became more demanding as they sank onto a deep pile of hay, and neither cared when the pins that held Jordy's hair in place fell into the mound. She was not a novice in the art of love-making, and when Hugh discovered that she was deliberately employing cunning, he abandoned all caution. Jordy was far more than a provocative girl whom he wanted; she was selfish and greedy, a typical representative of the callous breed responsible for all of his suffering. By conquering her he could compensate, at least momentarily, for his humiliation, and he took her savagely.

His possession was complete, though transitory, and when their passion was spent they recovered slowly, sprawling silently on the hay in the dark loft. At last Jordy stirred, and began to make herself presentable again, rearranging her hair and clothes so she could return to the great house without making it obvious to a casual observer that her conduct had been less than discreet.

Hugh felt dissatisfied with himself again, and the victory he had enjoyed had been so fleeting that his sense of depression almost overwhelmed him. In a sense, he realized, Jordy had won the real triumph, for she had come to him hoping to break down his resistance, and she had achieved her goal. Certainly his situation was no better now than it had been before their rendezvous, and there was little pleasure in taking a girl who granted her favors so readily.

Jordy's laugh interrupted his thoughts, and he stared at her in the gloom, aware of something in her attitude that put him on his guard.

"You thought you were clever when you wouldn't tell me about the girl you visited earlier today, but I didn't reveal everything I knew, either."

They were standing near the entrance to the loft, and in the half-light Hugh could see a hard smile on her face.

"I didn't tell you all of Papa's plans. If the rebellion in Virginia grows worse, he's going to form a regiment of men loyal to the crown. You've had experience as an officer, so he'll need you. He thinks you'll be pleased to join him, but I know you better than he does." She laughed again. "You won't have any choice now."

Hugh stared at her.

"Papa can't force you to take up arms for the king, but I can. When he offers you a place in his regiment, you'll either accept—or I'll tell him that you've seduced me."

VII / *July 1776*

THE king's ministers stubbornly refused to grant the demands of the colonies for greater freedom, public opinion in America hardened, and the crown responded by dispatching naval and military reinforcements to the New World. The situation continued to deteriorate steadily through the early months of 1776, and by spring even the moderates on both sides of the Atlantic knew that it would be impossible to avoid fighting a full-scale war. Volunteers from every colony joined General Washington, fresh contingents arrived to bolster General Howe's forces, and the Continental Congress, which had been slow to take action that would be irrevocable, prepared to sever relations with the mother country.

Militiamen were being recruited everywhere and the Tories, outnumbered but financially stronger than the rebels, built up arsenals, conferred with the royal governors, and made plans to defend their homes and businesses from "the rabble." It was impossible for anyone to remain neutral, to watch the developments without taking an active role on one side or the other, and tensions became almost unbearable everywhere.

Osbert Fleming, one of the few men in the Blue Ridge counties of Virginia who refused to change their attitude, prepared grimly for the struggle that would soon come. He converted his great house into a fortress, collecting rifles and ammunition, filling his cellar with potatoes, onions, and smoked meats, and deliberately defying his neighbors, flying the English banner of St. George from a pole that he erected on his roof. Visitors from the eastern counties of the province were frequent guests, and Fleming made no secret of his activities on behalf of the crown; it was common knowledge in Bedford County that he was supplying funds for the organization of a regiment of Tory provincials. Early in June he left his estate, accompanied by an armed escort provided for him by the royal governor, and returned late in the month, accompanied by his daughter and son, whom he had decided to bring home from New York, where riots and street fights were adding to the tensions of daily living.

Jordy paid only one visit to the stables after her return. She went for a brief canter, and when she rode back to the stables, she found an opportunity to speak a single word to Hugh. "Soon," she said, and he knew from her hard, bright smile that she was prepared to carry out her threat.

At the end of the first week in July the crisis came suddenly. Hugh was summoned to the great house, where a slave in livery was waiting to conduct him to Osbert Fleming's study. Jordy was sitting in a parlor a short distance down a corridor, pretending to be reading a book, and she raised her head for an instant as Hugh was led through the chamber. Her tight smile warned him that his hour of decision had arrived, and he braced himself as he paused and tapped at the study door.

Fleming was pacing up and down the room, and Hugh, who had seen it infrequently, thought it resembled an arsenal. Several muskets were stacked in a corner, a saber and two lighter swords hung from a wall peg, and a heavy pistol rested on the top of a stack of papers on the desk. Fleming paused at the desk, picked up a letter, and waved it angrily. "That congress of traitors in Philadelphia has done it," he said. "They've issued what they call a Declaration of Independence. The rebels have set up an independent nation they're calling the United States of America."

Hugh's temples throbbed, and he made a supreme effort to conceal his elation.

"But we're ready for them," Fleming continued, "and before we're done, we'll send the head of every last one of them to London!" He paused and looked sharply at Hugh. "What have you to say to all this, Spencer?"

"In my position I've had very little chance to learn much about politics," Hugh replied carefully.

"But you were once a soldier. You wore the king's uniform!"

If the pistol were loaded it would be the most effective weapon in the room, Hugh decided.

"You may be as indifferent as you appear, Spencer, but it doesn't matter. You're going to wear a uniform again."

Hugh waited silently.

"General Howe hasn't seen fit to send any of his troops to the southern colonies yet, so we've made plans to defend ourselves. A brigade of loyalists is being formed in Virginia, and there's a place for you in a cavalry troop as a sergeant. You and four of my other overseers will leave today for Richmond with two young gentlemen from Fairfax who have been visiting me. They'll be your superior officers, and both of them are pleased that you'll be serving with them, even though you're a bondsman. They believe you can perform a valuable function as a drill master."

Hugh's mind was working quickly, and he realized at once that, if he started east as a member of an armed party, it would be far more difficult to escape than it would be to make his way alone into the hills.

"The other overseers were delighted." Fleming's eyes narrowed. "I realize that I can't expect real patriotism from a man of your stripe, but I'm willing to offer you an incentive. If you serve faithfully, I'll reduce your indenture by five hun-

dred pounds after the rebels are beaten and you come back
here."

The seemingly generous gesture was meaningless, as the
sum Fleming had paid for Hugh was so large that even a
five-hundred-pound reduction of the total would be insuffi-
cient to cut Hugh's term appreciably. Even if he accepted,
he would be forced to work as Fleming's servant until he was
an old man.

"I've been authorized to accept enlistments and administer
the oath of allegiance to King George." Fleming moved to the
desk.

Hugh followed him, taking care to stand near the pistol.
His lack of enthusiasm annoyed Fleming. "Your ingrati-
tude surprises me, Spencer," he said harshly.

"Perhaps," Hugh replied quietly, "I'd be more grateful if I
had been given a choice."

"Oh, you have a choice." Fleming laughed unpleasantly.
"Either you'll accept or you'll become a stable groom again."

"There's a third choice," Hugh said, and picked up the pistol, which he pointed at the man on the far side of the desk.

Fleming astonished him by laughing again. "Now I know
how you stand."

"That's right."

"Unfortunately for you, I set a trap. And you've walked
into it. That pistol isn't loaded." Fleming reached down into
an open desk drawer and drew out a short, ugly whip. "You
need to be taught appreciation."

Hugh, still clutching the useless pistol, sprang at him
and caught Fleming's right wrist before the whip could be
brought into play. They grappled and fell together on the
desk, spilling papers, a jar of ink, and a silver container of
sand onto the floor. The unexpected attack had taken Fleming
by surprise, but he reacted vigorously, and in spite of his
corpulence he proved to be a man of considerable strength.
He struck Hugh a heavy blow on the side of the head with his
free hand, tried to free himself from his bondsman's grasp,

and, displaying surprising agility, rolled on top of the younger man.

If he called for help, there were at least a score of house slaves who would come to his assistance, and Hugh knew he had to win the fight quickly or abandon all hope. The pistol slipped from his hand as Fleming pinned him down, but he caught hold of it again after groping blindly for it on the polished surface of the desk. Fleming was so proud that he wanted to administer a beating to an insubordinate servant himself, but he would not hesitate to call out for assistance if he felt he was losing control of the situation, and Hugh became desperate.

His fingers closed around the barrel of the pistol, and, using it as a hammer, he raised it and brought the butt down sharply on the back of Fleming's head. For a moment the blow seemed to have no effect, and Hugh raised the pistol to strike again, but Fleming slumped, gasped, and slid across his foe's body to the edge of the desk. Hugh freed himself, and as he looked at the man whose head was hanging toward the floor, wondered if he had killed the master of the estate. He bent down, saw that Fleming was still breathing, and, aware that time was precious, started toward the door.

He was tempted to take one of the swords, but knew he would only create complications if he were seen with a naked blade in his hand, and he resisted the urge. Discovering that he was still holding the pistol, he threw it onto a chair and, remembering that Jordy had been sitting across the corridor, straightened his rumpled shirt, ran his fingers through his hair, and raised the latch. As he had suspected, Jordy was still sitting on a small divan from which she could see the entrance to her father's study. She raised her head when she heard the door open, so Hugh knew he had to play-act if he hoped to escape.

"I'll return at once, sir," he said to the unconscious man behind him. "And I'll be honored to serve His Majesty again." He closed the door and stepped out into the corridor.

Jordy rose quickly and came to the door of the parlor. "You've accepted Papa's offer?"

"I'd be foolish to refuse," Hugh countered.

"Very foolish. I was ready to swear that you seduced me, you know, and I would have worn my best silk dress to your hanging."

Every moment that Hugh lost increased the chance that he would be captured, but he didn't dare leave Jordy too abruptly. "Do you hate me so much?"

"Certainly not." She smiled at him intimately. "Surely you know by now what I think of you, and I'm prepared to prove it again at the first opportunity. But I loathe traitors, and if you had been disloyal to the crown, you'd have deserved hanging."

"Perhaps," Hugh said, edging away from the door, "we can find some chance to meet privately before I leave with the others for Richmond. It's dangerous to talk here." That, he thought, was a gross understatement.

An expression of undisguised lust appeared in Jordy's violet eyes. "I'll see what I can do. Perhaps if I tell Papa that I want you to saddle a horse for me yourself before you leave—"

"No." He knew he was replying too sharply, but his tension was almost unbearable. "Your father doesn't want to be disturbed until he rings. And most of the grooms are at the stables."

Jordy's pleasure turned to petulance, and she pouted sulkily. "What do you have in mind, then?"

"I've got to get my belongings and come back here. I'm supposed to return within a reasonable time, but it will take me only a few minutes to get my razor and spare boots."

She smiled slyly. "I understand. I'll be watching for you at the head of the stairs."

"Good. I'll hurry."

"All right, but don't run. We don't want to appear obvious, and we can't let Papa become suspicious."

"You're right. I mustn't run." Hugh bowed to her and hurried off down the corridor to the servants' entrance.

It was difficult, when he stepped into the open, to resist the urge to sprint, but he forced himself to walk at a brisk pace. Glancing over his shoulder, he saw Jordy peering at him from a window, and he grinned at her for an instant, then turned and headed for the stables, which were hidden from the great house by a small orchard.

Fleming might regain consciousness at any time, and Hugh had no false illusions about his fate if the master of the establishment caught him. Dr. Campbell had frequently recalled the bondsman who had responded to goading by striking Fleming and had been whipped to death. Hugh's shirt was clammy, but it would be stupid to look over his shoulder again, so he stared straight ahead and didn't break into a run until he reached the far side of the orchard and could not be seen from the great house.

Two slaves lounging in the sun near the entrance to the main stable building jumped to their feet when they saw Hugh, and they would have disappeared around a corner before he recognized them, but his shout halted them. "Saddle Toby!" he called, and the note of urgency in his voice was so strong that they obeyed without questioning him.

Hugh followed them into the stable and, ignoring the curious stares of two other indentured servants, took over the task from the slaves, who were slow and clumsy. Not bothering to offer an excuse for engaging in work that overseers usually allowed menials to perform, he ordered one of the slaves to open the stable door, and as soon as he finished adjusting the stirrups he vaulted into the saddle. The stallion, sensitive to his mood, lunged out into the open, and Hugh headed toward the woods.

Toby galloped up the path that ran parallel to the river, and Hugh, bending low in the saddle, let the mount set his own pace. They passed fields of tobacco, where slaves and overseers paused in their work to stare at the rider in shirt sleeves. Several of the indentured servants waved when they recognized a fellow bondsman; Hugh returned their greetings casually, but as he was uncertain which of the overseers were loyal to England, he was prepared to dig his heels into the horse's flanks and increase his speed if anyone tried to halt him. He heard no hoofbeats behind him, and, increasingly sure that no organized pursuit was under way, he dared to hope that his gamble would prove successful.

His spirits soared as he crossed the boundary of Fleming's property, and as he headed up into the Blue Ridge foothills, he patted the stallion's neck. "We're free, Toby!" he said hoarsely, and controlled an impulse to shout.

When he drew near the rocks where he had encountered the militiamen, he slowed his mount to a walk and advanced more carefully. The area seemed deserted, and his spirits fell when he realized that all of the militiamen who had been in training somewhere in the wilderness might have gone north to join the army. In that case, he thought grimly, his own plight would be serious. He was without funds or credentials of any sort, he carried no weapons, and his only clothes were the shirt, breeches, and boots he was wearing. He would have to make a wide detour around the Fleming estate if he hoped to find American troops, and even if he enjoyed extraordinary good luck, the possibility that he might be captured would be increased.

"Halt! Put your hands over your head and don't move!"

Hugh heard someone call out behind him and, uncertain whether he had been accosted by a militiaman or a pursuer, he twisted around in his saddle as he obeyed. He saw two men in linsey-woolsey, each armed with a long rifle, and felt infinite relief. "You've been expecting me," he replied. "My name is Spencer."

"I never heard of anybody called Spencer hereabouts," one of the men said suspiciously.

"I'm from Fleming's plantation."

"Then you're a damned Tory spy. Should we shoot him first or take the horse first, Del?"

The other man frowned. "Wait up. This here is the one Colonel Baxter told us about."

"I've just escaped from Fleming's, and I've come to offer my services to the American army." Hugh forced himself to speak calmly.

"How do we know you're telling the truth?" The first speaker kept his rifle trained on Hugh.

"If you stay out here on the road long enough, you'll find out. By now I imagine Fleming's whole staff is looking for me."

"Run off, huh? How'd you get away?"

"I knocked Fleming out with the butt of his pistol." Hugh was becoming impatient.

He was surprised when both of the men laughed heartily. "In our army they'll make you a major for that!" the friendlier of the pair declared. "Get off that there horse and come with us. We'll see what Lieutenant Talbot has to say about you."

Hugh dismounted, and the more suspicious of the men reached for the reins, but withdrew his hand quickly when Toby, craning his long neck, reached down to bite him. "My horse," Hugh said quietly, "doesn't like strangers." He took the reins himself, and, with one of the men leading the way and the other bringing up the rear, the party left the path and moved off into the forest of evergreens.

They walked for the better part of an hour, fording several small streams, and Hugh realized they were climbing constantly to higher ground. The forest was dense, and as it was difficult to lead Toby through the underbrush, progress was slow, but they came at last to a clearing behind the crest of a hill, and the leader paused, cupped his hands, and called, "Liberty!"

Several mature men, some armed with rifles, others with old-fashioned muskets, appeared from the forest surrounding the clearing. "Maybe we've got a new recruit and maybe we've caught a spy," the militiaman behind Hugh said. "We can't figure which he is, so we'll let Lieutenant Talbot decide. Leave your horse here with us."

Hugh didn't like the greed he saw in some of the men's eyes when they stared at Toby. "My horse stays with me," he replied curtly.

There was a moment's hesitation, and no one seemed inclined to argue with him. "This way," a heavy-set man in his forties said, and waved Hugh into the far side of the clearing.

They walked for a short time, then paused at the entrance to a cave. The pair who had captured Hugh had accompanied him, and both of them disappeared inside, emerging some moments later with a tall, frail-looking man with white hair. "This is him, Parson." The suspicious man jerked a thumb in Hugh's direction.

"I'm the Reverend Henry Talbot." The white-haired man extended his hand.

"Didn't I hear you called 'Lieutenant' Talbot?" Hugh asked in surprise.

"I hold a commission from the State of Virginia, so I won't be practicing my vocation again until the end of the war. Now I want to hear about you."

Hugh told his story succinctly.

Talbot listened, and remained silent until the newcomer had finished. "A question or two. When you first came up this way, how many men did you meet?"

"Three."

"Did they give you their names?"

"No, sir."

"You don't happen to remember the date?"

"I do. It was Christmas."

Lieutenant Talbot smiled. "I don't think there's any doubt that you're Spencer." He turned to the men who were still hovering nearby. "He's no spy, boys. You can leave him with me."

The men disappeared into the forest.

"I imagine you know you face a series of serious charges if the Tories catch you, Spencer. You're a runaway bondsman, you assaulted your master and you stole his property. Each of those crimes is a hanging offense."

"I'd better see to it that they don't catch me, Lieutenant." It was difficult for Hugh to think of the elderly clergyman in sober black as an officer.

"Is that why you've come to us? Are you looking for protection?"

"I just heard today that the colonies have formed an independent country. I want to fight for that country."

"That's what Colonel Baxter told me before he went north, but I had to make certain." Talbot looked at Hugh for a moment, then sighed. "I'd like to keep you here, but there's real trouble in the making up in New York, so I'd better send you there, if that's agreeable."

"I'll go wherever I can be useful."

"According to what I hear, General Washington is going to face Billy Howe's whole army on Long Island. I have instructions to send the younger men up to him. We're keeping a few platoons of older militiamen here in case any trouble develops, but I don't think you'll see much fighting in these mountains."

"When can I leave, Lieutenant?"

"In three weeks, two if you're lucky."

Hugh was dismayed.

"There are too many Tories between here and New York to send you off alone. Now that independence has been declared, some of the lads who have been reluctant to join the Continentals will be making their way up here, and I'll send all of you together. You'll have a better chance of getting there."

"Forgive my ignorance, but what are Continentals?"

"The nearest thing we have to a regular army. Those who join the Continentals will stay in the army until we've whipped the British. The militia of the states only serve for three months at a time, and are free to go back to their homes when their period of enlistment is ended."

"I have no home," Hugh said, "and as I've learned what independence means, I want to fight until America is free. So I'll volunteer for the Continentals."

VIII / *October 1776*

THE rebel army was disintegrating, Sir William Howe said in a dispatch to the War Office in London in October 1776, and he predicted confidently that within another three to six months the Continental Congress would be unable to put a full battalion of able-bodied men in the field. Admiral Lord Howe, the general's brother, who was commander-in-chief of the British fleet in American waters, expressed himself even more forcefully in a letter to the Admiralty. He refused to dignify the operation in which he was engaged by calling it a war, he declared; his fleet was stamping out the last, flickering flames of a minor insurrection. It was true, he conceded, that the rebels held Boston and Philadelphia, and that the British had been repulsed at Charleston, South Carolina, but he jauntily promised to deliver the leaders of the rebellion to His Majesty's ministers within the next half year.

There seemed to be ample reason for the optimism of the British commanders. General Washington's raw militiamen had suffered a humiliating defeat at the hands of British regulars and German mercenary troops on Long Island late in August. Entire regiments of Americans had become panicky and had run from the field, and Washington, who had enjoyed fox-hunting before the war, had been forced to endure the mortification of hearing the British rally their men with hunting calls played derisively by brigade buglers.

Washington escaped to New York, but Howe, who outnumbered him by more than four to one, followed him to Manhattan. The Americans fought spiritedly for the first time, and many of the raw militiamen discovered that their enemies were mere humans who could be wounded or killed. But the odds against Washington were too great, and when Howe, who privately disapproved of the war, failed to annihilate the rebels, the Americans retreated again. Howe completed his occupation of New York in mid-September, and Washington began to move slowly through New Jersey toward Pennsylvania.

Hugh, who had fought on Long Island and in New York as a scout for the Blue Ridge regiment of Continentals, had been granted a commission as a lieutenant a few days before the retreat from Manhattan. He was a veteran now, and had grown accustomed to the easy informality of the Americans, which was so different from the rigid discipline he had known in the British Army. His one uniform of threadbare blue and buff was soiled and torn, but he was grateful he had enough clothes to withstand the chilly winds that swept across New Jersey in mid-October. And, like all of his comrades, he had learned that the quartermaster was unreliable and that men who wanted to eat had to forage for their food.

One night, after a slow march across fields that were turning brown, Hugh and several other officers were gathered around a campfire, where Colonel Abner Baxter, the regimental commander, joined them. Baxter, the leader of the trio who had stopped Hugh in the hills the preceding Christmas, halted and sniffed, then peered at the fire. The officers grinned at each other, then at him, and Hugh had to curb a desire to jump to attention, as the British always did when a superior joined them.

"I thought I smelled chicken," Baxter said. "Did you steal those birds?"

His son, Lieutenant Ned Baxter, still clad in the buckskins he had worn when Hugh had first seen him in the Blue Ridge foothills, looked up reproachfully. "You know us better than that, Pa. We try to set an example for our men."

The colonel's smile was reproving. "I know you well enough to ask the question."

A company commander who was turning the roasting chickens on a spit glanced up from his labor. "You forgot that we got paid yesterday, Colonel, after the Continental Congress printed a new batch of money. Spencer and Ned were riding with the vanguard this morning, and they found a farmer who was willing to accept some of those paper dollars for the chickens."

"There aren't many damn' fools like that left in the country, Pa," Ned added, "but it's the truth."

The colonel glanced at Hugh, who nodded.

"In that case," Baxter said with a sigh, "I'll join you." He squatted beside Hugh and stared moodily into the fire. "Colonel Caruthers told me that half of his regiment is leaving tomorrow. Their enlistments have expired, so they're going home, and he's going with them. We've been asked to take the rest into our ranks."

A burly battalion commander with a deceptively soft drawl brightened. "That will bring us up to full strength, or blame near it!"

"I'm only accepting those who will leave the militia and join the Continentals," Baxter replied. "I want soldiers, not farmers and carpenters and shopkeepers who will go home in a few days or weeks."

"Then we'll be lucky if we get twenty or thirty men," the battalion commander said gloomily.

"Day before yesterday I tried to talk some New Englanders into transferring to us," a captain said, "but they wouldn't have any part of Virginians."

"We can't build a new nation overnight." The colonel was still staring into the fire. "Eventually they'll learn that being an American is more important than being a New Hampshireman or a Virginian."

There was a silence, broken only by the crackling of the burning logs and the sizzling of fat dropping into the flames. Suddenly Ned Baxter stirred. "Hugh, you used to be a redcoat, so maybe you understand the game that Billy Howe is playing with us. Why doesn't he attack us good and hard? He could end the war with one more battle."

"You don't have to be a redcoat to know what's in his mind," Hugh said. "Men are killed and wounded on both sides in battles. General Howe is beating us without fighting. It's enough for him to chase us across New Jersey."

"Spencer is right, I'm afraid," the colonel said grimly. "The army shrinks more and more every day, and the civilians are giving up hope. General Knox was saying at a conference of senior commanders last night that hundreds of citizens in these middle states are turning Tory and taking an oath of allegiance to King George."

The conversation was interrupted when a mounted courier whose white armband identified him as a member of the commander-in-chief's staff rode up to the fire. The officers thought he had come to summon the colonel to a meeting, and no one was more surprised than Hugh to hear the man ask, "Is Lieutenant Spencer here?"

Hugh stood.

"You're wanted at headquarters right away," the courier told him.

Puzzled, Hugh turned away from the fire. "Save me one of those chickens, Ned."

The colonel followed him a few feet. "You may not be eating one of them tonight, lad, but we'll remember that the Blue Ridge regiment owes you a roasted chicken." He gripped Hugh's hand. "I gambled on you when you joined us, and I won. So this isn't good-by. We'll meet again, I know."

Before the startled Hugh could question him, he returned to the fire.

"Ready to go, Lieutenant?" the courier asked impatiently.

"My horse is over there, at the vanguard bivouac." Hugh, more disturbed than he was willing to admit to himself, hurried to the place where Toby was tethered, quickly saddled the stallion, and mounted. "Lead the way," he said.

The courier started across an open field, skirting the area where a regiment of Pennsylvania militia had camped.

"Do you know who wants to see me and why I've been called?"

The courier shrugged. "I do what I'm told. The sergeant of the guard said somebody on the staff wanted you. That's all I know." Twisting in his saddle, the man studied Toby. "That's a mighty fine horse you've got, Lieutenant. There's an officer at headquarters—I'm not mentioning any names—who told me to keep my eyes open for a new mount for him."

"This animal isn't for sale," Hugh replied firmly.

"For a stallion like this one, he'll pay a thousand Continental dollars, maybe even more."

Hugh tried to terminate the discussion by laughing.

"I don't blame you, Lieutenant. A thousand Continental dollars isn't worth much today, and by tomorrow it'll be worth half as much. But this officer really wants a new mount, so you could persuade him to pay you in good English pounds."

The cause of the United States was dismal, Hugh thought, when a soldier on the staff of the commander-in-chief of the Continental army spoke scornfully of his country's money and referred to that of the enemy as "good."

The messenger, aware that he had made no impression, stopped talking and spurred his gelding. Hugh had to hold in the stallion, and after a ride of a quarter of an hour they approached a white frame farmhouse. Lights were burning in virtually every room of the three-story building, sentries were stationed at the front door, and another pair circled the house constantly, so it was obvious that this was Washington's headquarters for the night.

Hugh left his horse with one of the guards, and, following

the messenger inside, started down a corridor toward a flight of stairs. He passed a room in which an officer was copying a document, and recognized the commander-in-chief's aide, Captain Alexander Hamilton. Hugh knew him slightly and was tempted to see if Hamilton knew why he had been summoned, but he resisted the urge and followed the courier to the second floor.

The man halted outside the closed door of a bedroom. "This is where I leave you, Lieutenant," he said, and hurried away.

Hugh tapped at the door, and when a man with a deep voice told him to enter, he faced a captain in blue and buff, a serious, dark-haired officer in his early twenties. The captain returned Hugh's salute and extended his hand. "Ben Tallmadge of Connecticut, Spencer. You can sit on the chair over there or on the bed. Take your choice."

"I haven't felt the mattress of a real bed for weeks," Hugh replied, and moved to the four-poster that occupied half of the small chamber.

Tallmadge chuckled sympathetically. "When I was in the infantry and slept on the ground," he said, "I dreamed about beds constantly. Now that I'm on the general's staff I'm assigned a bed most nights, but I have so much work to do that I get very little chance to sleep." His smile faded and his eyes became solemn. "Maybe you've heard about my department?"

"No, sir."

"Good. The less that's said about it, the better I can operate. The general has made me the chief of his intelligence section." Tallmadge paused for a moment. "You first came to my attention when we were defending Harlem Heights, Lieutenant, and I've learned a great deal about you since then."

Hugh's face felt stiff, and he wondered whether he would be deprived of his commission because of his conviction by an English court.

"Is it true," Tallmadge asked calmly, "that you were a counterfeiter?"

"No!" Hugh replied vehemently. "I was the innocent pawn of some criminals who used me to save their own skins."

"I'm sorry to hear it," Captain Tallmadge murmured.

Too incensed to listen, Hugh told his whole story, openly admitting for the first time that he had allowed himself to be fooled by the girl who had called herself Sara Dean.

When he was finished, Tallmadge sighed wistfully. "Assuming that you've told me the truth, and I have no reason to believe otherwise, you know nothing about counterfeiting, I gather?"

"I'm no expert, Captain, but before I was deported and sold as a bond servant, I had the idea of finding the people who were responsible for my situation. So I made it my business to learn all I could from my cellmate, who had been a counterfeiter for years, and as we were deported together, I learned still more from him on board the brig that brought us to Philadelphia."

"That sounds interesting," Tallmadge said, brightening.

His attitude mystified Hugh, who watched him in bewilderment as he reached into his tunic and drew out a wallet.

Tallmadge handed Hugh the wallet. "There are two ten-dollar bills printed by the Continental Congress in the front portion. Tell me which of them is counterfeit."

Hugh extracted the bills and examined them closely by the light of a candle burning in a saucer on top of a chest of drawers. "They're both false," he declared at last.

"What makes you think so?"

"This one is obvious. It was crudely printed, and in places even the ink is smudged. The other is a better imitation, but if you study the signatures, you'll see they were written by the same man."

"You show promise," Tallmadge replied. "Now open the back portion. You'll find several Rhode Island three-pound notes. Which are real and which are counterfeit?"

Hugh inspected them, turning them over and holding them up to the light, but finally he shrugged. "If I knew which of these is genuine, I might have some standard of comparison. But I'm afraid I've got to admit I don't know."

"That's part of our trouble. Every one of the thirteen states is making its own money. A Georgian can't distinguish between a good Rhode Island bill and a bad one, and a Rhode Islander doesn't know real Georgia money from counterfeit."

"The man who taught me the little that I know could take one glance at these and give you the right answer, but my experience is too limited."

"Where is this counterfeiter?"

"He was sold as a bondsman to a Philadelphia printer, but I don't know what's become of him lately."

Tallmadge took the wallet, replaced the notes carefully, and stood. "I believe I've made the right choice. Come with me."

He led the way down to the ground floor and left Hugh waiting in the corridor while he conferred with Captain Hamilton. Then he disappeared into an inner office, and Hamilton, after a brief smile at Hugh, returned to the document he was copying. After what seemed like a long wait, the inner door opened, and Hamilton jumped to his feet. "Don't stand there, Spencer," he said urgently. "The general doesn't like to be kept waiting."

The commander-in-chief was seated behind a desk on which a large map of New Jersey was spread, and Hugh, who had seen him from a distance on numerous occasions, thought he looked even colder and more remote when he raised his head and glanced across the room. His blue eyes were piercing, his high forehead gave him a scholarly appearance, and although he was only forty-four years old, there were deep lines of fatigue in his face. However, his neckcloth was immaculate, there was no trace of dust on his uniform, and he had changed into a fresh white shirt and waistcoat after the day's march.

Hugh stood at rigid attention and saluted sharply.

General Washington's voice was surprisingly quiet and gentle. "Sit down, Mr. Spencer. It isn't often I see a salute like that. How I wish our army could be trained properly. Ah, well. All in good time." His tone changed, and he spoke more briskly. "I suppose you realize that Captain Tallmadge wants to use your talents for a special purpose."

"I've begun to suspect he might have something of the sort in mind, sir."

Tallmadge, who was standing near a hearth in which several hickory logs were blazing, grinned broadly.

"I have very few experienced officers, Mr. Spencer, so you can understand why I'm reluctant to detach one of them from military duty. However, this is a war without precedent. Our fortunes are at a low ebb at the moment, but they'll rise, and eventually we'll have an army of trained veterans who will expel the British from our soil. But all of our problems aren't military. Counterfeiting should be the concern of Congress, but the gentlemen in Philadelphia are too busy squabbling over petty politics of one sort or another to pay any heed to my requests. So I've got to take action myself. If we lose public confidence, we may lose the war."

Washington was sharp rather than cold, Hugh thought, admiring the commander-in-chief's incisive manner.

"I'm not suggesting that we may lose. Nothing will ever convince me that we're beaten, and if necessary, I shall fall back behind the Allegheny Mountains and establish a citadel in the Ohio Valley. But I prefer not to dwell on such a circumstance. At the moment, Mr. Spencer, you're my problem. Colonel Baxter has recommended you highly, and Captain Tallmadge wants you. Well and good. But I have a question or two. Suppose the crown granted you a complete pardon for the crime you say you didn't commit. Would you return to England?"

"No, sir. I've joined the Continental army, and I don't intend to leave it until we've become completely independent."

Washington's aristocratic charm became apparent on the rare occasions when he smiled. "And after the war?"

"I plan to settle down somewhere, sir. I know only two vocations, soldiering and farming, so I've thought of claiming some of the free land that the members of Congress keep promising us west of the mountains."

Washington's eyes seemed to cut through Hugh. "North America is a large continent, Mr. Spencer, and the French, who already own vast quantities of land, are offering very attractive inducements to settlers. You escaped from the Tory who bought your bond, and you're under obligation to no one. So why don't you go west now and accept land from the French?"

"My conscience and my principles wouldn't permit it, sir," Hugh replied firmly. "I don't take an oath lightly, and I swore a solemn one when I joined this army. And I agree completely with Mr. Jefferson's Declaration of Independence. I've read it many times in the past few months, and I prefer the American concept of government to the French system. I'm not partial to monarchies."

The commander-in-chief smiled broadly and nodded to Ben Tallmadge. "If he'll accept the assignment, you may have him, Captain."

"Thank you, sir."

"Do you want me to take this post, General?" Hugh asked.

"I think you could do the United States a great service, Mr. Spencer, but I have a conscience too, and I can't order you to give up military life in the field for work that may be unpleasant and hazardous."

"It's enough for me that you want me to take the assignment, sir. I'll accept it."

Washington stood and shook hands, terminating the interview. "I'll keep in touch with your activities through Tallmadge. Call on me if you need my help at any time. You might stop at Hamilton's desk on your way out and ask him to prepare an order promoting you to captain," he added casually. "You'll find the additional rank useful, and if our money ever has any value, I imagine you can find ways to spend the higher pay."

A short time later Hugh was closeted with Tallmadge again in the room on the second floor. "I suggest," the intelligence chief said, "that you try to find the counterfeiter you know and persuade him to enlist. I'll get some blank forms from Captain Hamilton so you can appoint your own sergeants and corporals. Build up a force of whatever size you may need. I don't care what caliber of men you recruit. All that matters is the results."

"I'll do my best," Hugh assured him, "but I don't know if you're serious when you suggest that I enlist rogues."

"I know no other way to catch counterfeiters, Captain Spencer."

Hugh flushed when he heard himself being called by his new rank; then he laughed. "Whether we succeed or fail, I'm sure the brigade of scoundrels will be the most unusual unit in the world's most unorthodox army."

IX / *November 1776*

"WE'RE the kind, you and me, who are lucky." Benjy sat near a window that looked out on a small sign reading, J. RICHARDSON AND B. FLAHERTY, PRINTERS.

"In your case it was skill that improved your situation, not luck." Hugh unbuckled his sword belt and rested his blade on a small table near his friend's desk.

"I'd still be a bondsman if it wasn't for Mr. Richardson being a patriot and America becoming independent. It's true that there aren't many printers who know more about their trade than I do, and that's why Mr. Richardson offered me a quarter interest in the business when he gave me my freedom. I brought in plenty of work, so it's been fair to both of us. But what if I hadn't been deported to America? I might still be sitting in a cell at Newgate. That's what I mean by luck."

Hugh worded a question carefully. "Have you found much time to practice your former profession?"

"I gave it up," Benjy said flatly. "I had to. It's odd, when you think about it." He gestured toward the presses and boxes of lead type at the rear of the shop. "I have all the equipment I need here, even engraving tools and copper bleach. But we have a contract to print all of the broadsides and pamphlets for the Pennsylvania Committee of Public Safety, and we do some jobs for other states, too, mostly Delaware and New Jersey. So I can't print their official papers and copy their money at the same time. It wouldn't be right, and besides, they could trace the notes to me too quick. Anyway," he added gloomily, "money hereabouts isn't worth much lately, so it isn't worth the effort to make counterfeit bills."

Hugh concealed a smile. It was clear that Benjy's standards of right and wrong were unchanged; what had prompted him to give up his criminal career was the small margin of profit he enjoyed. "I can see why you became discouraged."

"You can't earn a living here these days, no matter what you do." Benjy picked up a jar of Frankfort black, the best quality of printer's ink, and rolled it between his hands. "First we had to wait for months to get a new supply of ink, while our customers pestered us every day, begging us to get their work done. Then, by the time the ink arrived, people didn't want printing jobs any more. Philadelphia is so scared these days that nobody is doing normal business any more." He peered at Hugh anxiously, deep lines of worry between his eyes. "Do you think the British are going to take the city?"

"If Howe wants it, and I assume he does, I don't believe we can stop him," Hugh replied honestly. "But I can promise you that he won't keep it. General Washington won't stop fighting until he's driven every last redcoat out of the country."

"You sound just like all them other officers who work for him. How can he beat the best army and navy in the world? Is he some kind of magician?"

"Accept my offer, Benjy, and you'll find out for yourself."

"I got to admit I'm tempted. I talked to Mr. Richardson after I saw you this morning, and he's agreeable enough. There's barely enough orders these days to support one man, but he'll keep my partnership for me, and I can come back when the war ends."

"You won't earn much in the army," Hugh warned him, "and there are times when you may go hungry."

"I know what it feels like to be hungry." Benjy replaced the jar of ink on the desk with a thump. "Don't laugh at me, but I feel I owe something to this country. I can walk down the street and look square in the eye at anybody I see. That never happened to me in England. So if I can do something for the United States, maybe I owe it to myself. Nobody cares what I was before I came here. Nobody even minds that I was a bondsman. But if the English win this war, I'll be just a dirty little counterfeiter again."

Hugh was forced to revise his previous estimate; the change in his friend was far greater than he had imagined.

"If I join the army as your sergeant, I won't have to take orders from anybody except you, is that right? And I won't have to do any fighting?"

Hugh nodded and couldn't refrain from laughing. It was impossible to picture Benjy participating in a battle. "We won't face enemy troops in the field, but we might become involved in some nasty situations."

Benjy was relieved. "They couldn't be worse than some I've been in. I can take care of myself fine, even though it will feel peculiar to be chasing counterfeiters. All that worries me is what will happen if I've got to arrest a friend."

The possibility had occurred to Hugh, and he made light of it. "I hope that most of the men you've known will join our unit."

"Offhand, the only ones I can locate for certain are the Simpson brothers, down in Wilmington. They come to Philadelphia now and again, but their luck has been bad lately, and I haven't seen them for a couple of months. There's no better coin artist than Dave Simpson, not counting me, and Dick is as good as most at making paper money. They turned out some fair Delaware half crowns and two-shilling pieces a few years ago, and for a time they did a lively trade in four-pound notes. But they can't get the materials they need, so they went to work at the docks. Like I say, their luck has been bad. The British blockade has stopped most shipping, so there aren't any brigs to unload."

"What are they doing these days?"

"Any kind of work they can get."

"Then they might be willing to join us."

"I could find out. Mr. Richardson says he'll release me any time I want to go, but it will take a few days to have a uniform made." Apparently Benjy didn't realize he was committing himself.

Hugh gave him no chance to change his mind. "I'll administer the oath right now, and give you your sergeant's warrant."

There was no escape, and Benjy shook his head. "I never thought the day would come when I'd be a bailiff," he muttered.

Washington retreated into Pennsylvania, and Hugh, hampered by a lack of funds, set up a bivouac for himself and his unusual little unit at one end of the Continental Army's camp. Each day he and his men rode into Philadelphia, where they followed a set routine. Benjy, who had become acquainted with many of the city's businessmen, called on merchants and examined the money in their strongboxes. The Simpson brothers, burly men in their early thirties with scarred faces, looked like the desperadoes they were, and presented something of a problem, as respectable citizens were reluctant to deal with them. Hugh solved the dilemma, however, by giving each the rank of corporal and securing funds from Captain Tallmadge to provide them with neat uniforms which a Philadelphia tailor made for them. Dave Simpson, who drank no spirits, visited tavern keepers and the owners of inns, and Dick called on the proprietors of small shops. Hugh reserved the most delicate task for himself and made appointments with members of the Continental Congress, officials of the Pennsylvania Committee of Public Safety, and

the Tory sympathizers, most of them wealthy, who co-oper-
ated with him grudgingly.

At the end of each day Hugh made a careful list of all
counterfeit money that he and his men had found, but after
a month of painstaking labor he had little of importance to
show for the work that had been done. Counterfeit notes
from each of the thirteen states were numerous, but Dick
Simpson and Benjy agreed that they had been made by a
scattering of minor felons, most of whom were satisfied to take
a small profit and then destroy their equipment. Occasionally
one or another member of the unit found a forged Continental
Congress bill of excellent workmanship, and the men agreed
the money might have been manufactured by the same person. Some Rhode Island notes appeared to be the product of
a master craftsman, too, but there weren't enough of them
in circulation to offer Hugh any significant leads.

Suddenly, on December 11, the city was flooded with counterfeit money, and several irate congressmen were so incensed
they wrote a letter to the harassed Washington, demanding
that something be done immediately to stop the traffic. The
general, who was engrossed in plans to strike a counterblow
against the enemy in order to improve his army's spirits, replied in a brief note that he was confident the culprits would
be caught soon. Hugh received a copy of the communication
from Tallmadge, who saw no need to add a comment of his
own, and the unit redoubled its efforts to discover why so
much "bad money" had appeared simultaneously.

The Simpson brothers were inclined toward the belief that
a Philadelphia counterfeiter was responsible, but Benjy dis-
agreed. The Continental dollars and Rhode Island pounds
had not been made by the same people, he said; the ink and
paper were different, the dollars had been printed, but some
sort of tracing process had been used to reproduce the
pounds, and he suspected that the forger had used a fine
crow's-quill pen to copy the signatures of five Rhode Island
officials. Hugh was inclined to accept his friend's reasoning,

and tried to reconstruct every important event that had taken place during the two days prior to the sudden appearance of the counterfeit money.

At first the task seemed hopeless, as scores of people moved in and out of Philadelphia each day, and there was no way to investigate the background of every farmer, soldier, and merchant who had visited the city. However, as there had been too many notes for individuals to have carried them on their persons, it was reasonable to assume they had been brought to Philadelphia in vehicles, and Hugh's suspicions finally centered on a convoy carrying mail, food, and cloth that had been sent from New York and had passed through the British sentry lines.

"General Howe has been sending such a convoy every month," Hugh told Benjy thoughtfully. "He claims he's trying to be compassionate, and says he doesn't want civilians to suffer unnecessary hardships."

"I never got anything for nothing in England," Benjy replied sourly, "and I don't trust redcoat charity."

"It may be that Howe's only motive is the one that appears on the surface. He doesn't try to hide his dislike for crown policy, and he's made several public statements to the effect that he thinks a demonstration of leniency and tolerance will cause everyone except the radicals to take an oath of allegiance to the king."

"Nobody in New York sends me any letters, and I'd rather eat fresh-baked bread than soggy biscuits made by Tory sympathizers."

"So would I, Benjy. I'm just trying to understand the reasons for Billy Howe's generosity. It may be a coincidence that the last convoy arrived here on the afternoon of December tenth and the counterfeit money was passed into circulation on the eleventh. But someone on Howe's staff may be playing a diabolical trick on us. The value of the dollar has dropped again."

"I found that to be true this morning when I wanted to

buy some new boots from a man right down the street from Mr. Richardson's print shop. I know the owner and he knows me. He offered me a special bargain. I saw a pair of boots with soles as thin as the paper in a Massachusetts two-pound note, and he said he'd sell them to me for fifty dollars. Last month I would have paid half that much for them." Benjy stared down at his old boots. "I'll have to keep what I have."

Hugh was too absorbed to sympathize with him. "I may be following a blind lead, but we won't have to wait long to learn whether I'm right or wrong. I was told today that the provost has signed a permit allowing a special convoy to bring more food and supplies here for Christmas, so we'll be on hand to meet it."

The convoy of forty wagons arrived on December 23, and a large crowd gathered on the grounds of the Statehouse, which was now being called Independence Hall, to watch the unpacking of the merchandise. The day was cold and there were snow flurries in the air, but the people didn't mind the weather as they stared wistfully at the wagons piled high with barrels of English beef and pork. Food had been scarce in recent weeks because farmers were reluctant to sell their produce in return for the dollars that the Continental Congress was printing. A murmur of appreciation ran through the crowd, but the sound changed to dismay when a battalion of two hundred Continental infantrymen marched onto the lawn and surrounded the wagons.

A man with a deep voice protested loudly. "The British sent that food for civilians, not for the army!"

"Get your own meat!" a woman shouted. "My children and I are hungry."

Hugh, who had obtained the services of the battalion through Captain Tallmadge, conferred briefly with the unit's commander. "I'm reluctant to tell them why you're here, Major. If there are counterfeiters' accomplices in that crowd, they'd be scared away."

The commander looked for a moment at the people who

were beginning to surge toward the lines of his men. "You'll have to tell them something, Spencer, or we'll have a riot on our hands. And I'm damned if I want American soldiers firing at American citizens."

Hugh jumped onto the rear of the nearest cart, and, hanging on to the tail gate with one hand, he waved for silence. "You'll get your food!" he shouted, and had to repeat the statement twice before the people became calmer.

"Prove it, Captain!" the deep-voiced man called. "Get away from our property!"

Hugh made an attempt to grin and speak calmly. "General Washington hasn't sunk so low that he wants alms from Billy Howe!"

The crowd was pleased by his retort, and a number of citizens smiled up at him.

"We're here for a reason." Hugh paused and scanned the faces below him, but if anyone was waiting to receive a supply of counterfeit money, it was impossible to distinguish him from an ordinary, honest person. "We have cause to believe that some explosives may be packed in these carts."

Some of the wagon drivers laughed derisively, and Hugh couldn't blame them. His charge was absurd, and the drivers knew it, but the people accepted his statement without question and backed away from the line of troops.

"We intend to search every barrel and every package," Hugh continued. "But you're welcome to stay and assure yourselves that we aren't going to steal one biscuit or one piece of beef. If we find any bombs that might blow up half the city, I dare say you'll be happy to let us take them."

Several men smiled more broadly, but a few of the women inched toward the rear of the throng.

"Sergeant Flaherty!" Hugh called sternly.

Benjy stepped forward and, aware that he was performing before an audience, saluted clumsily. "Yes, sir?"

"Begin your inspection. As you pass each item, release it to the representatives of the butchers' and bakers' guilds."

"Yes, sir." Benjy beckoned to the Simpson brothers, and the trio moved to the cart at the head of the line.

The soldiers stood with their backs to the supplies and, their bayonets fixed, continued to watch the crowd. Everything seemed to be under control, at least for the moment, so Hugh joined his subordinates. They examined every box of biscuits, every roll of blankets, and opened every barrel of meat, but found no counterfeit notes anywhere, and when the citizens saw that the supplies were being delivered to officials of the various food guilds, who had assembled their own carts outside the military cordon, people lost interest in the search.

Hugh continued his examination doggedly, and it was late in the afternoon before he was prepared to admit to himself that his reasoning had been false. The Simpsons were looking at the pickled pork in the last two carts, Benjy was rummaging through a sack of mail, and the drivers of the carts, who had resented the investigation from the start, were becoming impatient. It would be humiliating to notify Captain Tallmadge that he had failed, Hugh thought, and that he had wasted the precious time of a battalion that the army needed elsewhere. But he had been mistaken, and as he plunged his cold hands into the pockets of his greatcoat, which he had purchased with his previous month's wages, he wished Tallmadge would release him and send him back to the Blue Ridge regiment. He was a soldier, not a counterfeiter-catcher, and he was as irritated as he was chilly.

"Hey, Captain, when are you going to let us go?" one of the drivers demanded belligerently.

Hugh was so annoyed he forgot diplomacy. "You'll leave when I release you!" The drivers didn't know it, but he planned to subject each of them to a personal search before he conceded complete defeat.

"We came through the lines on a safe-conduct pledge signed by three of your generals. Is this the way rebels keep their promises?" The man was shouting at the top of his voice now.

"Rebels?" Hugh stared at the man, and, forgetting the cold, let his anger take possession of him. "You're speaking to an officer in the army of the United States of America, you miserable Tory. The safe-conduct pledge doesn't grant you the license to insult the free citizens of a free nation!" He slapped the bare floor of an empty cart to emphasize his words.

The driver backed away, muttering apologetically, and hurried off to the far side of the cordon to join several of his colleagues.

Hugh realized that something odd had just happened, and was puzzled for a moment. Then, suddenly, he realized that the floor board had moved when he had struck it, and he turned to the wagon quickly. The board had slid the better part of an inch out of position, and Hugh knew instinctively that he had discovered the secret of the smugglers. He ripped the board aside, moved three others, and, in his excitement, completely forgot military etiquette.

"Benjy!" he called.

The note of urgency in his voice brought Benjy, the Simpson brothers, and four of the battalion's officers to his side.

Hugh pointed at the flooring, his face grim.

"I'll be damned," Benjy said. "We've spent hours looking for something that's been right under our noses."

"False flooring on carts is one of the oldest tricks in the world," Dave Simpson said. "A cousin of my father's spent four and a half years in Newgate because he was caught avoiding the customs tax collectors at Southampton that way."

Hugh recovered his breath. "Remove the flooring of every cart," he said sharply. "And Major, I'll be obliged if you'll assign a platoon to make certain that none of the wagon drivers escape. Maybe they knew what they were carrying and maybe they were innocent, but I want to talk to every last one of them."

The commander of the troops gave an order, and the drivers were surrounded by soldiers who paid no attention to outraged comments about "safe-conduct pledges."

Benjy and the Simpsons worked feverishly, prying up floor boards, and after an hour's intensive search they discovered counterfeit money in five of the forty carts. Hugh stuffed the notes into burlap sacks, keeping count of the sums, and the total was staggering. Someone had tried to smuggle more than two hundred thousand dollars in false Continental bills into Philadelphia. There were smaller denominations of forged notes from several states, too, including eight hundred pounds in Massachusetts pounds, nine hundred North Carolina dollars and almost two thousand Rhode Island pounds.

The drivers of all the wagons except those in which the counterfeit money had been carried were released. The five prisoners claimed they knew nothing about the false flooring and stubbornly insisted they had been hired to do a specific job; they neither owned the wagons nor had they been told the contents. Each swore that he was being paid three pounds to carry out his task, and that he had no idea how the money had been placed in the cart that had been assigned to him.

Hugh was unable to prove any of the men guilty, but took no chances and sent all five to Captain Tallmadge under guard. Then, exhausted but triumphant after winning his first victory, he divided the notes into four bundles, handed a sack to each of his men, and, carrying more than seventy-five thousand dollars in bogus Continental notes, he mounted Toby. Riding off in the gathering darkness toward his bivouac outside the city, he became immersed in thought, and one conclusion seemed obvious to him: the men who were responsible for making the money and smuggling it through the lines not only were professional criminals, but they threatened the future of the United States.

x / *March 1777*

WASHINGTON faced a cruel choice in the last days of 1776. His army had shrunk to a force of less than five thousand men, civilian spirits drooped, and even members of the Continental Congress began to speculate on the possible surrender terms they could obtain from the crown. Some senior officers believed that the only sensible course of action would be to retire across the mountains and force the British to follow the remnants of the army into the heart of the continent. But the commander-in-chief was reluctant to abandon the seaboard, and, feeling certain that a series of victories would revive public confidence, he struck boldly. On Christmas night he recrossed the Delaware and his surprise attack routed the redcoats and German mercenaries who made up the garrison at Trenton.

The Americans took more than one thousand prisoners in the brief but vicious fight, and Lord Cornwallis, General Howe's deputy, was sent from New York to disperse the impudent Yankees. Washington wisely avoided a pitched battle with Cornwallis, however, and instead struck another unexpected blow, overwhelming the enemy garrison at Princeton on January 3. The British, confused and frightened, withdrew their remaining garrisons from New Jersey, leaving Washington in possession of the entire state and temporarily relieving the threat against Philadelphia.

The people responded as enthusiastically as Washington had hoped, and volunteers came from every state to join him, bringing his total strength to twelve thousand men. But American independence had not yet been won and Ben Tallmadge, now a major, explained the situation candidly to Hugh when they met by prearrangement one evening in March at a Philadelphia inn. They sat together before a small fire in the bedchamber they had engaged for the night, and Tallmadge, rubbing his bony hands together, stared gloomily into the flames.

"Folks don't realize it, but the worst is yet to come," he said. "Howe is going to leave his winter quarters in New York soon, and at best we can delay him. Our new troops are untrained militia, and they'll need a few battle scars before they're worth much to us. Some supply ships are sneaking through the British blockade, but Admiral Howe has managed to cut us off from the world pretty effectively. You tell me that counterfeit money is starting to appear again, so people will become disillusioned with Congress and the governments of the states. Have you read that new pamphlet of Tom Paine's? He's right when he says, 'These are the times that try men's souls.' I'm afraid our worst year is ahead of us."

"When do you suppose we'll begin to pull ahead?" It didn't occur to Hugh, any more than it did to Tallmadge, that the Americans would give up the struggle.

"After we've won some major victories. We need the help of France, but Mr. Franklin has written from Paris to the general that we aren't going to get it until King Louis' ministers are convinced that we're strong enough to become a respectable ally. And we've got to prove that we're stable, capable of governing ourselves."

"We can't control prices, that's certain, not when so much counterfeit money is being passed. Did you notice the way the barmaid who served us our supper tonight acted when we paid her? She studied every note that we gave her. Every-one else is doing the same thing."

"Let's look on the bright side." Tallmadge forced a smile. "There have been only a few forged Continental dollars show up since you made your big haul just before Christmas."

"That's because Congress finally took our advice and changed the design of its money," Hugh replied. "I'm begin-ning to understand how the counterfeiters work, and I expect to see a whole crop of false notes as soon as the engravers have an opportunity to copy the new money."

"You have no idea who might be making the dollars?"

"None. Every clue I get vanishes into the air. Benjy Fla-herty and Dick Simpson are clever men, so clever that I'm glad we have them on our side. But they're every bit as con-fused as I am. Those coinmakers we arrested last month after Dave Simpson's investigation were petty rogues who had been clipping Milanese sequins and Spanish pieces of eight that they used to coat pewter coins, but their operation was a small one."

Tallmadge sighed, and his chair squeaked as he rocked back and forth. "I'm not asking you to perform impossible tasks, but we've got to put a stop to the flow of forged money. We can't win victories in the field without the support of the people."

"General Washington can't build an army overnight, and I need time to create my sources of information, too," Hugh said. "There's one good sign that I can report to you, Major. I've been corresponding with the provost generals and attor-ney generals of every state, and they've started to co-operate with me. So I should be able to trace the false Continental dollars to their source eventually."

Tallmadge laughed cheerlessly. "Whenever I take a new man into the department, I tell him that the quality an in-telligence agent needs most is patience. I ought to practice what I preach."

"Well, most of the states are reporting fewer forgeries now.

The counterfeiters are becoming more careful. Flaherty says it's because they realize that there's a real campaign under way to catch them."

"I'll report that back to the general. Maybe it will help to cheer him up a little, provided anything will improve his disposition when he knows that sooner or later Howe is going to take Philadelphia from him."

"I wish," Hugh said fervently, "that I could go back into the field."

"If you still feel the same way after you've caught the men who are making the Continental dollars, I'll grant your wish, Captain."

Hugh smiled wryly. "Thanks for your generosity. I think you realize that I haven't yet captured one important counterfeiter."

"You've done valuable work for the United States."

There had been a time when the praise would have pleased Hugh, but he was so engrossed in his assignment that nothing short of major results would satisfy him. "Maybe I'll have some better news to give you in the next few weeks, Major."

Tallmadge looked at him questioningly.

"I'm taking my men up to Providence in the next day or two. The roads are clear again, and I think I may catch a few fish up there."

"Do you have reason to believe the dollars are being forged in Providence?"

"No, sir. But there's a steady stream of Rhode Island pounds coming out of the state that have been stirring up mischief, so I'm hoping I can put at least one clever professional out of business. I've been corresponding with the Rhode Island authorities since early in January, and they're giving me their full support, so there's reason to believe we may make a significant arrest. I'm not forgetting that there was a considerable quantity of forged Rhode Island money in that haul we made just before Christmas."

"Do you have any reason to think there might be a connection between the Rhode Island forgers and the men who are making the Continental dollars?"

Hugh laughed again. "Common sense tells me to take one step at a time, Major, but I'm afraid I'm no more patient than you. I have hopes—but no real basis for them."

Thaddeus Green, the provost general of Rhode Island, stood with Hugh before a large state map that was tacked to a wall. "I had this prepared for you, Captain Spencer," he said. "I have a small staff and they're so busy helping ship captains run the British blockade that they haven't been able to spend much time on this job. But the work they've done shows a few results, I think."

Hugh was studying the map carefully. "You say that each one of these pins represents a letter or some other complaint that you've received, Mr. Green."

"Correct, Captain. I had no men to spare for a personal investigation, so I used the easiest system. It's logical to assume that most of the counterfeit money will appear somewhere near its source."

"If you're right," Hugh said slowly, "the people who have been cheated have done us a bigger favor than they realize. Their letters of complaint have come chiefly from one area."

Pins filled the southwestern corner of the map, obliterating the name of a town near the Connecticut border. "That's Westerly," the provost general said. "Folks there have been fooled by so much bad money they shy away from all Rhode Island paper. One week they've been taken in by false two-pound notes, the next by four-pound. We almost had a rebellion on our hands in February, and a company of militia that was going off to join General Washington had to go to Westerly instead. We restored order after a few days, but you won't find anybody in the town who'll take paper as payment for a debt. They insist on being paid in silver, and they test it first."

"Do the people there have any ideas that might be helpful to us?"

"They've got their suspicions, Captain, but the sheriff has no proof, and he doesn't want to get folks stirred up. Feelings run high in wartime, and it would be a black mark against the state's good name if somebody who is innocent got killed."

The trail seemed to lead in only one direction, and the following day Hugh and his three companions arrived in the sleepy town of Westerly on the Pawcatuck River. Most of the citizens, including the sheriff, Jed Lane, seemed to be engaged in smuggling merchandise through the British blockade, and Hugh had to wait at the sheriff's tiny one-room office for several hours because, as a woman who lived nearby explained, two ships carrying contraband from the West Indies had cast anchor off the neighboring seaport, Watch Hill, at dawn.

Lane appeared at noon, tired after spending a morning unloading cargo, and, contrary to Hugh's expectations, gave the visitors a hostile reception. "We've had enough trouble with the government up in Providence, and last month a delegation from Newport gave me no peace. Now you Continentals are shoving your noses into our business. It was bad enough when those militiamen ate us out of house and home early last month. We've learned to manage our own affairs by refusing to accept paper money, and we have our own fish to fry, so why don't you go back where you came from?"

"Sheriff," Hugh said firmly, "you have your duty to perform. If somebody commits a murder or a robbery, you've got to arrest the man. Well, I'm in the same position. I have my orders, and I've got to carry them out. I'm here at the personal command of General Washington."

The mention of the commander-in-chief's name impressed Lane, as Hugh had hoped it would. "I feel right sorry for General Washington, and that's a fact, Captain. He needs all the help he can get, but I don't see how you're going to do any good around here."

"Provost General Green told me in Providence yesterday that you might know who has been making the counterfeit Rhode Island money that's been showing up all over the country."

"I might, but I might not." Lane's smile was tight-lipped, and he rubbed the side of his face wearily. "I've raided Black Ox farm four times, but I haven't found one scrap of evidence to convict that fellow, Dale."

"Who?"

"August Dale, he calls himself."

Benjy, who was standing near the door, started to speak, but changed his mind.

"I don't want to act ornery, Captain," the sheriff continued, "but I'm scared of what might happen if I go out to the Black Ox again. Nearly everybody in town has been taken in, one time or another, by forged money, and there's been so much feeling against Dale that he hasn't dared come into town since the riots. People here are quiet, but they might take it into their heads to lynch Dale if they got to believing that he's the rogue who cheated them."

"Can you tell me anything about this man?" Hugh persisted.

"There's not much to tell, and that's a fact. He came here nearly three years ago from Boston and bought Black Ox farm, as nice a piece of property as there is in the area. He minds his own business, he never annoys his neighbors and back in the days before folks got to mistrusting him, he'd come to the Westerly Tavern for a drop of rum or a mug of ale and then go home again. Nobody ever saw him drunk, and he's never had a quarrel with anybody in town."

The Simpson brothers, who had been listening carefully, lost interest in the recital.

Hugh was less than satisfied, however. "What made you guess—or suspect—that he might be a counterfeiter?"

"I don't have any hard evidence, and that's my trouble. Dale bought a fine piece of land, but he doesn't farm it, he doesn't raise livestock and he's not in any trade. But he seems to have all the money he needs, he makes trips to Providence and Boston, and before the redcoats took New York, he went down there every now and again. He pays his taxes regular, too. So what bothers me is, if he doesn't work for his money, where does he get it?"

The sheriff's logic seemed weak, and Hugh was disappointed. However, he had traveled many miles trying to find the Rhode Island counterfeiter and thought he should complete his assignment. "You wouldn't object if I went out to Black Ox farm and had a talk with Mr. Dale myself?"

The sheriff shrugged. "If you got nothing better to do, help yourself. All I ask is that you don't tell anybody around town where you're headed. Folks might get excited, and I'm too tired to stop a lynching party." He told Hugh how to find the farm, shook hands, and added, "Stop off on your way back through town, Captain. You and your boys will be thirsty, and you'll need a glass of spirits to make you feel better after you've wasted your afternoon. I'm keeping a keg of rum we brought ashore this morning, and you're welcome to sample it with me."

Hugh thanked him and followed the Simpsons into the quiet, rutted road. "Where is Benjy?" he asked, as they walked toward the hitching posts where their mounts were tethered.

"He told me he had to go to the crib out back," Dave Simpson said.

Hugh was puzzled. "His horse is gone. You might look for him, Dick."

"All right, Captain." The younger of the Simpson brothers went to the rear of the house and returned quickly. "He ain't there."

A sense of uneasiness crept over Hugh. "Well, he knows where we're going, so he'll have to meet us there, or else we'll look for him when we're done." Spurring Toby, he started up the street.

Following the sheriff's instructions, he led his companions past a church and a small schoolhouse, then rode through a small patch of woods and emerged on a trail that meandered across the hills. The last snow had melted, and buds were appearing on red maples, oaks, and elms. The district outside the town was sparsely settled, and houses were located at least a quarter of a mile apart. Most of the homes that Hugh saw were small and unpretentious, so he was surprised when, after a ride of almost ten miles, he approached a substantial three-story frame building. A low retaining wall of gray field stones ran parallel to the road, and a carved black oxen was nailed to the gate, which was closed.

"This is the place," Hugh said, and realized why the people of Westerly had entertained suspicions about August Dale. Anyone who could afford to buy such a place was obviously wealthy, and a man whose source of income was unknown would inevitably draw attention to himself when he owned the finest house in the area.

Dave Simpson dismounted and opened the gate, then ran back to his horse, and the trio rode up a winding path to the front door. Hugh, uncertain what to expect, wouldn't have been surprised to see Benjy's horse, but there was no sign of the gelding, and he tried to put his sergeant out of his mind. It was possible that he had come to the Black Ox farm on a fool's errand, and he hoped the owner of the establishment would accept his intrusion with good grace.

He raised a polished brass knocker, and almost as soon as it fell, the door opened. A man wearing a suit of well-tailored green wool smiled and nodded, and at first glance his hair appeared to be powdered, but Hugh saw that it was white, although the man himself was in his middle years.

"Mr. Dale?"

"I've been expecting you, Captain Spencer." August Dale spoke with the accent of a London aristocrat.

Instantly alert, Hugh and the Simpsons followed the man into a small sitting room, where, to their astonishment, Benjy was sitting in a chair near the hearth.

Grinning apologetically, Benjy stood. "I thought I'd come out ahead of you and start the investigation. That's why Mr. Dale knew you were coming."

Hugh's reply was indirect. "Dave," he said crisply to the elder Simpson, "go around to the back and guard the rear entrance we saw from the road. Dick, stand guard at the front door. If anyone tries to leave, order him to halt, and if he disobeys, shoot."

The Simpsons raced out, and Dale looked chagrined. "Is such violence necessary, Captain?"

"Perhaps. That's why I'm here." Hugh turned to Benjy, his eyes hard. "Sergeant Flaherty, I ask you for an explanation of your disappearance from Westerly."

"You don't have to ask." There was a trace of a whine in Benjy's voice. "I'm telling you, all of my own free will, that I decided to start the investigation myself, so I rode out ahead of you."

"Flaherty," Hugh said crisply, "you're a liar."

There was a long silence, and finally Benjy hung his head sheepishly. "When you asked me to join the army, Hugh, you wanted to know what I'd do if I ever met an old friend. I didn't know at the time, but I gave you your answer this afternoon. August is somebody I knew in England a long time ago."

If Dale was an old acquaintance of Benjy's, it was probable that he was a counterfeiter, and Hugh quietly gripped the hilt of his sword. "Is there anything you'd like to say, Mr. Dale?"

"I know why you've come here, Captain. Benjy has told me, but that wasn't necessary. I've been hounded by the people of Westerly for months." Dale smiled bitterly. "You'll find no evidence of the kind that you're seeking, Captain, not in this house."

Hugh heard a sound behind a closed door at the far end of the small chamber. "Are you here alone, Mr. Dale?"

"You must have heard the fire crackling in the hearth in the parlor, Captain."

Hugh ignored the reply and, walking to the door, raised the latch. He halted in astonishment when he saw the red-haired, green-eyed girl he had loved and had been unable to forget, even after she had betrayed him. "Sara Dean!"

August Dale was alarmed. "Don't shoot him, Katie! He brought some soldiers with him!"

Hugh realized that Sara was holding a pistol, and that she was pointing it straight at him.

"Don't come any closer," she murmured.

Hugh laughed grimly, reached out, and caught hold of her wrist. She struggled, but was no match for him, and the pistol fell to the floor. He kicked it into a corner, drew his sword, and took his own pistol from his belt. "I've been waiting a long, long time for this reunion," he said.

XI / *March 1777*

"DON'T hurt her!" Benjy shouted. "Katie is harmless."

"My experience indicates that you're guilty of a gross understatement," Hugh replied coldly, keeping a wary eye on the two men while continuing to watch the pale, silent "Sara Dean."

"Benjy is right, Captain," August Dale declared earnestly. "My daughter has never used firearms."

"Your daughter—if that's who she is—shouldn't point a pistol, then, particularly at someone who has cause to believe that she's less than trustworthy."

The girl stood erect, her head high, and in spite of her predicament she maintained an air of dignity.

She was unable to look at Hugh, however, and averted her eyes when he stared at her. If he hadn't learned a bitter lesson, he thought, he would swear that she was feeling deep shame, but it was more likely that she was merely chagrined at having been caught by a man she had wronged. He could not allow himself to waste time trying to analyze a tenuous personal relationship when there was work to be done, so he roused himself. "How many others are in this house, Dale?" he demanded.

"There's nobody else, Captain. Katie and I live alone."

Hugh called Dick Simpson and ordered him to search the place.

"August is telling the truth," Benjy said anxiously.

"I'll ask for your advice when I want it, Flaherty," Hugh replied curtly, and did not speak again until Dick returned.

"I've looked everywheres from the attic to the cellar, Captain, and I ain't seen a living sign of anybody."

"Get your brother." Hugh realized he was alone with a group of acknowledged criminals, and braced himself.

Dave Simpson followed Dick into the room.

"Do you know these people?" Hugh asked.

"No, sir." Dick replied firmly and without hesitation.

Dave chuckled slyly. "It wouldn't bother me none if I got to know that girl, Captain."

She ignored the comment, but her eyes flashed angrily.

Hugh shifted his position slightly so he could fire at anyone who reached for a weapon. "I'll start with you, Flaherty. Explain your actions of this afternoon, and if you lie to me, I'll prosecute you as an enemy spy."

"I don't blame you for not trusting me, Hugh," Benjy said plaintively. "If we was wearing each other's shoes, I'd feel the same as you do. I didn't know August was here until the sheriff down in Westerly mentioned his name. We haven't set eyes on each other for five years, maybe six. He moved up out of my class long before I was sent to Newgate the last time. But we worked together years ago, and I—well, I was scared he was the man we've been hunting. So I came out here to warn him and give him time to get away."

Dale struck a pose and cleared his throat. "He's told you the whole truth, sir. All I can add is that I expressed my gratitude to him, but I assured him I had no reason to run. I've retired from my former profession, and I'm innocent of all wrongdoing."

The Simpsons, who were too simple to dissemble, were staring at him in wide-eyed awe. "That's Deacon Dale!" they said to each other solemnly.

"I believe I acquired something of a reputation during my active days," Dale said modestly.

Dave Simpson was breathless. "Captain, he was the best in the trade. Nobody else could make a five-sovereign note. He not only made them, but he fooled the Lord Treasurer himself with a pack of them!"

"That isn't quite accurate." Dale smiled self-deprecatingly. "It was the assistant director of the royal printing office who accepted some samples of my handiwork as genuine. The story has become exaggerated through the years, obviously."

"That don't matter," Dick Simpson said, envy and respect in his voice. "Everybody in the trade knew you were so good that you were never arrested, not once!"

"There's always a first time," Hugh said ominously.

"You'll have to find evidence against me, Captain," Dale replied, quietly confident.

"Quite right." Hugh decided to take a chance and trust the Simpsons; he needed help, and as there was no one else to whom he could turn, he felt he could obtain their enthusiastic co-operation by playing on their vanity. "Dave, Dick," he said, "do you want to become even more famous than this man you've been admiring?"

They nodded emphatically.

"You've just said yourselves that no one ever convicted him. Remember you're on the other side of the fence now, so locate his equipment. Go through this whole house, every room and every corner. Start in the attic and work your way down."

They ran out of the sitting room eagerly, and Dale smiled. "Let me congratulate you on your technique, Captain Spencer. You've acquired a considerable understanding of human nature. If you had been as wise a few years ago it would have been far more difficult to utilize your assistance for our benefit. Don't you agree, Katie?"

The girl forced herself to look at Hugh. "You won't believe this, and there's no reason you should, but I had no idea you'd become involved in such serious trouble the last time I saw you. I thought you'd find some way to prove you were innocent. And I couldn't help you without jeopardizing myself. Pa and I left England before you were brought to trial, and I didn't read about your case until I saw a small article in the Boston *Advertiser* months later." She paused, and there was a note of defiance in her voice as she added, "You'll think I'm lying, but that doesn't matter. I do want you to know I'm sorry."

Hugh glared at her, hoping he was concealing his feelings. It was absurd to discover that his old wounds hadn't healed and that he wanted, desperately, to believe her.

"Katie was miserable for months, I must confess," Dale said cheerfully. "You see, Captain, I hadn't planned to use you as a decoy to draw suspicion from me when I was bringing my most successful operation to completion. Katie had been ashamed of my profession and had invented a charmingly romantic background for herself when she met you. Sara Dean was a most ingenious device."

"Be quiet, Pa!" she cried furiously. "Captain Spencer doesn't care how I felt, and what I did was my business. It isn't any of his concern!"

Her father ignored the outburst. "Unfortunately, you had visited the house I was using as a headquarters, so it was necessary to take extraordinary measures to protect myself after you were taken into custody. I can reveal the details to you safely now because there's no way you can obtain legal redress, thanks to the Americans' attempt to cut themselves off from England. But I thought you'd like to hear that Katie wasn't responsible for your unfortunate situation. I gladly assume the full burden of guilt."

"Please, Pa! We ruined his life, so what does it matter how we did it?"

Hugh, still maintaining a stony façade, thought that Katie's feminine appeal was even stronger now than it had been when he had known her as Sara Dean. Certainly she had become more beautiful, if possible, and it was disturbing to know that she still had the power to upset his emotional balance, even though she had saved herself and her father at his expense. "The past no longer interests me," he said harshly. "I hold a commission in the army of the United States, and I fight her enemies. Counterfeiters who damage the spirits of the people hurt our capacity to wage a successful war, so they're enemies of America."

Benjy stared at his boots miserably.

August Dale patted his white hair carefully, and his poise deserted him for a moment. "You present the picture in a light I hadn't considered, Captain."

Hugh smiled cynically.

"Doubt me if it gives you pleasure, sir, but I have no love for England. I have developed a great fondness for the New World, however, and it would grieve me to see this infant nation lose her war for independence."

Tears appeared in Katie's eyes and she stamped her foot angrily. "Don't you realize that nothing you say is going to influence him, Pa? After the way we treated him, he wants to see us hang—and we can hardly blame him."

Dale looked pained. "A man can't be hanged for expressing his honest sentiments. I can state without reservation that I earnestly hope and pray that the United States will earn her freedom, and that I wouldn't harm her cause deliberately."

"Be quiet, Pa!" Katie cried furiously. "Can't you see he thinks you're just trying to influence him?"

Hugh inclined his head to her. "Your sensitivity to the feelings of others does you credit, Mistress Dean, or Miss Dale, or whatever you may call yourself," he said with heavy sarcasm. "You've convinced me that you grieved for me during the months when I was held in prison, particularly as it was in your power to arrange for my release rather than plot with your accomplices to ensure that I'd be convicted." He broke off abruptly, aware that he was hurting her, and was surprised to discover that he felt no sense of triumph. He had dreamed of the day when he would force her to pay for her trickery, but realized he was actually searching for some way to rationalize and excuse her conduct.

Katie, conscious of the intensity of his gaze, turned away from him and stared out of the window at the bare earth of the yard.

There was a long, uncomfortable silence, and finally Dave Simpson returned to the sitting room. "Dick is starting all over again, Captain, but so far we ain't found one crumb of evidence. We always figured we knew everything about hiding presses and such, and we've turned this house upside down, but there ain't even a jar of ink in the place."

August Dale chuckled benevolently. "The zeal of your associates does them credit, Captain, and you have good reason to be proud of your own devotion to duty. Now that you've satisfied your honor, perhaps you'll drink a glass of sack with me before you leave. I still have a bottle or two that I bought before the war began."

Benjy, who had been twisting the buttons on his tunic, shifting his weight from one foot to the other, and frowning unhappily, suddenly caught hold of Dale's lapel. "August," he said miserably, "I can't let you do this."

Dale was too startled to reply.

"I gave my word of honor to serve America as best I could, and if I go back on my promise, I don't deserve to be a free man living in a free country. I never had any honor before I came to this country, and if I don't pay her for giving me my self-respect, I might just as well be rotting in a Newgate cell."

"Don't be hasty, old friend," Dale said, trying to hide his alarm. "Before you do anything rash—"

"Pa, you shut up!" Katie was weeping openly now, but she seemed relieved. "You have real courage, Benjy, and I admire you. I wish I had your strength."

Benjy patted her awkwardly on the shoulder. "If I wasn't so little and ugly and ten years too old for you, Katie, I'd tell you what I think of you." He turned to Hugh, straightened, and stood at attention. "Captain, I can solve this case for you."

Color drained from August Dale's face. "No, Benjy! Think of the years we've known each other!"

"I'm thinking of the United States and the oath I swore." Benjy walked into the parlor that adjoined the sitting room, and, moving straight to the cold hearth at the far end of the chamber, squatted and began to sift ashes through his fingers delicately.

August Dale moaned softly.

After a few moments Benjy's search was rewarded, and, his hands coated with dust, he returned to the sitting room carrying several scraps of charred muslin, which he placed carefully on a table. "Here you are, Captain."

Hugh was proud of him, but the bits of cloth meant nothing to him.

Katie saw that he was puzzled. "You'll need more than the muslin," she said in a choked voice, and moved to a small sideboard on which several decanters of wine were sitting.

"My own flesh and blood is deserting me," August announced, but his attempt to achieve an air of tragedy fell flat. He looked old and pathetically crumpled.

Katie unhesitatingly reached for a decanter. "This looks like blackberry wine, but it isn't," she said, and, removing the stopper, handed the container to Hugh. "Smell it."

He sniffed, and the odor of ink was unmistakable.

"It's the finest quality of Frankfort black, diluted with water," she said. "Pa makes it thicker by boiling it until the water evaporates."

Hugh stared at her. "Miss Dale," he replied hoarsely, "it's only fair to tell you that your confession will be used against you."

"I know precisely what I'm doing," she declared, and raised her head.

They looked at each other steadily, and Hugh felt the pulses in his temples throb.

"You said enough, Katie," Benjy declared briskly. "Too much for your own good. I'll explain the rest. I'm not sure it matters, Captain, but the one thing I don't know is where August keeps his paper."

Katie started to cross the room, but her father halted her. "Permit me to contribute to my own downfall," he said. "As my daughter and one of my oldest friends have betrayed me, I shall walk the remainder of the path to the gallows alone." He halted at the wall, reached up, and tore off a long strip of the cream-colored paper that was used to decorate the whole chamber. "Here you are, Captain Spencer. I use only the finest quality of paper in the notes I make. The texture is infinitely superior to that used by Rhode Island, even after sitting on a wall for many months. My problem was finding a paste mixture that wouldn't damage the paper when I washed it off. I succeeded there, too."

Hugh took the strip, felt it, and realized that it was perfect for counterfeiting purposes. "You brought your supply with you from England?"

August bowed stiffly.

Dick Simpson had joined his brother in the entrance, and both were gaping at the master of their trade.

"The ink and paper aren't enough," Hugh said, unable to look at Katie again. "I'll be obliged if you'll give me your plates, Mr. Dale, and we can end this distasteful business."

"August never uses engraving plates," Benjy said, and pointed to the scraps of muslin. "There's his secret."

Hugh picked up one of the charred fragments gingerly, studied it for a moment, and shrugged.

"It's a very simple system," Benjy continued. "The printing on Rhode Island money is bad. The ink is always too thick. So August takes a bill—it don't matter what denomination, so long as it was printed by Rhode Island—and he puts a piece of muslin over it. Then he takes a medium-hot tailor's goose, a pressing iron, and he runs it back and forth across the genuine note until a print comes off on the muslin. The rest is easy."

"It grieves me to contradict an old associate who should know better, but the rest of the process is not easy," August said proudly. "There is only one artist alive whom I might call my equal, and the French authorities put him and his money out of circulation several years ago. Poor Bruyelle is an artist, and I am doomed to suffer his fate."

Benjy glanced at Dale contritely. "I'm sorry, August. I was never clever enough to do the trick, so I had no right to call it easy. Here's how he did it, Hugh. He took the muslin with the print on it and laid it on his own paper. Then he used the pressing iron again and transferred the print to the blank sheet. So he never had to use engraving plates. All he needed was ink and paper. And a supply of muslin."

"You've forgotten to mention the most important step, the last step that determines success or failure." August's eyes glowed for an instant, then became dull again. "Naturally, the final print was less than perfect. It invariably needed filling in here and there. So I made the necessary adjustments with a crow's-quill pen, using a slightly diluted Frankfort black. My secret will become public knowledge now, but no one else will ever be able to put the finishing touches on a note with my delicate artistry. That's a secret I shall take to the gallows with me, the secret of my natural talent."

"You won't be sent to the gallows, Mr. Dale," Hugh said. "However, I have no doubt that you'll be sentenced to a long term in prison." He paused and took a deep breath. "In the name of the Continental Congress of the United States, and acting under the powers deputized to me by the sovereign state of Rhode Island, I place you under arrest."

August recovered his dignity. "I am your prisoner, Captain," he said, and added bitterly to Benjy, "I imagine you'll want the pleasure of putting irons on my wrists?"

Hugh intervened quickly. "It won't be necessary to bind you, Mr. Dale."

Benjy thanked him silently.

Katie, who had dried her eyes, faced Hugh quietly. "Aren't you going to arrest me, too?"

"That won't be necessary," he replied painfully.

"Oh, but it will."

"That's enough, Katie," August shouted. "You told me to keep silent, and if you have any sense you'll follow your own advice."

She ignored her father's outburst. "Pa didn't mention to you that more often than not, I did the ironing for him. So I'm as guilty as he is."

Hugh's mouth and throat felt raw. "In that case, you give me no choice. You'll have to consider yourself under arrest too."

She dropped him a deep, mocking curtsy. "You must feel very pleased with yourself. It isn't often that someone gets such rich revenge."

Hugh couldn't tell her that he felt no satisfaction and that, on the contrary, he despised himself.

XII / *April 1777*

MOST of Connecticut's young patriots were serving in the army far from home, so few uniforms were seen in New Haven, and the patrons of the Mill Tavern, one of the city's oldest eating places, stared at the two young officers who sat in a secluded alcove overlooking the Green. Occasionally someone recognized Ben Tallmadge, who had been popular in New Haven when he had attended Yale College, but he responded absently to shouts and waves, so the diners made no attempt to disturb him. It had become common knowledge that he was engaged in secret work for General Washington, and as anyone who looked at him could see that he was pre-occupied, his acquaintances knew instinctively that he didn't want to be interrupted. The war was teaching even the most gregarious Americans new standards of tactful reticence.

Major Tallmadge cut his roast with relish. "I'm pleased for more reasons than one that official business brought me home to Connecticut," he said with a smile. "You haven't eaten army food lately, Spencer, but you can take my word for it that the quartermaster department is recruiting black-smiths and tanners. Most of the food we've been getting lately is inedible."

Hugh looked across the table solemnly. "There's nothing I want more than to rejoin the army in the field, Major."

Tallmadge eyed him shrewdly. "I've heard a rumor to the effect that you knew the Dale girl in London years ago."

"Yes." Hugh's curtness wasn't intentional, but he saw no need to elaborate.

"Will she be given a heavy sentence?"

"I haven't spoken to the justices of the Rhode Island Supreme Court, naturally, but the prosecutor plans to ask for a ten-year confinement. If the court is lenient, she'll be sent to prison for five or six years."

Tallmadge hesitated for a moment. "You'd be happier if the court shows her leniency?"

Hugh didn't answer directly. "I've been in prison. Even a month is a long time."

Tallmadge saw that his companion was disturbed, and, having learned what he wanted to know, changed the subject. "You realized I wouldn't have asked you to leave Providence if it hadn't been urgently important."

"Yes, sir."

"I didn't want to ask the Rhode Island court to postpone the trial of the Dales, but I had no choice. I couldn't take time to go up to Providence, and even though you're scheduled to be the principal witness for the prosecution, I had to see you."

"The Dales won't make any more counterfeit money, so a delay of a few days in their trial won't really matter." Hugh tried to speak in a matter-of-fact tone, but the knowledge that his testimony would send Katie to prison was an ever-present cause of depression.

"The commander-in-chief sends you his compliments on stopping the counterfeiting in Rhode Island."

"Thank you," Hugh replied dully.

Tallmadge guessed the reason his subordinate showed no enthusiasm, but refused to dwell on the matter. Many officers were struggling with grave personal problems, but the interest of the nation was paramount. "Unfortunately, we have few victories to celebrate."

Hugh heard the solemn note in the major's voice and tried to put Katie out of his mind for the present.

Tallmadge lowered his voice. "I don't know how much longer we can hold Philadelphia. The general hopes to keep Howe off balance until winter, when the British will go into garrisons again, but even Washington can perform only a limited number of miracles. And we have reason to believe that Lord Burgoyne may lead a column south from Canada to cut off New England and upper New York. But you and I have other worries."

"I served under Burgoyne for a time," Hugh said, "and I didn't like him. I'd welcome an opportunity to take part in a campaign against him."

"I'm afraid," Tallmadge replied with a short laugh, "that you've done too well as an intelligence officer. You're paying the price of success." Finishing his beef, he looked across the table sympathetically. "I know how you feel, Spencer. I'd like to fight in the open again too. But—if this will comfort you—I haven't forgotten my promise to you."

"That isn't why you called me down here from Providence."

"No." Tallmadge looked carefully at the nearest party of diners to make certain they couldn't hear him. "The flow of counterfeit Continental dollars into the territory we hold has increased. More and more people in every state are refusing to accept the Congress's money as legal tender."

"I'm afraid I've been out of touch with the situation lately, Major. I've never had much respect for lawyers, and I have even less now. The state prosecutor in Providence has been taking up all of my time helping him prepare his case against the Dales. As soon as the trial is ended, I'll be able to concentrate on the false dollars again."

"I have some information for you." Tallmadge spoke very softly. "It won't surprise you, I'm sure. The counterfeit Continentals are being made in New York."

"Are you certain?"

"Positive. I've had two reports on military matters from agents there in the past ten days. One slipped through the lines, and I interviewed him myself, and the other sent me a long letter in code. Both of them mentioned that they know New York is the source of the false dollars."

"Who—"

"They could give me no details. Their primary responsibility is checking on troop movements, and they could give me no details about the false money. What's more, their knowledge of counterfeiting is limited, so neither was in a position to investigate."

Hugh pondered for a few moments and sipped the coffee that Americans were learning to drink in place of the tea that had been imported from England before the war. "It won't be easy to stop all traffic from New York. Even if we had two or three regiments assigned to do nothing but catch smugglers, counterfeiters could send their money out of the city by boat."

"Precisely the conclusion I reached."

"It seems to me," Hugh said carefully, "that the only way to stop the flow is to cut it off at the source."

Tallmadge nodded, watching him intently.

"In other words, we'll have to send people into New York to catch the counterfeiters." Hugh took a deep breath. "My unit is the only American organization qualified to perform the task."

"I can't ask you to go into enemy territory, Spencer. Captain Nathan Hale, who was executed during the campaign in New York, was an old friend of mine, so I'm particularly sensitive, I guess. Not only would you run the risk of being hanged as a spy if they should catch you, but you're a fugitive from British justice. Your situation is even worse than that of Sergeant Flaherty, who was freed from his indenture."

Hugh smiled, but his eyes remained serious. "Can you suggest any alternatives, Major?"

"We have no agents in New York who know even a small fraction as much about counterfeiting as you and your men."

"Then it seems obvious that I have no choice." Hugh put his coffee mug on the table and turned it slowly. "August Dale is probably the most expert counterfeiter on earth."

"So I gathered from the written report that you sent to me, Spencer."

"The Simpson brothers are useful, and they have great physical strength, but they aren't very bright."

Tallmadge listened and waited patiently.

"Certainly Sergeant Flaherty has demonstrated his loyalty to us, so I'd trust him anywhere, under any circumstances. But he was a minor counterfeiter. He has a great deal of technical knowledge that he applied on a small scale, but he lacked the imagination to expand, as August Dale and his daughter did before we found them at Westerly. I don't know where Dale has hidden his money, but Flaherty assures me that he has a fortune. He was wealthy when he and his daughter came to America, and he's acquired even more since that time."

The major became tense. "Just exactly what are you trying to suggest, Spencer?"

"I'm volunteering to lead my unit to New York, find the counterfeiters of Continental dollars and destroy their equipment. Naturally, if one of my men doesn't want to take the risks involved, I'll excuse him from the assignment."

"That's understood, of course." Tallmadge poured himself another cup of coffee from a pewter pitcher. "I thought you were hinting at something more."

"I was, sir." Hugh steeled himself. "I have an unorthodox idea that would fool the British, I believe. The Simpson brothers and I are men of military age, and even Flaherty might conceivably be an American militiaman. But a pretty girl and a white-haired man with the manners of a great lord are the last people on earth the enemy would suspect. So I propose that Dale and his daughter be paroled into my custody and accompany the expedition."

Tallmadge stared at him for some moments. "To what extent is your plan motivated by personal feelings?" he demanded bluntly.

"I'm not sure I know the answer to that, sir. But I'll be frank with you to the best of my ability. There was a time, long ago, when I imagined myself in love with Katie Dale, whom I knew under another name. It was her perfidy that caused all of my trouble with the crown, and I imagined I hated her. I don't, as I discovered on the day I arrested her and her father in Westerly. Also, I don't like being directly responsible for sending her to prison, which may be weakness."

"I think not. I can sympathize with your position."

"Thank you, Major." Hugh's hand trembled as he poured himself another cup of coffee. "I'm still attracted to her. I can't and won't deny it. But I'm not in love with her," he added, and, aware that he was speaking too loudly, controlled his voice. "I couldn't love someone I don't respect, and it would be impossible for me to respect an adventuress who has spent her whole life as a counterfeiter's accomplice. I need hardly add that as she caused all of my woes, I find it difficult to look on her with favor."

Tallmadge weighed the reply, glanced around the room, and exchanged a bow with an elderly gentleman wearing the thick white stock around his neck that identified him as a senior lecturer on the faculty of Yale College. "What would be the advantage of using the Dale girl and her father in your venture, Spencer?"

"The success I've employed on a smaller scale utilizing the same tactics. Flaherty and the Simpsons have been valuable, but they're amateurs, relatively speaking. As I have good reason to know from personal experience, the Dales are a brilliant team. They're ruthless, they know every trick of the counterfeiting trade and they have an unmatched ability to escape from unpleasant situations. Our policy of 'using thieves to catch thieves' has proved effective so far, and I believe that the Dales would be the best of all possible reinforcements for the Scoundrels' Brigade."

"You present a strong argument," Tallmadge said, "but there's a question you haven't answered. Can you trust them?"

Deeply troubled, Hugh looked across the table at his superior. "I don't know, Major," he said frankly.

"They saved their own skins at your expense once before. They might be tempted to do it again."

"I've thought of the possibility. But if they hand me over to the British, they'll be placing themselves in jeopardy. August Dale isn't in a position to let the crown authorities examine his background closely. He doesn't want to be sent back to England for trial."

"What incentive might persuade him to work for you?"

"The hope of gaining his freedom."

Tallmadge shook his head dubiously. "We couldn't promise him that Rhode Island would drop its charges against him."

"No, sir, of course not. But let's assume that he and his daughter help us to break up the counterfeiting ring in New York. If they perform a real service for the United States, a letter from General Washington would influence the Rhode Island court."

"I can't speak for the general, so I don't really know whether he'd be willing to write such a letter."

Hugh hid his disappointment. "I understand, Major."

"I'll speak to him when I return to headquarters, and I'll ask for a further postponement in the trial of the Dales until we can clarify the situation."

"Thank you."

"I'm prepared to recommend that General Washington accept your plan, Spencer, although I believe you're taking on a fresh burden that may cause a disaster. However, I believe in giving a competent man the authority to solve his problems in his own way. And even though your scheme doesn't appeal to me, you give me little choice. If confidence in the Continental dollar continues to fall, and we're forced to evacuate Philadelphia, too, I'm afraid we'll lose public support everywhere."

"I believe the Dales can be a strong asset. Our chance of finding the counterfeiters will be improved by adding them to my unit."

Tallmadge took some coins from his purse to pay for the meal. "Surely you realize that you'd be taking a serious personal risk?"

Hugh smiled faintly. "It's a calculated risk. And if I should fail because of their treachery, I'd have no one to blame but myself."

No explanation was given for the postponement of the trial of August and Katie Dale, but the Rhode Island government reluctantly granted Major Tallmadge's request, and in the meantime the prisoners were kept under close guard in the old town jail on Benevolent Street in Providence. Hugh waited with mounting impatience for word from headquarters, and after three weeks he finally received a brief letter from Tallmadge. The commander-in-chief had been persuaded to accept the plan, the major wrote, and if Rhode Island agreed, action could be taken immediately.

Hugh went to the Rhode Island authorities and, without revealing any of the details of his scheme, asked that the Dales be paroled into his custody. The prosecutor was unwilling to release the prisoners, but the three justices of the court proved more amenable and made an appointment for Hugh to see the lieutenant governor, who supervised all criminal cases. Israel Stewart, the lieutenant governor, was a patriot, a hardheaded man who believed in using any means to win the war, and when Hugh convinced him that the Dales could help the United States achieve her freedom, he signed an order releasing them from prison.

It was necessary to gain the consent of the pair first, however, so Hugh went to the jail and, after conferring briefly with the warden, was admitted to August Dale's cell. The old man had lost his ebullience and listened apathetically as Hugh began to outline his plan, but gradually August brightened, and by the time that Hugh finished explaining his general idea, the counterfeiter's eyes were sparkling.

"You've come to the right man, Captain Spencer," he said. "You show remarkable perspicacity and wisdom for someone so young. I can give you a virtual guarantee that I can locate the people who are making Continental dollars in New York. You can rely on me, Captain."

"That's why I've arranged for your parole," Hugh replied quietly. "I want to make it clear, though, that Rhode Island isn't dropping the charges against you and your daughter. If we should succeed, the state might be persuaded to parole you permanently, but that's something I'm in no position to promise."

"I realize that your powers are limited, but I'm grateful to you for offering me an opportunity. I had given up all hope of obtaining my release, but you're giving me what may prove to be a fresh start in life."

"You realize that I'll be in a dangerous personal position, Dale." Hugh measured his words. "So it's only fair to warn you that if you try to trick me, I won't hesitate to kill you."

The old man, who had been sitting cross-legged on his pallet in the corner of his cell, stood and brushed straw from his breeches. "It is obvious," he said proudly, "that you have no concept of my code."

"I didn't know you had one." Hugh couldn't conquer the bitterness that rose up in him.

"I have never played a colleague false. You and I will be colleagues. What more can I say?" He extended his hand.

Hugh gripped it, conscious of the irony of shaking hands

with the man who was responsible for all that he had suffered. "If the enemy catches us, they'll hang us as spies, you know, so my offer is less than generous."

"I've taken gambles all of my life, and my record of success speaks for itself." August fingered the ruffled cuff of his shirt. "What specific plans do you have in mind?"

"I haven't made any as yet."

"Ah, then you'll be wise to give me a voice in your council. I've had experience in confounding authority, vast experience that will prove beneficial to our venture."

"I'm counting on your help," Hugh said with a smile. Then, suddenly, he sobered. "Naturally you'll want your daughter placed on parole too, but I doubt if you want her to risk being hanged as a spy, so you may feel that she shouldn't join us. If you wish, she can retire to some place where she won't be conspicuous and wait there until we either succeed or she becomes an orphan."

There was a ring of genuine admiration in August's voice as he said, "You claim you aren't generous, Captain. I beg to contradict you. When you started to outline your thoughts to me, I was prepared to hear you say that Katie would be held here as a hostage."

"I thought of that," Hugh replied candidly, "but I don't believe it would be fair to any of us. If we're taking risks together, we've got to work together. You'd resent me if your daughter remained in jail."

"I would, Captain." August hesitated for a moment. "Katie can be extremely valuable to us, if she can be persuaded to join us. However, she has a mind of her own, and she can behave in an infuriatingly stubborn fashion when she chooses."

"I'll talk to her."

August coughed delicately behind his hand. "With your permission, I'll speak to her first. Women let their feelings cloud their logic, and I regret to say that Katie's attitude toward you is extremely hostile at present." Brightening, he patted Hugh on the shoulder. "But I have confidence in my persuasive powers. Arrange a meeting with her in fairly pleasant surroundings, and give me a quarter of an hour alone with her before you see her."

Later that same day August conferred with his daughter in the warden's office at the jail, and Hugh waited impatiently in the corridor outside. It was difficult to control his indignation, and he thought it was absurd that he should be placed in the role of a supplicant. His temper was still rising when August, his manner that of a gracious host, opened the door and stepped into the corridor.

"Katie has consented to speak to you," he said in a confidential tone.

"Has she agreed to the plan?"

The old man looked less confident. "Children occasionally forget all their parents have done for them, and Katie is no exception to the general rule, I fear. In brief, she wouldn't give me her decision. She listened to me without saying a word, and finally told me she'd be willing to see you. I hope, for my own sake and that of your mission, that she'll be willing to forget her animosity toward you. There are times," he added plaintively, waving Hugh into the office, "when I wish I had been blessed with a son rather than a daughter."

Katie stood at the far end of the warden's office, behind the desk, staring out into Benevolent Street, and did not move when she heard the door close. Hugh saw that her gown was rumpled, but her hair had been combed carefully and was hanging in loose waves that fell across her shoulders and down her back. Curbing an impulse to move closer to her, he forced himself to lean against the door.

"Good-afternoon, Miss Dale," he said.

Katie turned slowly. "When I knew you in London I thought you were very innocent. I didn't suspect that you have a diabolically clever mind."

In spite of what her father had said, Hugh was surprised by her unpleasantness. "Nonsense," he replied brusquely.

"Is it? You seem to think I have no mind of my own." When Katie was angry, the green in her eyes became deeper and more opaque.

"I've thought many things about you, a great number of them unflattering," he retorted, "but I've always given you full credit for originality."

She became even more thoroughly aroused. "You felt sure I couldn't resist your offer. The prospect of freedom, even temporary freedom, is so tempting, and the knowledge that the alternative is a long prison term was bound to influence me." She laughed contemptuously, her hands on her hips.

When Hugh had known her in London she had always behaved like a lady, and he hadn't suspected that she had an earthy, violent temper. "I've made you a legitimate offer. If you're afraid of the enemy, reject my plan, and that will end the matter."

"Who is the enemy, you or the British? How easy it would be for you to denounce me as soon as we arrived in New York. Pa is usually so shrewd, but he can't see that you plan to hand us over to the crown and vindicate yourself."

The idea hadn't occurred to him, and he smiled scornfully; he knew, as Katie obviously didn't, that it was too late to exonerate himself in England. Even more important, he had learned, as had the Americans who were fighting for independence, that British justice was capricious, and he had no desire to be exposed to it again. "I've taken an oath to support the government of the United States, and I intend to remain faithful to the uniform I'm wearing," he said flatly, refusing to lower his dignity by giving her a fuller explanation.

"We're alone, so you needn't pretend to be so noble."

Hugh raised a hand to slap her, but let his arm fall to his side again. "When your father told me you're stubborn, he neglected to mention that you're also very stupid. Didn't he explain to you that I'm willing to let you stay somewhere on American territory while we go into New York? Does that sound as though I plan to turn you over to the British?"

"I believe you know just enough about me to realize that I won't let my father walk into a trap alone. After you've sent him to an English prison, you think I'll follow and try to help him." Katie's expression was mocking. "There. I've uncovered your little secret, haven't I?"

Exasperated, he grasped her shoulders and shook her. "Listen to me, you scheming, two-faced vixen. If I wanted revenge, you wouldn't be in Rhode Island now, and I wouldn't have to risk being captured myself. Prisoners are exchanged every week under a flag of truce. I could send you off to New York with a letter signed by the lieutenant governor of the state, if that's what I wanted. You'd be shipped to England, tried and sentenced there. We'd be completely rid of you." He shook her again.

Katie twisted away from him. "It's easier to hear you when my teeth aren't rattling," she gasped.

"Then behave sensibly!" He had felt the warmth of her body beneath his touch, and his anger was dissipating.

Katie hadn't realized he would resort to violence, and spoke more cautiously. "Is that true? Could you really send us through the lines?"

"Have you lied and cheated so much that you think everyone else is dishonest?" he shouted.

She backed away from him and edged around the desk.

"I don't ask you to take my word. You think I'm prejudiced against you. And you're right." Hugh heard footsteps outside and knew he had attracted an audience. Acting impulsively, he threw open the door. "Warden!"

The head of the prison staff, a militia veteran who had lost a leg in the campaign on Long Island, limped into the room.

"I believe you know the law regarding criminals who are in our custody but are also wanted by the enemy."

"Sure, Captain. We had a fellow like that about three months ago. He was a highway bandit who was making life miserable for folks in Newport. We caught him, but before we brought him to trial, we heard he was wanted in Liverpool for murder."

"I'm not familiar with the case, but I'll appreciate it if you'll tell Miss Dale the story, not me," Hugh said.

"Sure, but there's not much to tell." The warden couldn't understand what connection there might be between the parole of the counterfeiter's daughter and the fate of a highwayman, but he was aware of the tension in the room and was willing to oblige. "He ate like a wild goat, that fellow. He was costing Rhode Island a heap of money, and the court calendar was so crowded that the justices couldn't schedule his case right off. So we saved plenty. We got rid of him."

"How?" Katie's attitude was defiant, but there was a hint of uncertainty beneath her bravado.

"The usual way," the warden replied calmly. "When the exchange convoy came through here from Boston on the way to Westchester County in New York, where the truce meetings are held every month, we sent him along. The British were mighty pleased to have him." He chuckled. "They've had to feed him, and he'll keep right on eating until they hang him in England."

Katie seemed to be very busy smoothing a red curl that had fallen forward over her shoulder. "That's very interesting," she murmured.

"Thank you, Warden." Hugh nodded toward the door.

"Is that all you wanted me for?" Scratching his head, the warden left the room.

Hugh closed the door. "Well, Miss Dale?" he asked acidly.

"I—I'll accept your offer," she said, but could not admit defeat. "All the same, I don't trust you."

"As you can imagine, I feel precisely the same way about you." Hugh smiled coldly and gave her his arm. "Nevertheless, if we want to stay alive, we'll have to work together."

XIII / *May 1777*

A MILD spring breeze blew through the open windows of the large parlor, but the group gathered at the house at Black Ox farm outside Westerly was tense. Katie Dale tried to hide her nervousness by knitting, Benjy Flaherty slid a long hunting knife in and out of its thick leather sheath, and the Simpson brothers wandered around the room restlessly, picking up snuffboxes, statuettes, and other bric-a-brac, then putting them down again. Only August Dale was serene, and, seated in his favorite armchair near a window, he was engrossed in a copy of Thomas Paine's pamphlet, *The Crisis*.

"Is there any sign of him yet, Pa?" Katie discovered she had made a mistake and ripped out a row of knitting.

"I beg your pardon, my dear?" Her father didn't look up from the pamphlet.

"Captain Spencer said we could expect him no later than noon, and it will soon be dusk." She resumed her work, and her needles bobbed up and down energetically.

"Perhaps the messenger from General Washington's headquarters was late. This fellow Paine is a splendid writer, I must say. I knew nothing and cared less about the American cause until I began to read his work."

Hoofbeats sounded in the distance, and Benjy hurried to

the window. Katie stopped knitting, Dave Simpson dropped a silver snuffbox, and his brother held a vase rigidly in front of his face. Only August remained unruffled, and, nodding approvingly at something he had just read, sighed gently and turned the page.

"It's Toby," Benjy announced.

The hoofbeats grew louder, and at last they stopped in front of the house. A few moments later Hugh came into the room, his boots dusty and his uniform travel-stained.

August greeted him cordially. "Welcome back to Black Ox farm, Captain."

"Thank you. I've eaten nothing since breakfast," Hugh said, glancing at Katie, then turned to Benjy. "Toby needs a rub-down."

"I'm not leaving this room until I hear what's happened," Katie declared, flaring.

Benjy made no move, either.

Hugh smiled as he removed his gauntlet gloves. "The major has approved our plan to move into New York immediately."

"And the money?" Benjy asked eagerly. "Did you get the money?"

"Some of it, but not as much as I wanted. Funds at head-quarters are limited, and there's very little to spare for in-telligence."

August patted his white hair thoughtfully. "I could manu-facture a supply of excellent English ten-pound notes before we leave. I think their ten-pound bill is the finest work of art I've ever produced."

Hugh grinned, but shook his head firmly.

"Ah, well. If Major Tallmadge didn't give you enough, per-haps I can supply the difference myself, using legitimate cur-rency." August made the offer casually. "If we hope to succeed, we can't let a lack of money hamper us."

"That's very generous," Hugh replied, surprised.

"No, I'm anxious to ensure my own safety, so it's com-pletely selfish. I've learned that the greater the risk involved in an enterprise, the greater the need for a fat purse," August said candidly. "I've grown very fond of this property, and when the war ends I hope I'll be able to spend my declining years here and enjoy the fruits of a long life of hard work. I don't relish the prospect of languishing in a British prison any more than I enjoyed my existence in that foul cell in Providence."

Hugh had been nagged by doubts since the Dales had been paroled into his custody, but he was becoming increasingly convinced that the old man would prove to be the most valuable member of his unorthodox unit.

"Katie," August said vehemently, "bring the captain a platter of cold fowl and a bowl of French salad greens. Dave, you and Dick can help Benjy groom the stallion. The work will be finished more rapidly that way."

The group scattered and Hugh, secretly amused by the elderly rogue's habit of assuming command, made no protest.

"I wanted a few moments alone with you," August said.

"So I surmised."

"I've been devoting a great deal of thought to the plan you devised."

"I don't think it requires much thought," Hugh replied, nettled. "You and Katie will enter New York by one route, the Simpsons will take another and Benjy and I will travel by a third. We'll join forces at the Duke of Albany Inn near the Battery and start searching for the counterfeiters."

"I have no desire to usurp your authority, Captain, but the idea isn't sound. If any of the British in New York are aware of my existence, they'll connect me with my daughter. You and Benjy arrived in this country together as bondsmen, and you've been working together in the Continental army, so we must presume that the English civil and military authorities think of you jointly, if they think of you at all."

The argument, Hugh was forced to admit, made sense.

"As to the Simpsons, there is no way to disguise the fact that they're brothers. However, men with their obvious lack of breeding wouldn't choose of their own accord to stay at a hostelry like the Duke of Albany Inn. So I suggest that we make no attempt to disguise them, but I feel that the rest of us should shuffle our identities, so to speak."

"Do you have any specific thoughts?"

"Of course," August said loftily, "and I believe in adhering to the principle I've followed all of my life. I always use my own name and conjure up as few lies about myself as possible. That reduces the chances of being caught in a lie. Katie created grave problems for herself and caused me no end of trouble when she insisted on posing as Sara Dean for your sake."

He was interrupted by his daughter, who returned with a tray of food, which she placed on a table beside Hugh, who deliberately looked away. She ignored him, too, and took a chair on the far side of the room, where she resumed her knitting. Hugh started to eat, and the cold chicken and salad were delicious, but he thought Katie's manner had been so rude that he refrained from thanking her.

August, peering intently at one, then the other, nodded sagely. "I'm convinced that I've found the perfect solution," he said. "I shall travel to New York by way of Westchester County, and when I reach enemy territory I'll make it plain that I'm an Englishman who supports the king. Benjy will act as my secretary, and the Simpsons will pose as my retainers. I'll travel under my own name, for the reasons I've explained to you. Benjy will be the only member of my party who will be in any danger of discovery, thanks to his activity as an American soldier, but he'll enjoy my protection. And no one, I'm confident, will glance twice at the Simpsons."

Hugh put down the leg of chicken he was eating and smiled wryly. "You've taken good care to save your own neck, but you leave me exposed. If I arrive in New York alone, I'll be forced to undergo a whole series of investigations and cross-examinations."

"My dear lad," August said in horror, "I wouldn't dream of allowing you to go into enemy territory unaccompanied."

"Then you've forgotten how to count," Hugh said heatedly. "If you and Katie are going to take Benjy and the Simpsons with you, I'll be traveling alone."

"It would appear," the old man replied with a smile, "that you didn't hear me correctly. I didn't mention Katie."

The girl looked up from her knitting with a frown.

"I propose," her father continued, "that you make a slightly longer journey and arrive in New York from New Jersey. You will tell the British that you're an English gentleman, that you've been living in Philadelphia and that you've escaped through the American lines at the first opportunity."

"A flimsy story," Hugh said. "What would have prevented me from making my way to New York long ago?"

"Life is always more complicated for married men than it is for bachelors."

Katie jumped to her feet, letting her knitting fall to the floor. "No, Pa!" she cried.

August acknowledged her protest with a wave. "You're very perspicacious, my dear," he said, and turned back to Hugh. "What I'm suggesting, Captain, is that you and Katie travel as Mr. and Mrs. Hugh Spencer."

"I won't do it, Pa!" Spots of color burned in Katie's cheeks.

"I don't care for the idea either," Hugh said coldly, finding his voice.

August sighed and shook his head sadly. "I'm afraid you're allowing your unfortunate—ah—misunderstanding in London several years ago to cloud your thinking. Let us assume that the British high command is aware that a former officer in one of His Majesty's regiments is now serving as a captain in the Continental Army. Let us even assume that someone in New York knows that an indentured servant named Spencer ran away from his master in one of the southern colonies. States, that is to say. I'm inclined to doubt that anyone in the city will be aware of the incident, but it's always preferable to assume the worst when making preparations."

Katie put her hands on her hips and stamped her foot vigorously. "You're very persuasive, Pa, but I refuse to listen to you."

The old man regarded her sternly. "It shouldn't be necessary to remind you, my dear child, that we wouldn't have been forced to leave England if you hadn't insisted on playing your little charade with Captain Spencer. You forced me to take extraordinary steps to save us from prison, you may recall. Mrs. Radway had to lie, a waiter who had been in my employ for years was of no further use to me, and after I sold the house that had been my first real home, I was compelled to flee from my native land. I've never taxed you or complained, but the fault is on your shoulders, and I regret that your memory is so short."

Her face flaming, Katie sat down again and gripped the arms of her chair.

Hugh wanted to change the subject quickly. "I fail to see how any of us would benefit, August."

"You're too intelligent to let your hatred for Katie warp your powers of analysis, Captain. Think of the impression you'd create. A charming young couple, members of the gentry, arrive in New York. They've fled from their home, leaving all of their possessions behind. They have enough funds to take up residence at the Duke of Albany Inn, to be sure, and they ask for no charity, but they're loyal subjects of King George who are innocent victims of the rebellion."

Hugh's meal was forgotten and he rubbed his chin thoughtfully.

"Don't listen to Pa!" Katie said, addressing him for the first time.

August ignored her protest. "You'd be received with great sympathy. You'd be passed through the lines without difficulty, and Katie would be an enormous asset."

"I'm familiar with her work," Hugh said dryly.

"What's more, the Tories in New York would welcome you. Your disguise would be brilliant. Who in his right mind would suspect that an American officer would come to the enemy capital posing as a married man and bringing his lovely partner with him?"

"Who in his right mind would ever do such a thing?" Katie asked.

Hugh looked down at the tray and weighed the matter carefully. He knew his former countrymen, and he had to concede that Katie would be a perfect shield for him. British officers would extend every courtesy to a pretty refugee, Tories would open their doors to the couple, and the chance of discovery would be diminished enormously. "Your plan has certain merits," he said at last, cautiously.

"I knew I could rely on your good sense." August beamed at him.

Katie clenched her fists and pounded the arms of her chair. "I've already said I won't be a party to any such scheme. Don't I have a voice in this matter?"

"You do not," Hugh told her firmly. "You'll do what you're told."

She glared at him, and for a moment he thought she intended to throw a snuffbox at his head.

"You agreed to certain terms before you were released from jail in Providence," Hugh said, goaded by her opposition. "You're in my parole, and I'm not permitting you to change the terms now in order to suit your convenience."

"There was no mention of any personal relationship between us!" she cried.

"The idea didn't occur to me any more than it did to you," he said, "and I don't look forward to a period of enforced intimacy, even a sham one, with any pleasure. My only concern is to find the men who are making counterfeit Continental dollars and destroy their plates. And I'll do anything necessary to achieve that end."

"This is splendid," August said, chuckling.

"Not so fast." The lines in Hugh's face hardened as he turned back to the old man. "I trust you aren't suggesting that Katie and I actually live together as husband and wife."

August cleared his throat delicately. "The welfare of my daughter has always been one of my first considerations, and I trust I'll be a good and loving father as long as I live. Captain, I've been observing you and Katie whenever you've been together since we've returned here from Providence. I take justifiable pride in my understanding of people, which has been as essential to my profession as my artistry, and your own behavior is responsible for the birth of my idea. You and Katie act like a married couple who can't tolerate each other but are still bound by invisible ties. I'm confident that the British will believe that you're man and wife."

"That isn't what he meant, Pa," Katie said in a low, embarrassed voice.

"You're capable of defending your virtue, my dear child," August replied soothingly. "As for you, Captain, I believe you've become impervious to Katie's charms."

"I have no personal interest in her," Hugh said flatly, wishing he felt as confident as he sounded.

"Then you agree to my plan?"

Hugh realized that the masquerade might distract him from his mission, but on the other hand he knew that the unreliable August would be less likely to defect if his daughter were a hostage. "The scheme is sound, but I can accept it only on one condition." Hugh stood, crossed the room, and stood in front of Katie.

She looked up at him stonily, a challenge in her eyes.

"The success or failure of this expedition will help to determine the fate of the United States. I'll need your active co-operation."

She folded her hands in her lap demurely. "You told me I'm to follow orders," she said, "so you give me no choice."

The faint but distinct note of mockery in her voice warned Hugh that she was reserving the right to defy him.

After a final evening of frenzied preparations, Hugh and Katie left Black Ox farm shortly after dawn. They would make a longer journey than the other members of the Scoundrels' Brigade, so August, Benjy, and the Simpson brothers planned to remain at the farm until the following morning, and if everything went according to plan, the two groups would be reunited in New York in four days. Katie, who was an accomplished rider, had her own mare, and Hugh, who was mounted on Toby, led a gelding carrying boxes of clothing and bric-a-brac that had been packed under August's supervision.

Hugh, marveling at the old man's cunning, could understand why he had been so successful in his career as a counterfeiter. August had insisted that the baggage should substantiate the claim that the couple were refugees, so Katie had taken more clothing than she would need, and Hugh, who had purchased only two civilian suits since he had decided to invade enemy territory, had been told by August to invest in other items of apparel before he reached British-held territory. Several pieces of silver, a cut-glass vase, and a pair of battered pewter mugs were stuffed into one of Katie's leather boxes too, and Hugh approved heartily of August's foresight. The household items were precisely the sorts of objects that a woman leaving her home would take with her.

"We'll avoid Westerly and ride across open country to the Connecticut road," Hugh said to Katie as they waved to the men who watched them from the entrance to Black Ox farm. "I think it wiser if people who would recognize you don't see us together."

"I'm not known in Westerly." She sat in her saddle easily, staring straight ahead.

"How is that possible?"

"Pa thought it might be safer for us if local people weren't aware of my existence. It was one of the precautions he took to protect us. I made trips with him to Boston and New Haven, and before the war I went to New York with him several times, but I've never set foot in Westerly. The only person who would recognize me would be the sheriff. I'm sure you'll remember that he arrested us at the farm and that you took us straight to Providence because he was afraid the people of Westerly might become unpleasant."

Hugh recalled the incident vividly. "I think we'll work together more harmoniously if we don't drag up painful memories of one sort or another."

"If those are your orders, I'll obey them."

Her exaggerated meekness irritated him, but he wanted to avoid a quarrel at the outset of the journey, so he ignored the provocation. "Is it true that you've never visited Westerly?"

"You and I will have to reach an understanding right now, Hugh." She addressed him by his Christian name for the first time since he had seen her in America. "My father loves adventure for its own sake, but I don't. I like living quietly in my own home, and I certainly don't enjoy the prospect of being hanged in New York as a spy. I've come with you for two reasons. Naturally, I hope Pa and I will win a pardon. And if I can, I want to repay my debt to you. I was unkind to you in London, so I'd like to help you now. Please let me finish. I don't expect to win either your friendship or your respect, but I'm not stupid, and I know we'll be caught if we don't work together. So, even though this may be hard for you to believe, I won't lie to you." Giving him no chance to reply, she spurred ahead and took the lead on the road to Westerly.

They didn't converse again all morning, and Hugh, after trying to evaluate Katie's alleged desire to help him, decided it would be in his best interests to give her no credit for the statement. She had fooled him once, and he would be courting disaster if he allowed her to influence him again.

Shortly before noon they reached the Thames River, and dismounted on the ferry that carried them across the stream to New London. They stood together at the rail of the clumsy, broad-bottomed boat, and Katie startled Hugh by laughing.

"Pa thinks he's so clever, but he's forgotten the most obvious token of all, and so have you." She held up her left hand.

Hugh looked at her blankly.

"We're going to pose as a married couple when we reach British territory, but I have no wedding ring."

He said he would rectify the oversight immediately, and found a silversmith's shop on the High Street in New London. The proprietress, a plump, taciturn woman, brightened when she saw Hugh's uniform and announced that her husband was serving with a regiment of Connecticut militia.

"We'd like to buy a wedding ring," Hugh said, and the woman smiled broadly.

"I like your taste, Captain," she replied. "You've sure picked yourself as pretty a bride as ever I've seen."

Katie flushed, and Hugh realized that his task might prove to be more difficult than they had anticipated.

They stopped for the night at a small inn on the western bank of the Connecticut River, where Hugh asked for two rooms at opposite sides of the building. The next day they reached New Haven, followed the Post Road through Bridgeport, and then started to move inland. It was after dark when they arrived at a tavern in the small town of Wilton, and the innkeeper gave them one room. Hugh protested, much to the man's surprise, and, as no other space was available, gave the chamber to Katie and spent the night in a hayloft. She thanked him at breakfast the following morning, and he accepted her remark with a curt nod, which left the innkeeper even more puzzled. Hugh offered no explanation, but knew the luxury of avoiding Katie would soon come to an end.

On the third day of the journey they crossed the Connecticut-New York line, cut across the upper portion of Westchester County, and were ferried over the Hudson River several miles above the British sentry outposts. Hugh knew precisely where he was going, but offered Katie no explanation, telling her only that the enemy frequently raided the district and that if they were attacked he would try to hold off the foe while she rode on ahead. They were tense and exceptionally quiet during the latter part of the day, but no incidents marred their journey, and Hugh pressed ahead long after night fell, pausing occasionally to study a map by the pale light of a half-moon.

At last they came to a large, dark farmhouse, and Hugh dismounted at the entrance. Katie watched him curiously as he tapped five times on the door, and after a long pause a chain rattled, the latch was raised, and the door was opened a crack.

"Liberty or death. Patrick Henry," Hugh said.

A man grunted approval softly.

"All men are created equal and independent. Thomas Jefferson. First draft of the Declaration of Independence." Hugh paused for a moment, then asked, "Countersign?"

"Put none but Americans on guard tonight. General Washington."

Hugh relaxed, and the door opened.

"Who are you?" The gaunt, elderly man in the entrance looked like a simple farmer.

"Captain Spencer, of Tallmadge's staff, and a lady."

The old farmer called out an order, and Katie was surprised when four or five other men came out of the house. She was helped to the ground, and the horses were taken to the rear. An old woman who was waiting inside the dark house conducted her to a bedroom, brought her a plate of cold food, and told her that under no circumstances should she light a candle.

Hugh disappeared until the following morning, and when he tapped at Katie's door shortly after the sun rose, he was dressed in a suit of dark green wool with velvet lapels. His neckcloth was made of the finest grade of linen, an edge of lace showed at his cuffs, and his military sword had been replaced by a lighter blade of the type that civilians carried. "This is the first time I've appeared before the world as a member of the gentry since you and I dined together in London," he told Katie with a quiet smile when she admitted him to the chamber.

She flushed and turned away.

"I'm sorry. I shouldn't have brought up the past on the most critical of days."

Katie could hear the note of genuine contrition in his voice, and her anger faded. "I assume that we're going into New York today?"

"Yes. I've now changed my identity, and I won't come back for my uniform until our mission is completed."

"Where are we?"

"In New Jersey. It's better for you if you don't know any details. Butcher Billy Cunningham, General Howe's provost, has developed a remarkable technique for forcing prisoners to reveal information."

She was grateful for his thoughtfulness.

"Are you ready to leave?" There was a trace of impatience in Hugh's voice as he glanced through the window at the sky. "We'll eat quickly while the horses are being saddled."

Katie looked down at the dusty, creased dress she had been wearing since they had left Black Ox farm. "If I'd known we were going to cross the lines today, I'd have changed into something more appropriate for the occasion."

"You look fine to me," he replied, and meant it.

"I don't! You're a dashing gentleman, and I look like a frump."

He realized they sounded like a couple who had been married for a long time, and couldn't help grinning.

As soon as Katie saw he was in a good mood, she moved to the one leather box that had been brought to the room. "I'll find something more suitable in here, and I'll join you in a few moments."

"There's no need for you to change." It was absurd to waste valuable time primping, Hugh thought, and wondered how to persuade her that her vanity was the least important of their considerations.

"You've told me that we'll be facing danger when we cross into territory occupied by the English," Katie said stubbornly.

"We will. And that's why I want to leave this area before too many people are stirring. I don't want us to be seen near this house."

"The longer you stand there, arguing, the longer we'll be delayed."

He had tried to persuade her to behave reasonably, but she was giving him no choice, so he had to remind her to obey his orders.

Katie saw his expression. "You have your weapons," she said. "I know how to use mine."

Recalling vividly how she had dazzled him in London, he flinched and had to admit she was right. A beautiful girl, as August had pointed out, was worth more than a sword and a brace of pistols. "All right," he said grudgingly, "but hurry."

Katie's smile was quiet but self-confident. "You can rely on me."

XIV / *May 1777*

MAJOR the Honorable Kenneth Frederick, commander of the outposts on the lower Hudson, stared in unconcealed admiration at the girl in the handsome traveling gown of thin, dark yellow wool, who wore a huge matching feather in her broad-brimmed hat. "Are you sure you've never been painted by Gainsborough or Sir Joshua Reynolds, ma'am?"

"You flatter me, Major, but I'm quite sure." Katie toyed with the end of her plume, readjusting it artfully so it nestled in a mass of long red curls.

Hugh, aware of the perfection of her technique, stood beside his stallion, and as he watched Katie flirting expertly with the enemy officer, he felt an unexpected stab of jealousy. But it was ridiculous to allow his own emotions to become involved; he knew she was making the task of crossing the lines into New York infinitely easier. Nevertheless he resented her obvious enjoyment of the major's attention and her consciousness of the ogling red-coated soldiers who stood at either side of the barricade that blocked the road.

"You should have her painted!" Frederick said emphatically to Hugh. "Such beauty should be reproduced on canvas for future generations to enjoy."

Hugh remembered to smile, but his tone was frigid. "I'll try to arrange a sitting as soon as we return to London."

Katie smiled at the major quickly to counteract Hugh's coldness. "You're very gallant, sir. I don't feel like someone who should be painted, I assure you. We were accosted by rebel patrols so often on our ride from Philadelphia that I lost count of the number of times."

"They didn't harm you, I trust?" Frederick tugged at his bristling mustache and glowered fiercely.

Katie, continuing to smile, shook her head.

"We'll clear the colonies of that rabble in the next few months, ma'am!"

"I hope," she said sweetly, "that we'll be back in England by then."

"When do you sail for home?"

Hugh, realizing that he had nearly provoked a quarrel with the officer, decided to remain silent and let Katie, whose charm was working miracles, answer the question.

"We have no definite plans yet," she said vaguely. "At the moment I can't think of anything, I'm so grateful that we've escaped from the rebels. I know that my husband feels as I do," she added pointedly.

"It's a great relief," Hugh said.

The major pulled at his mustache again. "Where do you intend to stay in New York?" He beckoned to a junior officer, who came forward with a printed form pinned to a board. "General Howe's orders," Frederick explained. "I'm required to make out a dossier on you."

"I'm afraid we don't really know where we'll go." Katie sounded distressed.

"You aren't going to the home of friends?"

The situation was delicate, so Hugh intervened swiftly. "Everyone we know has suffered such great losses in this idiotic rebellion that we don't want to be a burden on our friends."

"Quite true," the major muttered. "I can understand your

feeling completely." He looked at Katie appreciatively, and his voice was oily as he said, "I have a small house in Manhattan, a place I requisitioned last year. The senior officers have taken all of the imposing houses, of course, but mine is quite comfortable, and you're welcome to share it. It would be almost like having a house of your own, as I spend most of my time on outpost duty."

Katie's warning glance silenced Hugh, who was tense beneath his gracious façade.

"I believe that's the kindest offer that's ever been made to us," Katie cried, and when she clapped her hands together the gesture looked impulsive. "But we wouldn't dream of imposing on your hospitality, Major."

Frederick tried to protest, but she gave him no chance.

"Besides," she continued, "I don't believe I could cope with the problems of keeping a house in order at the moment."

Hugh was fascinated by her play-acting, and almost forgot the crisis caused by the major's offer. She looked sad, and sounded forlorn.

"We had such a lovely little house in Philadelphia." Her voice wavered. "It broke my heart to leave it." Recovering, she smiled pathetically. "I'm sure you can understand why I don't want to be reminded of a place I shall never see again."

"We'll take Philadelphia soon, ma'am," Frederick said earnestly.

"I'm sure you will, sir, but I'm putting my domestic life in the colonies behind me." Katie spoke firmly now, and appeared courageous and strong. "Perhaps you could suggest a hostelry where we might stay until we sail for home, a place that isn't too expensive. Then," she added brightly, "we might all dine together when you come into the city."

"Splendid." The major beamed at her, then tugged at his sword belt. "All of the better inns are crowded with refugees these days, of course, and most of them are quite expensive. You might try the Lion and Sceptre."

"I'll remember that." Hugh was relieved that Frederick

hadn't mentioned the Duke of Albany Inn. "Thank you for your help, sir."

"It's the least I can do," Major Frederick replied, paused, and reddened in embarrassment. "Now, then. Accept my apologies in advance. I'm afraid I must subject you to a rather humiliating experience, but I have no choice. Headquarters of the general-officer-commanding has ordered me to inspect the luggage of all travelers."

"How dreadful for you," Katie said sympathetically.

The major murmured his thanks and shifted uncomfortably as several red-coated soldiers unstrapped the leather boxes. "I'm sure you're carrying no contraband, but I must follow regulations."

"What is considered contraband?" Katie asked innocently.

"Explosives, ma'am. And rebel literature."

Hugh decided it would be wise to join the conversation again, and laughed heartily. "Do you mean rubbish like those pamphlets written by that fellow—what's his name—Paine?"

Frederick laughed too.

"I am carrying my small arms and a supply of ammunition." Hugh went to one of the cases and, digging beneath a pile of clothing, brought out a leather case, which he opened.

Frederick looked inside enviously. "I've never seen a finer pair of dueling pistols."

"I'm lucky to have them," Hugh said honestly. They had belonged to one of Howe's mercenary Hessian officers whom he had made prisoner in one of the last, fierce battles in which he had fought.

"You're fortunate the rebels didn't find them and confiscate them on your journey from Philadelphia," the major declared.

"The rebels are incredibly stupid."

Frederick pulled at his mustaches. "They are." He walked to the leather boxes and gazed down at them reluctantly.

"You will be careful of my things, won't you?" Katie asked anxiously. "I could bring so little with me."

"You may trust me, ma'am." The major took a vase from the

top of one case, looked at a snuffbox, and examined a pair of carved mahogany book ends. "These are quite handsome," he said.

"Don't." Tears appeared in Katie's eyes. "I'm reminded of all the books I had to leave behind."

The major replaced the objects. "Close the cases," he told his men. "I've completed my inspection." He removed his helmet and bowed gallantly to Katie. "You're free to proceed. I hope to enjoy the pleasure of your company some evening in New York, ma'am. And yours," he added belatedly to Hugh.

Katie continued to smile steadily while the barricade was moved, and Hugh tipped his hat as they rode down the hill to the ferry that would take them from New Jersey to the city across the Hudson.

"Congratulations," he said, when they could no longer be overheard. "You handled that pompous fool brilliantly." She had manipulated him as easily when he had courted her in London, he thought bitterly, and the victory they had just won lost its savor.

Norton Walker, proprietor of the Duke of Albany Inn, studied his new guests surreptitiously. Both were dressed expensively, their manners were patrician, and their horses, particularly the stallion, were animals that only wealthy people could afford to own. Walker, whose business had thrived since the British had occupied New York, considered himself an excellent judge of character and an even better one of his patrons' ability to pay the prices he demanded. He bowed, smiled ingratiatingly, and stood aside to let them enter the inn ahead of him.

"You'll want some tea after your exhausting journey," he said, "so I'll have some sent up to you at once."

"Thank you," Hugh replied with the air of one accustomed to such treatment, and Katie, playing the great lady to perfection, smiled distantly.

"I assume, Mr. Spencer, that you'll want one of our better suites?" Walker rubbed his hands together.

"What is your charge for such accommodations?" Hugh managed to convey the impression that any discussion involving money was distasteful.

"Ten shillings per day, sir."

The price was outrageous, but Hugh maintained his poise. "I'm afraid I can't afford a suite at the moment," he said regretfully. "I'll have to wait until we capture Philadelphia and my property there is recovered for me." He turned to Katie apologetically. "We'll have to make do with less, my dear."

She stifled a sigh and contrived to look heroic.

Walker's attitude changed immediately. The Spencers weren't English aristocrats, as he had assumed, but Tory refugees. Loyalists from every colony had come to New York, and the proprietor of the Duke of Albany knew from long experience how to handle them. "The only other quarters I can give you cost three shillings per day, or one pound at the weekly rate."

"We'll pay by the week."

"I'll have a boy show you upstairs. If you'd care for tea, the taproom is on your left." Walker turned away abruptly.

"One moment," Hugh called. "I'd like to see for myself what care is being provided for my horses, and I want a word with your principal groom."

The owner of the establishment hastily revised his new estimate. Most of the Tories who came to the inn neither knew nor cared how their horses were treated, but members of the English gentry frequently inspected the stables. Perhaps his first appraisal of this handsome couple had been correct, in which case it would be wise to treat them with deference. The refugees from Boston and Charleston might not recover their property for a long time, but there was a persistent rumor that Sir William Howe might take Philadelphia soon, and the Spencers would be delighted to move from a cramped garret room to an expensive suite.

"I'll escort Mistress Spencer to your chamber myself,"
Walker said, "and the boy can show you to the stables, sir."

Hugh had two reasons for going to the stables; he wanted
to make certain that the stallion Toby, the mare, and the pack
horse received proper treatment, but even more important, he
could tell by looking at the other mounts whether August,
Benjy, and the Simpsons had arrived. The stable was located
on the far side of a small courtyard, and the chief groom, eager to impress a client who made it clear at once that he understood horses, offered to take the guest through the place.
Hugh accepted, and was disappointed when he saw none of
the familiar mounts from Black Ox farm. Cutting his inspection short, he gave the groom crisp instructions, and, returning to the inn, was shown to a room on the top floor.

Katie was unpacking the contents of the leather boxes
when he entered, and he looked around in dismay. The chamber was tiny, with a sloping ceiling that made it impossible to
stand erect on the left side. A large four-poster bed was the
most prominent piece of furniture, and the only other items
were a small dressing table, a chest of drawers, and a straight-
backed chair. It was too late for regrets, but Hugh realized he
should have accepted the offer of a suite regardless of the
price.

"Rather cozy, isn't it?" Katie giggled as she folded a cloak
and put it in the chest.

It would be virtually impossible to maintain any sort of
privacy in such a cramped room, and Hugh started back toward the door. "I'll tell Walker we've changed our minds and
that we want the suite."

"You can't. You were very emphatic when you said we
couldn't afford the price, which we can't. And he offered me
his sympathies at great length when he brought me up here.
I suspect that Walker has a sharp mind behind that round,
red face, and we don't want him to speculate too much about
us."

"You're far more clever at this sort of thing than I am, as

I discovered earlier today when you had that fatuous major at the outpost fawning all over you." The incident was distasteful, and he put it out of his mind. "Your father isn't here yet."

"Oh dear."

Hugh shared her concern, as August should have arrived no later than noon had he met no unexpected obstacles. But there was no need to worry Katie unnecessarily. "He's only a few hours late."

"You don't know Pa. He's never late."

"He didn't have you to help him through the lines." Hugh tried to sound jovial. "It's possible that he's been delayed by an officer who wanted to question him or Benjy at some length."

"I suppose you're right."

"I suggest we go down to the taproom for dinner."

"I'd rather wait for Pa."

"As you wish." Hugh started to unpack his own belongings.

He finished in a short time and, with nothing else to occupy him, sat on the edge of the bed and watched Katie. She was the last woman on earth with whom he would have imagined himself sharing such intimate quarters, and a sense of unreality gripped him as he watched her taking petticoats and stockings, nightdresses and negligees from the leather boxes. She took her time, deliberately dragging out the process, but at last she came to the bottom of the one remaining box.

It was obvious that she was thinking about her father, but she refrained from mentioning him again, and instead looked at her reflection in the silver-backed mirror she had brought with her from the farm. "I'll have to do something about my face," she announced, breaking the silence, and sat down at the dressing table.

Hugh jumped to his feet immediately. "Shall I wait for you in the taproom?"

"If you disappear every time I do something about my ap-

pearance, it's going to be terribly inconvenient for both of us."
She smiled absently as she began to take pins out of her hair.
"Please sit down."

Hugh obeyed, and watched in fascination as she brushed
her hair, which almost reached her waist. A sense of excitement began to mount in him, and he had to remind himself
that this was the girl who had betrayed his love. He had
chosen to work with her for the benefit of the United States,
but it would be insane to let himself become involved with
her too deeply, and he tried to look away, but found it impossible to take his eyes from her as, holding her mirror in
one hand and manipulating her hair with the other, she
twisted and patted and coaxed. Order finally emerged out of
chaos, and her hair was piled high on her head, with one long
curl dipping over her right shoulder.

She was aware of Hugh's scrutiny, but said nothing until
she was satisfied with her hair. "It's growing dark," she said.
"Would you light some candles, please?"

He struggled briefly with a tinderbox and flint, then
lighted three candles and an oil lamp, which he offered to
Katie.

She was pleased that he had discovered it, and he went
back to the edge of the bed while she applied a delicate green
salve to her eyelids, outlined her mouth with rouge, and
dusted her nose, forehead, and chin with rice powder. Katie
studied herself closely and was pleased with what she saw,
but her smile faded as they heard a bell in a nearby church
tower chime seven times.

"Was that the curfew?" she asked.

He nodded and looked away from her. Civilians were required to remain indoors after seven o'clock in the evening,
so August could not arrive until the following day.

"You're worried too, aren't you?"

"Yes," he admitted, "but your father has taken care of himself for a long time. And Benjy can manage anywhere. They'll
be here tomorrow." Rising, he walked to the room's one win-

dow and stared out at the British warships that choked the mouth of the East River. The sight of so many men-of-war and frigates, sloops and bomb ketches depressed him; there was no fleet on the high seas stronger than Admiral Lord Howe's command, and for a moment Hugh allowed himself to give in to despair.

Katie joined him, saw his expression, and understood when she glanced out at the ships. "I'm sure Pa and Benjy will make out all right," she said. "And so will the United States."

He was surprised, and grinned at her. "You sound as though you mean that."

"I swore that I'll never lie to you."

"I've told you no untruths, and I don't intend to begin now." He looked at her for a long moment. "I haven't told you for a very long time that I think you're lovely."

Katie laughed lightly. "You can say that after watching me use pomades and salves and pasting this velvet patch on my cheekbone?"

"That," Hugh replied with mock severity, "is a less than subtle attempt to win another compliment." He realized he hadn't allowed himself to enjoy a conversation with her since he had first discovered her at Black Ox farm.

"If you think I won't disgrace you, we should go down to eat before the food is gone." She slipped her arm through his, and they walked together into the corridor and down the stairs.

The taproom, a large chamber with oak beams, an open hearth, and tables of unpainted maple, was crowded, but Walker, who hovered near the entrance supervising his employees, had formed the definite conclusion that the handsome Spencers were aristocrats and, beaming, led them to a table in a far corner. Conversation halted for a moment, then began again vivaciously as people stared at Katie. The women watched her with narrowed eyes, but the majority of men, including several British officers, made no secret of their admiration for her. She was accustomed to creating a stir and paid no attention to the commotion, but the stares made Hugh uncomfortable, and after he had ordered two glasses of sack, he turned to her with a wry smile.

"I think I may have made a mistake by bringing you with me," he said in an undertone so the overdressed party of wealthy Tories at the adjoining table couldn't hear him. "I blame your father as much as myself. He knows that you cause a sensation when you walk into a public place, but the first rule in our sort of work is to remain inconspicuous."

"I could try to make myself look drab, if that would make you less apprehensive, but Pa always found my appearance was a help."

His own experience had taught him that no one would suspect her, so she was probably right; General Howe's intelligence officers wouldn't imagine that the enemy would send a ravishing beauty to the city which they made their occupation headquarters.

A barmaid brought the sack, and when she had gone, Katie leaned forward. "An officer sitting against the wall to your left is staring at you, not me," she murmured.

Hugh raised his glass in a toast and, twisting slightly in his chair, glanced obliquely over his shoulder. "We served together in the same regiment."

"Then he knows you?"

"As well as I know him. I expected something like this might happen, so I'm prepared for it."

"I hope so," Katie replied somberly. "He's coming over here."

The officer in the gold-braided red coat, white breeches, and polished boots approached the table, halted, and peered suspiciously at Hugh. "You're Spencer of the cavalry, aren't you?"

Hugh pretended to see him for the first time. "Captain Talbot! I'm delighted!"

The cavalryman's face remained stiff. "Didn't I hear that you had trouble with the law?"

"There was an unfortunate administrative error in the office of the crown prosecutor, but it turned out to be a blessing in disguise," Hugh replied easily, having rehearsed a speech for such a situation. "I did rather handsomely in Philadelphia before the rebels made life impossible there, and I won an even more important prize. My dear, I'd like to present Captain Talbot of the Fourth Dragoons. My wife, Captain."

Katie's smile was dazzling, and when she extended her hand, the flustered officer bent low to kiss it.

"An honor, ma'am," he said, and when he straightened it was easy to read his mind. A criminal could not have persuaded such a charming creature to marry him, nor would he be dining with her in one of the occupation center's fashionable gathering places. "I'm very pleased for you, Spencer." Talbot thawed, and his conquest was complete. "Are you living in New York now?"

"We just came through the lines today."

"Ah. Then you'll probably be eager for a bit of sport. I'm with a new regiment that's been formed recently, and we need men like you. The rebels have a nasty habit of shooting officers. I'm sure if you applied to Sir William for a renewal of your commission, he'd grant it. I'm rejoining the regiment tomorrow for some rebel-hunting, and there are several of us who'd be happy to stand as your sponsors. Major Kirkwood, who was your old troop commander, is the regimental adjutant, and—"

"Captain, I wouldn't permit him to do it!" Katie appeared agitated.

Hugh was grateful for her intervention, as the unexpected suggestion had caught him off guard.

"We hope to sail for home as soon as we can take care of some business matters here," she continued. "If he wants to rejoin the army after we arrive in England, I can't oppose him, naturally, nor would I want to prevent him from serving. But we've been so miserable in this rebel-infested wilderness that

I couldn't sleep if I had to sail alone and left him behind to fight the Yankee rabble."

She sounded so upset that Hugh's grin was natural. "You can see my problem, Talbot. Every time I've mentioned the idea of rejoining the army, she becomes hysterical."

"Please, darling," Katie begged. "Don't even talk about it. If you love me, you'll come back to London with me."

Captain Talbot sighed enviously. "I must confess that if I had a wife like Mistress Spencer, I'd find such a plea irresistible. My apologies, ma'am, for disturbing you." He chatted for a short time longer, and finally returned to his own table.

Hugh sat down again, looked soberly at Katie, and lifted his glass to her. "This is the second time today that you've saved me. It's obvious that I was wrong when I said you were too flamboyantly attractive for this sort of work."

She preferred to ignore his flattery. "It's my duty to help you," she said, ending the discussion by turning away from him and studying the list of the evening's dishes chalked on a board that hung from a wall behind the cooks' hearths and spits.

Deliberately choosing English specialties, they ate veal and ham pies and shared a sour-plum tart. They exchanged an occasional word for the benefit of the other patrons, who would have believed they were quarreling and therefore would have paid more attention to them if they had remained silent. The tension mounted, and Hugh found it increasingly difficult to talk about impersonal matters. This meal was different, and he knew Katie felt as he did, that a new and delicate phase of their relationship had begun. Not only were they compelled to pose as a married couple in public, but the problems of maintaining barriers between them would be complicated before the evening ended, when they would retire to the tiny chamber they had rented.

A sense of panic assailed Hugh, and he doubted whether he was strong enough to resist Katie's charms. At last he admitted to himself that he had no real desire to avoid her; on the contrary, he still wanted her. She no longer appealed to him romantically, and he certainly wouldn't marry a girl who had been responsible for his arrest, imprisonment, and deportation from England on a false charge. Nevertheless she was still the most attractive creature he had ever known, and he saw no need to exercise unnecessary self-control. An affair would not hamper the mission that had brought them to New York.

They finished their meal, and Hugh ordered two glasses of port. He drank his wine quickly, but Katie sipped daintily, and it occurred to him that she was taking her time purposely. However, when a group of British naval officers arrived and sat at a nearby table, she realized it would be dangerous to delay too long. The men had already drunk more than was good for them, and all of them stared at Katie, nudged each other, and talked about her in loud voices. Hugh bristled, so she drained her glass and he paid for their dinner with English money he had acquired at the farmhouse in New Jersey. The naval officers continued to comment about her as she made her way out of the taproom and Hugh followed her, stiff-necked.

They didn't speak until they reached their chamber on the top floor, and when Hugh bolted the door, Katie giggled. "If we had stayed there any longer," she said, "you would have had a fight with those officers, particularly the dark-haired lieutenant with the dueling scar."

"He was rude and vulgar," Hugh said curtly.

Katie tried to humor him. "I must admit that he was blunt."

"Any man who sees you is certain to gape at you. But a gentleman doesn't discuss a lady's anatomy at the top of his voice." He was still seething and didn't realize he had referred to her as a lady.

She was pleased, but thought it better not to thank him.

"I'll remember that lieutenant," Hugh said, lighting several candles and the oil lamp from the single taper they had left burning.

"Please don't get involved in unpleasantness because of me. The authorities become terribly unpleasant when a civilian quarrels with a British officer, and I prefer to suffer a few minor indignities than call ourselves to the attention of the provost's office."

Hugh knew she was right, but he was still irritated. "It would be odd if a man failed to appreciate the way you look, but I won't tolerate crude leering."

"You sound like a real husband," Katie said, and realized her mistake instantly.

Hugh placed the candle on top of the chest of drawers, stared at her for a moment, and smiled. "How fortunate for the sake of our work that I react instinctively in the right way."

She thought it wiser to drop the subject, and, turning to the dressing table, began to remove pins from her hair.

He stood behind her, watching. "I assumed," he said, speaking slowly, "that when we arrived here we'd have quarters large enough to ensure each of us some measure of privacy."

"So did I." Katie did not turn around.

"Would you have agreed to come with me had you known we'd be given a chamber like this?" he asked suddenly.

She shrugged, removed a large comb, and shook her hair free. "You seem to forget that I had no real choice."

Hugh, unable to see her face, was uncertain whether she was mocking him. Her tone had been bland, almost too innocent. "Katie!" he said harshly.

She was removing her beauty patch gently, and gave no indication she had heard him.

"Look at me."

"Is that an order?" She made no attempt to conceal her irony now.

"Yes."

She turned slowly, and her eyes were expressionless. "I don't know whether it will be enough to say, 'Yes, sir, Captain,' or whether I'm supposed to salute, too."

The knowledge that she was goading him helped him to curb his temper. "We have an obvious problem, and it will be easier to solve if we discuss it without bitterness."

Katie smiled mischievously. "The solution is obvious," she said flippantly.

"Is it?" He hoped she didn't know that his heart was pounding.

"Of course. One of us will have to take a blanket and sleep on the floor."

"That isn't necessarily the only solution," he replied flatly.

Color rose in Katie's face, and suddenly she stamped her foot. "Is that why you insisted I come with you and pose as your wife?"

Her unexpected anger startled him.

"I understand now." Katie glared at him. "You've wanted revenge since the day you discovered me at the farm, and you've planned to treat me like a bawd. I haven't blamed you for hating me, but I didn't think you could be so vicious."

Hugh looked at her in silence.

"You're contemptible! You think you've outmaneuvered me, but you're wrong. I'll go to the British with the whole story, and I don't care if they send me to prison. They'll arrest you, too."

Hugh took a step toward her, and she raised a hand to strike him, but he caught her wrist and pinned her arm to her side. "I have no intention of treating you like a bawd," he said firmly.

Katie laughed wildly.

She was so furious that words wouldn't convince her that he had no desire to humiliate her, so he took her in his arms. She struggled violently to break away from him, and when she realized that she couldn't move her arms, she started to kick his ankles and shins. But Hugh gripped her more firmly and bent to kiss her. She tried to twist her head to one side, but he forced her against a wall, then pressed his lips against hers. She continued to fight for a time, then became limp, and he released her for an instant, grasped her by the shoulders, and kissed her again, gently.

"Maybe that will convince you," he said, and was surprised by the hoarseness he heard in his own voice.

Tears appeared in Katie's eyes, and she tried to reply, but couldn't speak.

"We've waited enough years, don't you think?" Hugh moved toward her again.

Katie made no attempt to evade him, but raised her face to his, and when he embraced her, she curled her arms around his neck. His desire was overwhelming, and he began to caress her; she shuddered and pressed close to him, and when his hand touched her right breast, she responded instantly. They broke apart, breathing hard, and stared at each other. Neither spoke, and there was no need for words as Hugh blew out the nearest candle and Katie deliberately extinguished the flame in the lamp.

XV / *May–June* 1777

A TAP sounded at the door, and when there was no response, it was repeated, more insistently. Hugh stirred, opened his eyes, and saw Katie's red hair on the pillow beside him. Bright sunshine was streaming in through a crack in the heavy drapes, and when the rapping on the door became still louder, he leaped out of bed, found his dressing gown, and searched in the dark frantically for the case that contained his pistols. He found it, removed one, and cocked it.

Katie was awake now too, and sat up, clutching the bed-clothes to her. Hugh silently handed her a negligee of pale yellow silk, then gave her the other pistol, which she concealed under the sheets. Bracing himself, he walked to the door and opened it a crack.

"I thought I had come to the wrong room," a familiar voice said.

Hugh was too embarrassed to reply, and he blinked at August, who grinned cheerfully and pushed his way into the chamber. He opened the drapes, and as sunlight flooded the room he smiled at his daughter. "Good morning, my dear," he said calmly.

Katie was so abashed she averted her face.

"Let me explain," Hugh said, and although he could think

of nothing reasonable, he was prepared to accept full responsibility.

"When facts are self-evident," August declared blithely, "explanations are tedious. I've spent sixty years observing people, and human behavior neither surprises nor disturbs me."

"How can you be so calm, Pa?" Katie cried. "You've always sworn you'd kill any man who—"

"Now, now." August stroked her hair. "The gentleman in question isn't just 'any man,' my dear. I could have predicted the future, if either of you had cared to seek my advice."

She was still upset. "If you had been here last night, this wouldn't have happened."

August chuckled and shook his head as he sat in the room's only chair. "It pains me to hear my own flesh and blood speak such gibberish. Like the ancient Greeks, I believe that the fate of every individual has been predetermined."

Hugh realized he was still gripping a pistol, and, feeling foolish, put it into its case. Then he retrieved the other from Katie and tried to comfort her with a look. He was rewarded when she smiled up at him tremulously.

August serenely ignored the intimate byplay, and, taking a snuffbox inlaid with mother-of-pearl from a waistcoat pocket, helped himself to a generous pinch. "We were delayed by events over which we had no control." He lowered his voice. "The member of your esteemed Major Tallmadge's staff who arranged to pass us through the lines was aware that a band of frontiersmen from western New York planned to attack a British garrison in the vicinity, so we were forced to spend an extra day and night at an inn in Norwalk. However, I believe there's good in everything, and I hate idleness." He removed a thick sheaf of fifty-pound notes from the inner pocket of his coat, and handed one to Hugh. "This is one of my better works of art, though I must give credit where it's due. I've rarely had more efficient assistance, even though Benjy opposed the idea when I first proposed it."

Hugh put his personal embarrassment out of his mind as he examined the counterfeit bill. "We're taking enormous risks without complicating our situation," he said, frowning.

"I'm reluctant to pay our common enemy genuine money," August replied, untroubled, and handed a note to his daughter. "I defy you to find any flaws in this."

Katie, propped up on the pillows, studied the note closely, turning it over several times and holding it up to the light. "You've made a perfect reproduction, Pa," she said at last, grudgingly. "But I—I can't help wishing you hadn't done it."

"Your respectability pleases me, my dear. It's something I've always sought for you. But don't condescend to me, if you please, and don't feel ashamed of me." August turned back to Hugh briskly. "When we arrived this morning, I told the proprietor I had heard a rumor that my good friends, the Spencers of Philadelphia, had escaped from rebel territory. I asked him if he knew how I might substantiate the story, and you can imagine my delight when he said you were guests under the same roof."

Apparently there was no limit to the old man's ingenuity. "Very clever," Hugh said.

"I thought so," August replied. "Now you can visit me in my suite without creating suspicion."

"You've engaged a suite, Pa?" Katie looked at her father in astonishment.

"The habits of a lifetime are difficult to break, and I've become accustomed to certain small luxuries." August riffled the counterfeit British notes lovingly, then put them into his pocket and stood. "We needed a meeting place, and I can imagine none more convenient. Had we given the matter more thought and planned more carefully, you might have engaged a suite too. But," he added with a faint smile, "you might not care for such an arrangement."

Hugh didn't know what to say, and glancing obliquely at Katie, saw that her face was flushed.

August looked at the heavy gold watch he carried in a lower

waistcoat pocket. "It will seem strange if I tarry here. What's more, I ate a tasteless breakfast at dawn this morning in the miserable Tory inn where we stayed last night in Westchester, and it's time for me to soothe myself with a substantial meal. Join me in my suite later for a drop of brandywine. What could be more natural than the celebration of dear friends who are reunited?" He sauntered out of the room casually, but took care to close the door carefully.

Hugh bolted it, turned to Katie, and walked to the bed. "I'm sorry I was so careless. I certainly didn't expect your father to walk in and catch us together this way."

"You and I were surprised, but Pa wasn't." She hesitated for a moment. "I know how his mind works. It was his scheming that brought us together, and he undoubtedly expects us to marry when we've completed our mission here."

A few days earlier, at Westerly, the idea of marrying Katie would have been inconceivable to Hugh. But now, looking down at her in the bed in which they had spent the night together, the prospect of spending the rest of his days with her seemed completely reasonable, even though he felt certain he had not fallen in love with her again.

"This is one time Pa won't get his way," Katie said emphatically. "He thinks you'll feel obligated to propose to me because you're a gentleman. But even if you do, I'll refuse. You'd believe I was a party to the trick, and after what I did to you in England, I wouldn't blame you. We'd be miserable together."

Hugh bent down and kissed her firmly. "We've come to New York for a purpose, and it's time to go to work."

"This brandywine comes from Admiral Lord Howe's private stock," August said, "and his orderly sells it for an outrageous price. But it's worth every penny. In fact, I wouldn't mind paying real money for a cask. It's superb."

"None for me, Pa, thank you. We've just finished breakfast." Katie spoke without thinking, and blushed.

Hugh shook his head and, glancing around the sitting room of August's suite, avoided looking at Benjy or the Simpson brothers. However, their realization that he and Katie were lovers had no bearing on the task that confronted the group. "Benjy, you've spent several hours roaming around the city. What have you learned?"

"As near as I've been able to find out, the situation is exactly what Major Tallmadge told you to expect." Benjy tallied the points he was making on his slender fingers. "First, most people prefer to deal in British pounds. Second, there are plenty of Continental dollars in circulation. Third, nobody likes to accept them, but General Howe hasn't issued an order forbidding the use of them, so you see dollars as well as pounds everywhere. Fourth, anybody who has dollars tries to get rid of them."

"That should make it easier for us," Hugh said, and August, who was sniffing a small glass of brandywine appreciatively, raised his head and nodded.

"Forgive my stupidity." Katie smoothed her skirt of pale brown silk. "I don't understand, probably because I've never been on the hunting end of this game."

"Everything depends on a systematic approach." Hugh broke off when he saw the elder of the Simpsons take a glass and approach the small cask that stood on a table near August. "Dave, you're a soldier on duty."

"That ain't easy to remember when I'm not wearing a uniform." Dave grinned and tugged at his coachman's coat.

"There's a noose waiting for you any time you forget it."

Dave sobered and stood at attention. "Yes, sir," he replied gravely.

Hugh rose and faced the group. "Each of us will concentrate on a different arena. Benjy, you'll visit printers and tailors and small merchants. Find your own reasons for calling on them, buy some inexpensive item wherever you go, and always accept Continental dollars when they're offered to you. Examine every dollar you receive. When one is counterfeit, make a detailed notation of the place and be sure to mark down the name of the man who gave it to you. A description of him will be helpful, too."

"I'll start this afternoon," Benjy said.

"Dave, you and Dick will work together. Go to the waterfront, drop in at the taverns that are popular with the British sailors, and visit the inns near the military garrisons, too. But don't drink anything stronger than beer, and at all costs avoid arguments or fights with men who wear King George's uniform."

Katie, remembering Hugh's anger at the lieutenant in the taproom, hid a smile behind her hand.

"August, I prefer to let you roam where you please rather than give you a specific assignment."

"Very wise of you, my lad." The old man tugged at his waistcoat. "I've already made the acquaintance of a colonel, and I've met a distinguished couple who own a magnificent house on the Broad Way near Trinity Church. I'm confident I'll receive invitations to dine from all of them and will be able to broaden my friendships rather quickly. Naturally, I intend to entertain a great deal, too, and I have every reason to expect that I'll be asked to spend evenings attending the theater and playing whist. I prefer card-playing, of course."

Hugh was puzzled. "You aren't going to cheat at whist?" he asked sharply.

"This is the second time today that you've failed to credit me with sufficient intelligence. I'm an excellent whist player, and could win honestly. As a matter of fact, I could earn my living at the game. But I'll win more friends if I lose." August paused and looked at his daughter. "You understand what I have in mind, Katie?"

"No, Pa."

The old man sighed plaintively. "There was a time when I hoped you'd follow in my footsteps, but it becomes plainer every year that you'll never have a distinguished career." He turned back to Hugh patiently. "I shall always lose small amounts, but I'll be carrying notes of large denominations, so the winners will have to give me change in return. I discovered long ago that aristocrats are as greedy as poorer people, so my new friends will try to get rid of dollars by giving them to me in return for what they think are good pounds. It will be interesting to learn whether anyone who associates with the Howe brothers or moves in wealthy Tory circles is passing the counterfeit dollars."

Hugh was inclined to doubt that British officers or the ultraconservative New Yorkers who had remained loyal to England were engaging in criminal activities, but a thorough investigation was essential. "I approve," he said. "I'll go to the inns and taverns that are somewhat less expensive than the places you'll visit, August, and as I presumably need new clothes and equipment of all kinds to replace the property I supposedly left behind in Philadelphia, I'll visit bootmakers, tailors and the like who deal with the less wealthy members of the gentry. Between us, I think, we'll see the money handled by every class and group in the city."

Katie, who had been listening quietly, bridled. "Have you forgotten me?"

"Certainly not," Hugh told her. "You'll come with me to the various inns I test, and as your father doesn't like the theater, we'll go together to all three playhouses as soon as we can arrange for a permit allowing us to ignore the curfew."

Her impatience was obvious. "What do you expect me to do the rest of the time, while all of you are roaming about New York? I don't intend to spend my days reading and sewing. Pa forced me to hide from the world long enough at Black Ox farm."

Hugh realized he wanted to protect her, that he was reluctant to let her conduct an independent investigation. "I see no need for you to expose yourself to danger unnecessarily. If the rest of us do our work thoroughly, we'll take care of everything."

Katie smiled condescendingly. "Do you plan to visit the

dressmakers and the ribbon shops and the cobblers who make women's shoes? Are you going to call at the places that sell petticoats or rice powder or bonnets? Presumably I lost almost all of my possessions when I escaped with you, so I'll need replacements for the better part of my wardrobe."

Her logic was unassailable, and Hugh could find no rebuttal.

"It's fortunate," August said dryly, "that I was delayed in Connecticut. Otherwise our funds would be exhausted in a week." He grinned at Hugh.

Katie, warming to her theme, ignored the interruption. "I'll go to the bookshops and the furniture- and cabinetmakers, and I really enjoy browsing in the shops that sell bric-a-brac. It's natural for a woman to want to replace things she's lost, but I'll confine my buying to small objects that could be packed into cases and be stored in the hold of the ship we'll take to England."

She spoke so earnestly that Hugh was surprised, and only the amused gleam in her eyes convinced him that she wasn't actually planning to leave the New World.

"There are greengrocers and butchers who might be passing false Continental dollars too," she continued. "I'll shop around for some raw fruits and vegetables that we can keep in our room, and when I see a particularly juicy cut of beef or a fresh fish steak that takes my fancy, I'll buy it and persuade the cook here to prepare it for us."

Hugh knew she was right, and made no protest; she could visit places where none of the men could trade. He realized, too, that his fears for her safety were groundless and that she was less likely to get into trouble than any of the men. As she had demonstrated in the past, she could take care of herself.

Hugh and Katie ate an occasional meal with August, but were careful not to be seen in his company too frequently, and whenever they encountered Benjy or the Simpson brothers in public, they nodded distantly. The group met at irregular intervals in the suite that August and Benjy shared, and Hugh analyzed the data the others had collected while scouring New York. The group remained alert, and there was no indication that the British suspected them. August, who had become friendly with a number of high-ranking officers, was positive that no one had guessed that enemy agents were making their headquarters at the Duke of Albany Inn.

There was ample evidence that counterfeit dollars were circulating freely in the city. Hugh charted each discovery carefully while August burned the notes in his sitting-room hearth, and they hoped a pattern would appear that would help them to identify the counterfeiters. They found no substantial clues, however, and by the end of June Hugh began to feel discouraged.

He hid his growing pessimism from the other men, but made no attempt to conceal his feelings from Katie. They were continuing to live together, their relationship was growing deeper, and although neither of them realized it, they were reacting to each other like a couple who were really married. Katie, returning to the tiny chamber on the top floor of the Duke of Albany Inn late one afternoon, was in a gay mood as she deposited several parcels on the bed and smiled at Hugh, who was using her dressing table as a desk.

"I've had a completely successful afternoon," she said happily. "My new gown was ready, and it's the prettiest I've ever owned, I think. I found some gloves to match it at a little shop on Wall Street, and at both places I was given some counterfeit dollars as part of my change."

Hugh continued to scowl at the long columns of closely written notes on the sheet of paper before him. "Are you sure the money is counterfeit?"

"I couldn't swear to it. Pa will have to check for me the next time we see him, but I'm reasonably certain."

He threw down his quill pen and cursed under his breath. "That's our problem!" he said explosively.

Katie looked at him in concern. "What's wrong, darling?"

Neither of them thought it strange that she used a term of endearment when she addressed him.

"Ordinarily you can tell at a glance whether a note is false or real. But these dollars confound you, and Benjy admits that he has to study them for a long time before he knows whether they're genuine. We've seen three-dollar bills, ten-dollar and fifteen-dollar notes, and all of them are almost perfect. Your father says he's never seen better."

"He's never made better." Her attempt to alleviate his distress failed, and she became serious. "The gang that's making this money is professional. There's no doubt about that." Reaching into the silk pouch that dangled from her left wrist, she took out several Continental bills and spread them on the table.

Hugh examined them, sighed, and, suddenly angry, threw them down. "I hate to admit defeat, but they're too clever for us."

"How long have you been studying those notes?" Katie asked calmly.

"All afternoon, and the more I look at them, the less sense they make to me."

"You didn't go out this morning, either."

"I had to write some letters to Philadelphia. It's important to our security that I keep up the pretense of negotiating for a cash settlement in return for our nonexistent property. The censors read the mail before they dispatch it, remember, and our only excuse for staying in New York and not sailing to England is my correspondence. Tallmadge is doing splendidly, of course, and the man he's assigned to write replies and negotiate with me has a talent for inventing new complications that drag out the whole procedure, but we can't stay here on this basis indefinitely."

"You need some fresh air. You brood too much when you spend a day alone."

"I need results!" he retorted. "General Washington is maneuvering brilliantly against a superior force, and I live here in luxury, doing nothing for our cause."

"No man could work harder or more conscientiously, so stop blaming yourself." Katie was too concerned to realize she sounded like a wife.

Hugh picked up the sheet of paper containing his notes, flourished it, and then read at random. "Bookshop near King's College. Counterfeit three-dollar bills on two occasions. Since then, only legitimate money. Bric-a-brac shop across the street from the Van Cortlandt mansion. A counterfeit fifteen-dollar Continental, a counterfeit three-dollar Continental. Source has now dried up. Greengrocer in the Bouwerie. Counterfeit ten-dollar notes on two occasions for you and one for Benjy. You've gone there almost every day for the past fortnight, and they haven't tried to pass any more false bills."

"Oh, it's confusing. Even Pa says so." She decided to distract him and relieve his tension by wearing her new gown that evening. She knew he would be pleased with it, and she would insist that they attend a pantomime at the Prince of Wales Playhouse.

"These counterfeit dollars are like the plague. No one knows where they're made, they appear everywhere, and people of every class pass them. Even General Howe himself paid a whist debt to your father the other night with some false fifteen-dollar notes." Hugh stood, his eyes hard and his expression grim. "We're losing our battle, and if we don't develop new tactics, we may lose the war."

XVI / *September 1777*

LATE in the summer Hugh finally came to the conclusion
that British seamen were members of the counterfeiting ring
and that they were responsible for passing the false Continental notes into circulation. His tedious, unending task of
charting the reports of his colleagues and himself indicated
that sailors stationed on some of Admiral Lord Howe's warships were guilty. At least half of the powerful fleet was anchored in the East River, and when a pattern began to emerge
from the haze, it became evident that most of the bills first
appeared in the taverns, shops, and mercantile establishments
that catered to naval personnel.

Hugh assigned his subordinates to new tasks immediately.
August became friendlier with rear admirals and senior captains, Benjy began spending all of his time at the establishments frequented by petty officers, and the Simpson brothers,
who had visited the favorite eating and drinking haunts of
the common seamen from time to time, now concentrated all
of their attention on these taverns. Hugh and Katie ate most
of their meals at inns that catered to junior officers, and Katie
modified her appearance in order to call less attention to herself, wearing a scarf over her head to cover her bright
hair, dressing modestly, and using cosmetics sparingly. Hugh

spent most of the daylight hours in the area too, wandering from one place of business to another.

Shop owners and tavern keepers who had suffered losses were now refusing to accept any Continental dollars because it was too difficult for them to distinguish between genuine notes and counterfeit, Hugh learned, and the other members of his unit brought him similar reports. What puzzled him was that the bills appeared sporadically; new notes circulated for a short time, then there was a lull. But the areas occupied by the Americans were less fortunate, according to a letter written by Major Tallmadge that was smuggled into the city. The United States was being inundated with counterfeit bills, he wrote Hugh, and confidence in the money printed by the Continental Congress had dropped to a new low. Citizens everywhere preferred silver and the notes issued by the individual states, and many staunch patriots refused to take Continental dollars.

Hugh redoubled his efforts to find the men who were making the counterfeit bills, and his colleagues worked feverishly too. Katie, however, was inactive, for Hugh had refused to permit a young, unusually attractive woman to roam through the waterfront district alone. August agreed that she would be courting trouble, so she was forced to spend most of her time at the Duke of Albany Inn and idled away her days reading and sewing. She complained bitterly that she was doing no good and should have remained at Black Ox farm, but Hugh refused to reconsider his decision, and their relations became increasingly strained.

Personal complications were forgotten on September 28, however, when news reached New York that Washington had been compelled to abandon Philadelphia the previous day and that General Howe had occupied the American capital. The Tories rejoiced and held an impromptu victory parade, warships fired their cannon, and the citizens who had been praying for Washington's success remained behind the locked doors of their homes.

Hugh heard the news shortly after he and Katie finished eating their breakfast, and hurried down to the Tory news-paper offices near the Battery to see if he could glean more detailed information. The crowds were so dense that it was late morning by the time he was able to make his way back to the inn, where Katie was waiting for him in their room. She wasted no time observing ordinary civilities.

"A messenger brought you a letter," she said, handing him a small, folded sheet of parchment, "but he was taking a frightful risk coming up here, so I didn't try to question him."

Hugh broke the seal, scanned the brief communication quickly, and then buckled on his sword, which he had stopped wearing in order to create the impression that he was harm-less. "We're going to your father's suite," he said.

Katie heard the note of excitement in his voice and snatched a scarf from a peg.

August and Dave Simpson were alone in the sitting room. "Where are Benjy and Dick?" Hugh asked.

"Down in the street, watching the parade," Dave replied.

"Get them."

August was aware of Hugh's agitation too, but controlled his curiosity.

When the entire group had been assembled and the door had been bolted, Hugh took charge crisply. "Katie, pour some brandywine for everyone. If we should be interrupted, it will look as though we're celebrating General Howe's victory." He opened the letter. "I've heard from Major Tallmadge, who doesn't share our gloom. He says the fall of Philadelphia was expected, the British lines are now too thin to be protected, and he predicts that we'll force the redcoats to retreat within six months to a year."

August's expression was dour. "I know very little about military matters, but I think American independence is a lost cause."

"In that case," Hugh replied crisply, "you're excused from

taking part in our coming operation. I believe the major's estimate is correct."

"I didn't know we were going to engage in an operation," the old man said cautiously.

"Neither did I until a few moments ago." Hugh glanced at the letter. "Tallmadge has sent us news that he considers more vital than the temporary loss of Philadelphia. Our mystery has been solved."

The others stared at him, and Benjy, who had been sitting quietly near the windows, jumped to his feet. "Who has been making the money? Is it people we know, maybe?"

"The counterfeiters," Hugh said, "are officials of the British government who have been acting on direct orders from King George's ministers."

The men stared at him incredulously, and Katie gasped. Only August remained unperturbed. "Very clever," he murmured. "Judging by the excellent techniques they've used, I'd guess that the money has been made by men who have been employed by the royal mint."

"Correct. The plates were engraved in London, and the notes are printed by experienced government workers."

August was pleased that his own status had not been threatened. "Anyone who enjoys official sanction, even a clumsy bungler, can make excellent copies of money. I don't consider such people true artists."

Benjy was bewildered. "Why would the British government print counterfeit bills. The ministers are rich men. They don't need the money."

Hugh smiled broadly. "They haven't been seeking personal profit. They've been engaging in a campaign more harmful to American liberty than all of General Howe's victories." He became tense again as he explained. "Their purpose has been a simple one. They've tried to create an atmosphere of despair, to induce the people of the United States to lose faith in the Continental Congress. So far they've succeeded, and they've sapped our will to fight. But we're in a position to strike back."

"That's what I like to hear," Benjy said eagerly.

Hugh consulted the letter again. "Major Tallmadge writes that American privateers recently captured two small British warships, the *Blacksnake* and the *Morning Star*. Both were carrying large quantities of counterfeit money, which they had intended to pass on to English agents operating behind our lines."

"That's disgraceful!" Katie said indignantly, sitting erect in her chair.

She was revealing her true sympathies, and Hugh was heartened, but this was not the time to pause for a private word with her. "The notes," he went on, "are being printed right here in New York, and it's no wonder that sailors have been passing some, which they undoubtedly stole. The presses are located on board the H.M.S. *Phoenix*."

"I know that ship," Benjy declared. "She's anchored on the near side of the East River, close to a patch of woods upstream."

August stroked his chin thoughtfully. "I dare say I've met her captain."

"The *Phoenix*," Katie said quietly, "carries forty-four guns."

"How did you know that?" Hugh demanded.

"I told you I didn't intend to hide meekly while the rest of you went out on your investigations every day," she replied smugly. "So I've made it my business to find out everything I can learn about the British army and navy here. I hoped my information might be useful someday."

"How—"

"I've gone down to the taproom occasionally for a cup of tea. It's astonishing how freely officers will talk."

Hugh was wildly jealous, but couldn't let his emotions interfere with his duty. "Your information is correct," he said coldly. "Major Tallmadge writes that the *Phoenix* is a frigate of forty-four guns and that the presses are located in a cabin near the stern of the ship, next to the captain's quarters." He paused, and his voice became somber. "Our orders are to destroy the equipment at all costs."

There was a silence, and August cleared his throat. "Although you've excused me from participating in this enterprise, I hope you'll reconsider your decision."

"Certainly," Hugh said promptly. "We'll need all the help we can get."

"No, Pa, you're too old." Katie was distressed.

Her father silenced her with an eloquent gesture.

"There's work for you to do, too," Hugh told her, still annoyed by the discovery that she had been gathering information when he had believed she had been safe behind the bolted door of their chamber. His temper soared when he thought of her smiling at British officers, coaxing them to talk, and he shut the picture out of his mind so he could concentrate on the urgent problem that confronted him. He threw Tallmadge's letter into the hearth, and as he watched it burn to ashes on the glowing coals, a plan began to form in his mind. He walked to the window, then started to pace up and down the room, his hands clasped behind his back. August, who found it difficult to remain quiet for any length of time, cleared his throat preparatory to making an observation, but Katie silenced him with a fierce gesture. Benjy and the Simpsons waited tensely, and it was so still in the room that Katie was startled when a gust of wind that blew in from the bay rattled the windows.

At last Hugh faced the group, halted, and hooked his thumbs in his sword belt. "It's essential that we act quickly," he said. "When Lord Howe learns that the *Morning Star* and the *Blacksnake* have been captured—and he's certain to hear the news soon from spies working behind our lines—he'll probably move the printing presses from the *Phoenix* to another ship, and as he's a wise and efficient officer, he'll undoubtedly take the precaution of mounting a strong guard to protect the counterfeiting equipment. We've got to strike first."

Again August tried to interrupt.

But Hugh gave him no opportunity, and, speaking firmly, made it clear that only one man was in command of the expedition. "There's another reason we can't delay. Katie and I no longer have a valid reason for staying in New York. Under the circumstances it would be natural for us to return to Philadelphia, reclaim our property, and dispose of it. If we tarry here, the British will become suspicious, and even a cursory investigation will prove to them that our whole story is a fabrication. So we'll have to notify the proprietor that we're leaving for 'home' tomorrow, and that means we'll attack tonight."

"I've always made it my policy to avoid violence," August declared, unable to curb himself any longer. "I bow to your greater experience in such matters, but I've always found that it pays to weigh a plan carefully before moving."

"We can't afford the luxury of waiting," Hugh said, "and I don't think circumstances will favor us more than they will tonight. As I came back to the inn a short time ago, I saw large numbers of British soldiers and sailors in the crowds. It's traditional in the armed services to grant leaves of absence for a day and night after a major victory has been won, and I feel certain that both the army and the fleet are observing the custom today."

Benjy, who had been beating a restless tattoo on a table with his fingertips, relaxed slightly. "That's clever, Hugh. You're saying that there will be a weaker guard on board the *Phoenix* tonight than there will be tomorrow or the next day."

"Precisely. And my scheme is very simple. We'll disguise ourselves in British naval uniforms, commandeer one of the small boats that are tied to the East River docks, and after we row ourselves out to the frigate, we'll destroy the equipment."

His daring stunned the others. "Where will we get uniforms?" Benjy asked uneasily.

"There's a naval storehouse behind the gardens of the Bouwerie. We'll have to steal seamen's clothes for you and the Simpsons there."

Dick grinned. "You leave that to me, sir. There won't be many men on duty at the storehouse today, and I can walk off with all the uniforms you want. There ain't a place I've seen yet where I can't steal whatever I want."

His brother was annoyed. "I taught you everything you know about burglary. You ain't as good as I am!"

Hugh was pleased that his band consisted of conscience-less scoundrels. "You can prove your boast by finding me a naval officer's uniform at one of the tailoring establishments, Dave. I've seen several on Maiden Lane that cater to the fleet, and I suggest that you force your way into one that has closed to celebrate the holiday."

"You can depend on me, sir," Dave said happily.

"I presume you'll want me to appear in the disguise of an officer too," August said briskly. "I'd be too conspicuous as an admiral, but in view of my age, I should think a captain's uniform would be suitable."

"You'll wear civilian clothes," Hugh told him. "Dress in a dark suit."

The old man was outraged. "Are you denying me the right to take part in this raid?"

"We'll need someone to wait for us in the boat so we can escape after we've accomplished our task," Hugh replied. "What's more, you aren't familiar with the regulations of the armed services, and if someone dressed as a senior officer should reveal his ignorance of the protocol that's observed on board His Majesty's ships, you'd give all of us away."

August subsided grudgingly. "I've always thought I'd look distinguished in a naval captain's epaulets, but I suppose you're right."

Katie, who had listened carefully but said nothing, decided to intervene. "Your scheme isn't sound, Hugh. Where will you change into the uniforms, presuming some can be stolen?

And where will you change into civilian clothes again? You can't do it here without calling attention to yourselves."

Hugh looked less sure of himself and hesitated for a moment before he replied. "Our ability to slip in and out of disguise will depend on your willingness to assume an unsavory role."

She thought he was challenging her. "Do you think I'm afraid?"

"No, but I am." He smiled wryly, then took a deep breath. "There are a number of houses on a street called the Queen's Walk near the East River waterfront that can be rented for a single night."

The men, who realized what was in his mind, glanced at each other uncomfortably, but Katie listened innocently.

"You aren't familiar with that part of the city, and for good reason," Hugh continued. "The rooms are rented exclusively by harlots."

"I see." She controlled herself without visible effort.

"What I propose is this. I'll escort you to the Queen's Walk this afternoon, but you'll have to negotiate for the room yourself. Then I'll go there with you tonight, and the rest can join us, one by one. No one pays any attention to the men who go in and out of those places all night, but make certain you engage a room on the ground floor so we won't waste any time."

Katie overcame her embarrassment. "You plan to change your clothes there. Then I'm to wait until you return from your raid, and you'll change again."

"Yes. I'm sorry to ask you to play a distasteful part, but—"

"I'll enjoy it," Katie said, interrupting him. "Anything is preferable to sitting upstairs or drinking tea in the taproom and picking up scraps of information from fatuous young officers."

Hugh didn't like to be reminded of her frivolous escapades. "There will be enough action tonight to satisfy you," he said grimly. "We'll make the attack shortly before dawn, and as soon as we return to the inn, we'll leave New York, ostensibly for Philadelphia. If we don't encounter too much trouble," he added, turning to the men, "it will be wiser for you to remain here for an extra day or two. It might seem odd if we leave on the same morning."

August stood and bowed. "I owe you an apology, sir, and I make it gladly. You've been forced to improvise a plan in a very short time, but you've done it brilliantly. I can find no flaws in it."

"If there are flaws," Hugh replied brusquely, "we'll learn them tonight."

The Simpsons lived up to their promises, and early in the afternoon Dave appeared at the Duke of Albany Inn carrying a complete uniform of a senior lieutenant, but he apologized because he had been unable to find a naval officer's sword. He had opened a window of a Tory tailor's shop that had been left unlocked, and he had taken the precaution of leaving by a rear window that faced an alley. The place had been deserted, he said, so the tailor wouldn't discover his loss until the following day.

The uniform fitted Hugh reasonably well, but the tunic was snug, which hampered his movements, so Katie, who had been packing her belongings for the next morning's departure, interrupted her work, took her sewing basket from one of the leather cases, and adjusted the sleeves. She was finishing the task when Dick arrived, triumphant, and piled an assortment of seamen's blouses, trousers, and stocking caps on the bed. Only two sailors had been on duty at the warehouse, he reported, and both of them were drunk, presumably because they had not a holiday leave, so Dick had roamed through the establishment, a converted barn, at will.

When Dick hurried off to August's suite with the clothes, Hugh looked at his watch. "It's time for us to go down to the Queen's Walk," he said. "The trollops are going to be busier

than ever tonight, and we want to make certain you engage
a room before all of them are taken."

Katie nodded as she dropped a small container of rouge, a
pot of black antimony, and a comb into her pouch bag.

Hugh, still angry with her, wanted to express his indignation, but realized this was an inappropriate time for a quarrel. If they succeeded in carrying out his plan, there would
be ample opportunity at a later date to tell her that he disapproved of her conduct. However, he knew he had no right to
lecture her; she had done no harm when she had conversed
with various British officers in the taproom, and Hugh was
not in a position to claim any prerogatives. She was still a
paroled prisoner of Rhode Island, and if they escaped, Hugh
could do no more than request that clemency be granted her
because of the services she had performed on behalf of the
United States.

They left the inn, and when Katie slipped her hand through
Hugh's arm, he knew, certainly and irrevocably, that he
wanted to marry her. But he couldn't propose to her on a
crowded street, and decided to wait until they reached
American-held territory. She would be in a more receptive
mood then, and in the meantime he didn't want romance to
distract her.

British soldiers, sailors, and happy Tories filled the streets,
and although Hugh was impatient, he and Katie were forced
to stroll as they crossed the Broad Way and turned east on
Park Row. The middle of the road was a jumbled mass of
horsemen, sedan-chair bearers, and carriages, and pedestrians were forced to walk close to the buildings to avoid
being struck by a rider or vehicle. Katie clung to Hugh's arm
more tightly, but so many people were shouting and singing
that it was almost impossible to converse. Suddenly her fingers dug into his arm, and she raised her face so she could
speak into his ear.

"Someone is staring at you."

Hugh tensed. "Where is he?"

"It's a woman. She's riding in that little carriage being pulled by the matching bays."

As Hugh turned, the woman withdrew from the window of the carriage, and he caught a momentary glimpse of dark hair. It was unlikely that anyone had recognized him, but it was wise to take no chances, even though he was acquainted with no women in New York. He watched the carriage obliquely while walking at the same pace, but the woman in the carriage apparently lost interest in him, and didn't look out of the window again. The carriage moved ahead in the traffic, and when it disappeared Hugh breathed more easily.

"Can you describe her for me?"

"I'm sorry, no. She realized I saw her staring at you, and she pulled back as soon as you turned."

"You don't know whether she was young or old?"

"I caught only a glimpse of her, but I'm inclined to believe she was young."

Hugh laughed and shrugged. "I don't know any young ladies here."

"Perhaps," Katie replied acidly, "you've neglected to tell me everything you've been doing when you've wandered around the city alone. It may even be that some of your private activities have been less innocent than mine."

Her jealousy delighted him, and he grinned at her.

Katie realized he was teasing her and, tossing her head, looked straight ahead.

Hugh forgot the incident when they reached the end of Park Row, walked through the Bouwerie gardens, and approached the waterfront. The streets in the district bordering the East River were quiet. There were no carriages or horsemen here, and only a few pedestrians could be seen. The area wouldn't join in the celebration until after dark.

"The Queen's Walk is only one square ahead," Hugh said at last.

Katie made no reply until they reached a narrow, empty alleyway that stood between two silent houses. "Keep watch for me," she said, "and let me know if you see anyone coming."

She worked swiftly, and her transformation astonished
Hugh. She removed the pins from her hair, combed it, and let
it fall freely. Then she applied a heavy application of rouge
to her lips, dabbed her eyelashes and lids with black antimony, and, as a final touch, pulled her gown low on her shoulders so the cleavage between her breasts was visible.

"How do I look?"

"Like a bawd." Her disguise was so effective that he wished
he hadn't thought of it.

Katie laughed, and as they resumed their walk she swung
her hips with exaggerated abandon. A sailor, moving in the
opposite direction, slowed his pace, licked his lips, and ogled
her, but finally averted his face when Hugh scowled at him.
He was gone by the time they reached the first of the old
houses that stretched out behind an unpaved street overlooking the East River, and Hugh halted.

"The places that have vacant rooms advertise them with
placards on their door knockers," he said. "I'll wait for you
here."

Katie sauntered off down the street confidently, her hips
swaying, and her manner was so brash that anyone seeing her
would be convinced that she was a trollop. Hugh, one hand
on the hilt of his sword, watched her enter a house, return
to the street a short time later, and meander toward another.
His nervousness increased, but it was too late for regrets, and
he forced himself to remain at his post as Katie left the second house she had visited and walked into a third.

After a long, tense wait she finally reappeared and started
back toward him. When she drew closer he could see by the
expression in her eyes that she had been successful in her
quest, but before he could join her, two red-coated soldiers
brushed past him.

"Ah," one of them said, "there's the juiciest plum we've seen
all day."

The other caught hold of her arm. "We've been looking

for you, sweetheart. Which of us strikes your fancy? If you can't decide, we'll toss a coin for you."

Hugh moved quickly, and, extricating Katie, placed himself between her and the soldiers, who, he noted, were Dragoons. "The lady is engaged," he said sharply.

The taller of the men glared at him. "We saw the bawd first, and we mean to have her."

A brawl might prove disastrous, so Hugh made no attempt to draw his sword. Instead he looked the soldiers up and down slowly. "I've never known members of the Seventh Cavalry to be guilty of insubordination, but even if you're new recruits, your conduct is intolerable."

The men blinked at him in amazement.

"Stand to attention when a superior addresses you," he said, his tone rasping.

The soldiers drew themselves up stiffly.

"Your names, ranks, and battalion numbers," he continued. "I shall send a report on your conduct through my adjutant to your regimental commander."

The taller trooper was no longer belligerent. "Please, sir," he asked, "how was we to know you're an officer?"

"It's true I'm not wearing a uniform today, but Dragoons know their own!" Hugh paused and pretended to ponder for a moment. "In view of the circumstances, I shall excuse you."

"Thank you, sir." The man who had clutched Katie's arm was vastly relieved.

"But remember hereafter that gentlemen who hold His Majesty's commission are privileged to dress as they please when they're not on duty."

"Yes, sir." The taller cavalryman was perspiring.

"We'll remember, sir," his friend declared earnestly.

"You'll find all the women you want there." Hugh waved in the direction of the houses, then suddenly put his arm around Katie. "But this doxy is mine."

The men continued to stand at attention.

"Dismissed!" Hugh said curtly, and they hurried off up the street.

Still holding Katie firmly, he led her away from the area. "Your imitation," he told her, "was too accurate."

There was an undercurrent of hysteria in her laugh. "I was so shocked I didn't know what to do. But you were wonderful."

"The years I spent in the Dragoons weren't wasted." He glanced over his shoulder and was relieved to see the soldiers entering one of the houses.

They paused at the alley where Katie had altered her appearance, and she went through another transformation, piling her hair high on her head, wiping cosmetics from her lips and eyes, and pulling her gown up over her shoulders again.

Hugh watched her apprehensively. "If that incident was an omen," he said gloomily, "we're going to have trouble tonight."

XVII / *September 1777*

THE more respectable districts of New York became quiet after midnight, but Englishmen and Tories, military men, sailors, and civilians who still had enough energy and desire to celebrate the capture of Philadelphia came to the Queen's Walk, where trollops paraded boldly. Hugh, standing behind a dusty window blind, peered through a crack into the street, and so far had every reason to feel satisfaction. He and Katie had finished packing their belongings when they had returned to the inn, and after they had eaten dinner he had paid their reckoning, so if the venture were successful, they could leave New York early in the morning.

Katie, her face heavily painted with cosmetics, sat on the edge of an old bed, the only piece of furniture in the room, and shivered. Cold air from the river was seeping into the room, and she was chilly in the sleazy, bare dress she was wearing, so she picked up the shawl she had worn earlier in the evening, when it had been necessary to hide her nudity. She wrapped herself in it, taking care not to disturb her father, who was stretched out on the bed, sleeping soundly. As always in an hour of crisis, August Dale was serene.

Dick Simpson, attired in a seaman's uniform, stood near the flimsy door, and Dave, similarly attired, lounged against the far wall. In the corridor a bawd and her drunken client made their way slowly up a flight of creaking stairs, and every word they said could be heard plainly in the chamber on the ground floor. Elsewhere in the building a couple haggled loudly over price; in the room directly overhead, a soldier began to sing a regimental artillery song, and his companion joined him in an off-key contralto. Privacy was not one of the pleasures available to patrons of the establishments on the Queen's Walk.

August snored gently, and Hugh turned away from the window quickly, but before he could signal to Katie, she nudged her father and he became quiet again.

The wait seemed interminable, but at last Benjy appeared in the street outside, and when he identified the house, strolled toward it. Hugh waited until he disappeared through the entrance, then waved to Dick, who opened the door. A taper that was set in a rusty candelabrum suspended by a nail from a wall, providing the chamber's only illumination, fluttered briefly, but revived after Benjy slipped inside and Dick closed the door.

Hugh greeted the newcomer with a single word of command. "Whisper!" he muttered in a low tone.

Benjy nodded and tried to catch his breath. "I'm late, but I'm lucky I got here at all."

If British intelligence agents suspected that something unusual was taking place, the scheme would have to be abandoned. Hugh was dismayed.

Benjy shook his head. "It isn't what you're thinking. A strumpet who was marching up and down outside a house down the street took a liking to me. She was twice as tall as I am, and the strongest woman I ever seen. I tried to get away from her, but she grabbed hold of me and lifted me up into the air. A whole crowd of soldiers and sailors gathered around us and started to cheer her. Too many lobsterbacks were watching me, and that wasn't good, so I stopped fighting to get away and let her carry me inside. After that, it was easy. I argued with her about price so long that she got discouraged. I never heard a woman who could swear as hard as that big strumpet when I told her I couldn't afford to pay more than three shillings. Anyways, I'm here."

Katie's nervous giggle seemed to shake the room, but her laugh was not incongruous in the place, and when she clapped a hand over her mouth, Hugh smiled reassuringly.

Dave handed Benjy his seaman's clothes, and Katie looked the other way while he changed. August opened his eyes, stretched, and, sitting up, straightened his coat, adjusted his lace-edged neckcloth, and reached for his sword.

Hugh inspected his brace of pistols to make certain they were in good working order, glanced at his pocket watch, and saw that it was two o'clock in the morning. It was time to leave.

August patted his daughter fondly, brushed his lips against her cheek, and walked out into the night. The other men said brief farewells to Katie and followed him, one by one, but Hugh lingered behind. "Bolt the door behind me, admit no one, and wait for us," he told her.

She looked up at him tremulously.

"I swear to you, I'll come back," he said earnestly, and, taking her in his arms, kissed her fiercely.

Katie clung to him for a moment after he released her, and her eyes were luminous. She reached out again, but knew it was wrong to detain him and withdrew her hand quickly as he started out of the door. "I love you," she whispered as the door closed.

Hugh wanted to turn back, but restrained himself. He waited until he heard Katie bolt the door behind him, then he clapped his cumbersome naval bicorne hat on his head, loosened his sword in its sheath, and left the building. The Queen's Walk was growing less rowdy and the crowd had become thinner, but enough Tories, men in uniform, and trollops were still abroad to force Hugh to proceed with caution. He walked south along the street slowly, quickening his pace only when he drew near a tavern where celebrants were still drinking toasts to General Howe's victory. A slattern lurched out of the place and clutched Hugh's arm, but he shook her off without pausing. Another trollop called out to him, but he didn't glance in her direction, and soon he reached the end of the street.

Commercial warehouses formed a long, solid line on his right, and he walked more rapidly now. The ships of Lord Howe's fleet rode at anchor in the East River on his left, and somewhere, upstream, was the *Phoenix*. The last act of his wild adventure was about to begin.

Several figures were clustered in the shadows of a warehouse, and Hugh put a hand on his hilt as a precautionary measure, but relaxed when he recognized the members of his band. "Keep a sharp lookout for a boat at one of these commercial wharves," he said when he joined them. "If we can find one, I'd prefer to steal a civilian craft."

He took the lead, with Benjy and August close behind him. The Simpsons, carrying short lengths of lead pipe, brought up the rear. It soon became obvious that boat owners were taking no chances on a night when Tories were celebrating, and all of the wharves were deserted. A merchantman, the *City of London*, was berthed alongside a quay, and evidently her cargo had not yet been unloaded, for a man sat on her stern deck, a heavy musket across his lap. He peered at the men in the dirt road, but they pretended to be unaware of his existence, and when he felt certain they had no intention of boarding the brig, he sat back in his chair.

At last Hugh saw the naval boatyard ahead, and called out softly over his shoulder. "We'll have to act boldly. August, you'll walk with me. And remember, all of you, try to avoid a fight." He linked arms with the old man, who tilted his hat rakishly over one eye.

Two royal marines armed with muskets and bayonets were standing sentry duty at the wharves where the boats that carried men of the fleet back and forth from their ships were tied. When the marines saw the gold braid on Hugh's uniform, they stood at attention and presented arms in unison.

"Stand at ease," he told them.

"Aye aye, sir."

"What boat can you give me?" He tried to make out the sizes and shapes of the crafts in the dark.

"You can take your choice, Lieutenant," one of the marines told him with a broad smile. "Most officers are staying ashore tonight."

"Splendid." Hugh didn't turn as he called arrogantly, "Flaherty."

Benjy stiffened. "Sir?"

"Find a suitable boat."

"Aye aye, sir." Benjy saluted smartly, and walked toward the nearest dock.

One of the marines went to a small shed and returned with a sheet of paper, pinned to a board, and a dripping quill. "Your signature, if you please, sir."

"Of course." Hugh took the board, was pleased to see that only a few officers had signed their names, and as he scribbled illegibly on the paper, he reflected that with any luck the *Phoenix* would be lightly guarded.

"I've found a boat for you, Lieutenant," Benjy called.

"Go aboard," Hugh told the others.

The marines looked at Hugh, then at August. "If you please, sir," one of them said, "we need this gentleman's permit to visit the fleet."

"I'm taking a friend to my quarters to share a bottle of port that I've been saving." Hugh spoke crisply, but his heart sank. A procedural technicality could ruin his entire scheme.

August met the emergency calmly. "I have the permit," he said. Paper crackled after he reached into the inner pocket of his coat, and the marines presented arms again.

The band climbed into a small gig, Benjy untied the line that held her fast, and the Simpsons began to row. Hugh, sitting in the stern with August, looked at the old man curiously. He had been prepared for a brawl, but August had solved the problem. "What in the devil did you give the marine? You had no permit."

"You're wrong, my dear lad. It was a universal permit, a two-pound note."

Hugh stared at him.

"Oh, never fear, it was genuine."

It was useless to explain that, had the marine been less avaricious, the entire party might have been placed under arrest for trying to corrupt members of His Majesty's armed services. Hugh sighed and shook his head silently.

A brisk wind was blowing from the west, but the current was not strong, and the Simpsons soon reached midstream. They steered a devious course to avoid the ships riding at anchor, but they were powerful oarsmen, and the boat slid past towering ships of the line, sleek frigates, and swift sloops. The night was dark, and only a few lights burned on the quarter-decks of some of the larger vessels, which was encouraging, but Hugh did not allow himself to dwell on the risks that he and his comrades were taking.

It was enough to remember that the United States, which possessed no navy of its own, had challenged the most powerful nation in Christendom. Privateers and Yankee brigs managed to elude the enemy every day, and even though half of Lord Howe's fleet was at sea, the Americans were breaking the blockade. David was defying Goliath on both land and sea, and a determined band of rogues was intent on destroying a counterfeiting operation that had official British sanction.

There were two sets of unused oars in the boat, and Hugh was tempted to change his seat and work, but he thought it wiser to refrain. Sailors standing watch on the decks of the warships had become accustomed to the dark, and if anyone saw an officer rowing a gig, an alarm would be given immediately. August was incapable of performing manual labor, and it did not occur to Benjy, who was half standing in the prow, to man a pair of oars. His task was vital, however: he had spent part of the afternoon scouting the fleet from the shore, and only he knew the precise location of the *Phoenix.*

"There she is," he called at last. "Off to starboard."

The gig changed direction, slid toward her goal, and finally hovered beneath the ship, which looked enormous from the water line. The portholes and windows were too high to reach, the line in the gig was insufficiently long to enable even the most agile member of the band to board the *Phoenix,* and the Simpsons were dismayed.

Benjy shared their bewilderment. "How do we get up there?" He gestured helplessly, reached out, and almost fell into the water as he tried to touch the hull.

Hugh examined the ship carefully and saw no lights burning anywhere, but he knew that a forty-four gun frigate would not be left unguarded. "We've got to take a chance," he said, "the greatest of all." Cupping his hands, he called loudly, "Ahoy."

After an almost interminable wait a man appeared on the main deck high above, carrying a lantern. "Ahoy," he replied. "Bo's'n of the watch here."

"Gunnery officer here," Hugh called. "Lower a ladder for me."

"Well. Lieutenant Perkins. We wasn't expecting you tonight, sir."

The bluff was succeeding, so Hugh became even bolder. "I am here, as you can see, so lower a ladder, damn you."

"Aye aye, sir. But it will take a bit of time. I'm all alone, sir, but if you wish, I can call the officer of the watch—"

"No, don't disturb him. But hurry." Hugh watched the lantern bob down the deck. "If he suspects anything, he'll return with reinforcements, so be ready to shove off quickly. But if he allows us to come on board, I want one of you to silence him. You'll have to act quickly and quietly."

"I don't like them bo's'ns," Dave said. "We had a cousin

who was one, and he bullied us something awful when we was youngsters."

"All right, Dave, I accept the offer. Follow close behind me, and don't be afraid to use that lead pipe."

Dave laughed savagely.

The lantern reappeared, moved slowly down the deck, and a ladder was lowered. "I'll have to ask you to tie up your boat, Mr. Perkins," the bo's'n called. "But I won't have a work crew on hand until afternoon, sir."

"Very well," Hugh replied, and gave final instructions to his subordinates in a low voice. "Dick, you'll follow your brother. Benjy, you'll bring up the rear. Don't use firearms unless it's essential to destroy the counterfeiting equipment. August, slip that line through the ladder and wait for us. If all goes well, we'll return soon."

Steadying himself, he started up the ladder, with Dave at his heels. It was fortunate, he thought, that he had crossed the Atlantic on a frigate and had been carried to Gibraltar on another when he had been a Dragoon officer. The *Phoenix* was a recent addition to the fleet and was probably more modern in some respects than the frigates Hugh had known, but he felt reasonably sure the naval architects who had designed her had made no major changes. Straining to see as he climbed to the main deck, he caught a glimpse of the mainmast beyond it, and when he saw the shadow of the quarter-deck's superstructure, he was reassured. It would be a tremendous help to know where he was going, but there was a more immediate crisis to face, and he swung one leg over the rail.

The bo's'n stood at attention and saluted. "Will any of the other gentlemen be coming back tonight, sir?" Suddenly he realized he had been fooled. "You ain't Lieutenant Perkins!"

Dave Simpson leaped onto the deck, and before the British seaman could shout for help, brought his lead pipe down on the back of the man's skull. The bo's'n, his mouth still open, slumped forward and fell to the deck.

"He won't wake up for a spell," Dave muttered.

Wasting no time, Hugh began to drag the unconscious man toward the base of the mainmast, where several coiled lines, a block and tackle, and a spare anchor chain were arrayed in an orderly semicircle. Dave hurried to help him, and together they hid the limp bo's'n behind several pieces of equipment. It was difficult to determine whether the sailor was still breathing, but Hugh was more concerned with the noise the lantern had made as it had fallen to the deck. The *Phoenix* was swaying in the tide, which was growing stronger, and her hull creaked in protest, but there was no other sound, and none of the frigate's officers or men seemed to have heard the brief scuffle.

Dick was on the deck now, with Benjy close behind him; they saw what had happened and Dick ran to the mainmast, but Benjy scooped up the lantern, a heavy sea lamp. Its wick was still burning, so Hugh told Benjy to keep it and started aft. The first obstacle had been overcome, but the officer of the watch was still at large, and it was reasonable to assume that at least three other officers and seventy-five members of the crew out of a total complement of more than five hundred were asleep in their bunks.

Benjy, unaccustomed to the erratic movements of the frigate, lost his balance and lurched forward, but Hugh caught him before he fell, and they moved together into a narrow passageway directly below the superstructure of the quarter-deck. Hugh paused, took the lantern, and raised it as he peered down the deserted passage. The door at the far end, which stood at the stern, was the entrance to the captain's quarters, so the suite on the portside probably housed the equipment he had been seeking for so long.

The Simpsons crowded into the passageway, and Hugh handed the lantern back to Benjy, drew his sword, and opened the door. By the feeble light of the lamp they saw a printing press beneath a square window on the far side of the cabin. The search was ended.

"Close the door," Hugh said. "Open that window and throw the presses overboard. But save the engraving plates. We'll take them with us."

The door to an inner cabin opened, and two burly men in civilian breeches and shirts glowered at the intruders. Apparently they were either printers or guards. "Get out!" one of them said angrily. "You know Sir Thomas's orders. No members of the ship's staff or crew are allowed in these quarters." Too late he saw Hugh's naked sword.

The blade sang as it cut through the air, and in spite of the bad light, Hugh's aim was true. He saw the point enter the man's throat, and knew there was one enemy less with whom he had to deal.

Dick Simpson, always anxious to prove he was as strong and intelligent as his brother, attacked the other civilian with his lead pipe, but the man side-stepped, and they grappled with each other, then tumbled onto the deck, where they continued to fight fiercely. Dave came to his brother's assistance, and one short, sharp blow was enough; the civilian moaned, then slumped on the deck.

Someone stirred in the inner cabin, and Hugh decided to investigate immediately. "Get rid of that equipment," he said. "Benjy, I hold you responsible for the plates." He dashed into the adjoining quarters, where two lamps that swung from bulkheads were burning, and he was surprised to see at least ten double bunks lining the exceptionally large cabin. Two tables were nailed to the deck, and it was obvious that the men who made the counterfeit dollars ate and slept here.

At first glance all of the bunks appeared to be empty, but Hugh heard a stealthy, scraping sound, and, looking up, saw a heavy-set man in an upper bunk frantically loading a pistol. Hugh raced across the cabin as the man finished his task, raised his weapon, and cocked it. Hugh lunged desperately, and the blade penetrated the man's wrist before he could fire. He screamed, and as he fell back onto his narrow mattress, the pistol dropped to the deck.

Hugh kicked it under one of the lower bunks, realizing he should kill his enemy, but he couldn't force himself to murder a foe who was wounded and could not protect himself. Nevertheless it was vitally important that the man be given no chance to scream again, so Hugh drew one of his own pistols from his belt, and, using it as a hammer, held it by the barrel and brought the butt down sharply on the civilian's left temple, knocking him unconscious.

Feeling ill, Hugh shoved the pistol back into his belt, and belatedly became aware of a scuffle in the outer cabin. He turned just as a slender man in a blue, gold-braided uniform came through the door.

"Officer of the watch here. Drunken revelry will not be tolerated, sir."

Hugh recognized the lieutenant with the dueling scar who had aroused his anger in the taproom at the inn by commenting loudly and vulgarly about Katie.

The lieutenant came into the cabin, halted when he saw Hugh's sword, and drew his own blade. "I know you," he said, paused, and shouted, "I have it! You're the fellow who has been escorting that red-haired wench."

Hugh kicked the door closed and braced himself.

"You're a damned Yankee spy!" the officer declared, and called for help, but apparently realized that his voice would not carry through the thick timbers of the bulkhead. "It would appear," he said, raising his sword in a mock salute, "that I shall have to dispose of you myself." His sword cut through the air unexpectedly.

Hugh parried the thrust, but the officer lunged a second time, then a third, and Hugh retreated slowly. He knew at once that he faced an opponent who was an experienced duelist, and he guessed that the Englishman had probably acquired his scar in a sword fight. Hugh was confident of his ability to take care of himself, but the lieutenant had an advantage of major importance; the *Phoenix* was pitching and rolling in the rising wind, and a man who had been living on board a ship could balance far more easily than one who had spent several years on land.

The officer attacked repeatedly, and Hugh, constantly on the defensive, backed around the cabin, giving ground while he studied his opponent's technique. The *Phoenix* shuddered, Hugh lost his balance for an instant and raised his blade just in time to deflect a thrust aimed for his face.

The lieutenant laughed. "You should know better than to cross swords with an Englishman, Yankee," he said scornfully. "You stupid farmers and trappers need to be taught a lesson, and I'm grateful to have you for a pupil. What will your wench do when you don't return to the Duke of Albany Inn?" He laughed again. "Never fear, she'll forget you when I offer her consolation."

Hugh saved his breath, and continued to retreat. The *Phoenix* was bobbing and tossing unpredictably, and the officer was pressing him so closely that he knew he would be finished the next time he staggered. Only an act of outrageous daring could save him, and he acted as soon as an idea occurred to him. The nearer of the two tables was several feet to his right, and, hoping it was strong enough to bear his weight, he leaped onto it.

The lieutenant was startled by the unorthodox tactics, and, halting cautiously, struck a defensive pose. "Very dramatic, Yankee, but what are you going to do now?"

Hugh jumped from the table and, using his sword as though he held a cavalry saber, slashed wickedly at his foe. The lieutenant was unable to protect himself against the fierce onslaught, and when he sustained a deep cut on the side of his neck, a look of astonishment appeared on his face. He leaned against the bulkhead and made an attempt to speak. "Fought twenty duels. Never lost one yet." He crumpled slowly, slid to the deck, and sprawled there.

Hugh, still breathing hard, knew it was premature to rejoice. The sounds in the outer cabin had subsided, and he opened the door fearfully, prepared for another battle. Dave was winning a fist fight with a brawny sailor, and the bodies of several other seamen were on the deck. Dick and Benjy were heaving the last pieces of printing equipment, felt rollers, and jars of Frankfort black ink out of the open window into the river. To Hugh's amazement, August Dale stood in the middle of the cabin clutching several thick steel engraving plates.

"Excellent imitations," he said, smiling weakly. "I couldn't have made better myself."

"What are you doing here?"

"I thought you and the lads needed help."

Benjy turned away from the window just as Dave knocked the groggy sailor to the deck and, for good measure, bent down and hit him again. "That's the last of it," Benjy said breathlessly.

It was unnecessary for Hugh to give an order; the members of the Scoundrels' Brigade followed him through the passageway to the deck and ran to the ladder. Benjy was the first to descend, and steadied August, who followed him. "They had a strong watch," Dick said before he climbed over the side.

"There was four sailors and an officer, and we took care of the sailors," Dave explained hastily, and started down the ladder.

Hugh took a last look around the deserted, dark deck of the *Phoenix* and lowered himself to the boat, which was bouncing in the water. The current was so strong that he took a pair of oars and told Benjy to do the same. He directed August to sit in the prow and warn them if they rowed too close to a warship, and he removed his bicorne and gold-braided coat so he wouldn't be recognized as an officer if they were seen from a quarter-deck. "Hold her as close to the Manhattan shore as possible," he told his companions. "We can't risk being swept over to Long Island."

Waves soon drenched the party, and there was no opportunity to talk again as the oarsmen battled the wind and current. August was strangely silent and twice failed to warn his comrades that they were drifting too close to a British ship. Benjy became aware of the danger the first time, but the second resulted in an accident that almost proved fatal. The gig struck the hull of a mammoth ship of the line with such force that she almost capsized, and she hit the man-of-war three more times before the oarsmen could pull away.

August smiled apologetically when Hugh twisted around for an instant, and the old man looked wan, desperately tired. The adventure had drained his strength, Hugh thought, but there wasn't time to dwell on the state of August's health.

Reviewing the incident on board the *Phoenix*, Hugh knew that an alarm would be given as soon as the bodies of the dead and injured were found. The lieutenant was still alive and so were several members of the watch, so the entire British occupation apparatus, military, naval, and civilian, would begin an intensive hunt for the band almost immediately. Benjy, August, and the Simpsons were in greater danger than he had anticipated, so he changed his plans and decided that all of them would leave New York at once. Minutes were precious, and while he was grateful that the current was sweeping them downstream rapidly, it would be hazardous as well as time-consuming to return the gig to the naval boatyard, as he had intended. Improvising as he rowed, he concluded that the best course of action would be to dock at one of the civilian wharves near the Queen's Walk. Later in the morning, when someone found the gig, the discovery would be unimportant as the authorities would have started their search in any event.

The first dirty gray streaks of dawn were appearing in the sky, and when Hugh caught sight of the first commercial docks off to his right, he called to his companions, but the wind was so strong they couldn't understand him. He gestured violently, almost losing his oar, and the Simpsons responded quickly. Benjy, who was exhausted, tried to help, but Dave and Dick managed, with Hugh's assistance, to veer toward the shore.

August made a feeble attempt to throw the gig's line over a stake attached to one of the wharves, but he missed, and the rope dragged in the water. Hugh made his way forward, and the Simpsons tried again, straining with all of their might to force the craft closer to the land. Hugh threw the wet line accurately, the boat held, and a few moments later the bedraggled group climbed onto a stone quay.

Hugh explained the change in plans briefly, and the men started up the waterfront road toward the Queen's Walk, which was now silent. Benjy soon recovered his breath, but August continued to lag behind, so Hugh took his arm and, remembering that the old man still had the counterfeit plates in his possession, took charge of them. The taverns were quiet now, their shutters closed, and the street that had been so full of activity a few hours earlier was deserted. Lights still burned in a few rooms, but the civilians had returned to their homes and the soldiers and sailors who were spending the night in the district were asleep.

Hugh wanted to walk more rapidly, but August continued to lag, so he had to adjust his pace to the old man's. At last they reached the rendezvous, and, not bothering to enter the building one at a time, moved together down the narrow corridor. Katie had been watching for them, and when they approached the chamber she had rented, she opened the door, greeted Hugh with a fervent kiss, and, embracing her father, looked at him anxiously.

"Are you all right, Pa?" she asked solicitously.

"Certainly," August replied hoarsely. "I can't recall enjoying a more exhilarating experience."

"He disobeyed orders and did too much." Hugh gave her a brief account of the raid while the men changed from their soggy uniforms into their civilian attire, and she was elated when she learned that the mission had been successful. She agreed heartily when Hugh explained the change in plans, and he was relieved when she said that no one had disturbed her during the hours she had been waiting.

When the group was ready to leave, Hugh beckoned, and they gathered around him. "Give me your uniforms," he said. "I've kept a small box in our room at the inn for them." He saw no reason to explain that he intended to take the naval attire to Major Tallmadge, who might find it useful for other agents on other occasions. "Katie and I sent all of our belongings except that one box to the stables last night, so we'll be ready to leave as soon as we get there and I pack the uniforms."

"There will be time for me to scrub my face and change into the gown I kept out for the journey, I hope." Katie looked with distaste at her sleazy harlot's costume.

Hugh nodded. "You can't travel in those clothes. Dave, when we reach the inn, go straight to the stables, harness the team, and drive the carriage into the courtyard. Benjy, you and August will pack your belongings as quickly as possible, and Dick will help carry them down to the carriage. August, if you should see the proprietor, I'll trust you to think of some logical reason you can give him for your sudden departure."

The old man smiled absently.

"I'll concoct a story we can tell the sentries when we reach New Jersey, but there's ample time for that." Hugh gathered the wet uniforms into a bundle. "We'll discuss the details while we're leaving."

Katie took his arm, and they left the shabby house, the men at their heels. Again August, who appeared to be in something of a daze, seemed unable to hurry, and the sun was rising by the time the party reached the Duke of Albany Inn. "If we're seen," Hugh cautioned as they parted at the entrance, "we've spent the night celebrating."

Dave Simpson went directly to the stable, as he had been instructed, and while August made his way up the stairs slowly, with Benjy and Dick following him impatiently as he clung to the bannister, Hugh and Katie hurried ahead to their chamber on the top floor. The inn was quiet, and Hugh was thankful that the patrons had eaten and drunk too much the preceding evening. If Katie changed her clothes quickly and didn't primp, they would be ready to leave in a quarter of an hour.

The bedroom door was unlocked, and Hugh felt a twinge of uneasiness as he raised the latch.

But he was totally unprepared for the shock that awaited him. Katie preceded him into the room, but halted abruptly when she saw Norton Walker, the proprietor, and beyond him a man, wearing the sash of a Tory bailiff, and a dark-haired young woman.

"I knew I recognized him!" Jordy Fleming said triumphantly. "That's my father's runaway bondsman!"

XVIII / *September 1777*

THE bailiff carried a thick staff and Walker was wearing a sword, but before either could use a weapon, Hugh reacted to the emergency. Throwing the bundle of wet uniforms at the bailiff to prevent the man from using the staff, he drew his pistols and cocked them in a single motion. Katie, realizing what he was doing, stepped nimbly to one side.

"Raise your hands, all of you," he commanded.

Walker, horrified to discover he had been giving refuge to a runaway indentured servant, obeyed meekly, and the bailiff complied too, after he had extricated himself from the tangle of uniforms. But Jordy, laughing contemptuously, made no move.

"You wouldn't dare fire a pistol," she said. "You'd awaken the whole neighborhood."

A relief watch would be reporting for duty soon on board the *Phoenix*, and even the slightest delay could prove catastrophic. "You underestimate me," Hugh replied curtly. "Do as you're told."

"I prize you highly, as you have good cause to know," Jordy said slyly, and, striking a defiant pose, folded her arms. "I was positive I knew you when I saw you from my carriage in Park Row yesterday, and we've been waiting here for hours to take you into custody. I don't intend to be cheated. I'm going to take you before a magistrate as soon as the law courts open their doors. You're my father's property, and as he can't travel through rebel territory, you'll be given to me. Don't scowl, my dear. I can remember when you enjoyed my company."

It was pointless to argue with her. "Katie," Hugh said, "take the staff and sword, and search the men for other weapons."

Walker moaned. "My reputation has been spotless. What will Sir William Howe say when he hears I've been harboring a fugitive from royal justice?"

No one answered him, and Katie, working quickly and efficiently, seized the bailiff's staff and unbuckled Walker's sword belt. Then, running her hands lightly over both men for concealed weapons, she took a cumbersome, old-fashioned pistol from the tail-coat pocket of the bailiff's uniform. "This isn't even loaded," she said, and threw it onto the bed.

Jordy looked the other girl up and down slowly. "I'm surprised that you've been consorting with a bawd, Hugh," she declared scornfully. "Have you no taste or discrimination?"

Katie, realizing she still wore the clothes and cosmetics of a strumpet, flushed angrily.

Hugh, still holding the trio at bay with his pistols, refused to be drawn into a discussion. "Katie, tear the sheets into strips and bind their hands and feet. Hurry."

Although Katie was furious, she lost no time ripping the linen.

The bailiff was outraged. "I shall recommend to the magistrate that you be publicly whipped," he said, "and the wench will be flogged for helping an escaped bondsman. I warn you, when you mistreat me, you defy the dignity and authority of His Majesty himself."

A shaft of sunlight brightened the room. "Gag them, too," Hugh said. At any moment alarm gongs on board the warships might arouse the entire city.

Walker, still groaning, submitted meekly to the indignity of being trussed, and Katie silenced him by stuffing a large scrap of linen into his mouth. The bailiff protested and tried to edge away, but Hugh jabbed him in the ribs with a pistol and he subsided. Katie, working feverishly, bound his hands behind his back, tied his ankles securely, and shoved a gag into his mouth.

Jordy, who had been watching disdainfully, looked disgusted. "I shall ask the court for the privilege of administering the flogging to both of you myself."

"Bind her, too," Hugh directed.

"Gladly," Katie replied, her eyes stormy.

Jordy backed away. "I will not allow a filthy harlot to touch me!"

The enraged Katie approached her, holding several strips of linen. She was so angry that she stepped between Hugh and Jordy, blocking the line of fire.

Hugh realized the danger instantly, but before he could tell her to move, Jordy, who had been waiting for an opportune moment, acted swiftly. Reaching into her bodice, she drew out a bodkin, or "lady's knife," a tiny dagger no longer than a woman's thumb. It was fashionable for young ladies to carry such weapons for their self-protection, and Jordy was no novice. Not wasting a motion, she stabbed at the other girl viciously.

Katie was unprepared for the attack, but defended herself with an agility that surprised the dismayed Hugh. She ducked, caught hold of Jordy's wrist, and, twisting it with all of her strength, forced her antagonist to drop the bodkin. With her free hand she slapped Jordy's face, then struck her again across the mouth when Jordy tried to scream.

Before Hugh could intervene, Jordy broke loose; the two girls started clawing and kicking at each other, and suddenly they fell to the floor, arms and legs flailing, petticoats swirling. A dress was torn, a button rolled across the floor, and Jordy said thickly, "You dirty harlot!"

They were the last words she spoke. They rolled over twice,

and Katie was clearly the winner; she sat on the brunette's stomach, slapping her repeatedly as Jordy lay on her back, unable to retaliate. Hugh called a halt by picking up the strips of linen and, pushing Katie aside, tied Jordy's hands and ankles. Katie took a piece of cloth and shoved it into the other girl's mouth with greater force than was necessary.

"She was your mistress!"

Hugh was collecting the naval uniforms and throwing them into the leather box he had kept in the room for the purpose.

Katie was still breathless. "Well, wasn't she?"

Before Hugh could reply, the door opened and Benjy stood in the frame, blinking.

"We've had a little trouble," Hugh told him, "and we've got to leave before there's more." Katie had picked up the bodkin, and he kept a wary eye on her as she glared at the prostrate Jordy.

"We got more already," Benjy said tersely. "August was wounded in the fight."

Katie gasped.

"He didn't help with the packing, and when Dick and me got back to the suite after taking things down to the carriage, we found him just plain sitting in a chair. He looked like he was sleeping, but when I went to wake him up I saw that one side of his shirt was covered with dried blood. One of the sailors stabbed him, it seems like."

Katie raised the flimsy skirt of her costume and ran out of the room.

Hugh listened to her footsteps as she hurried to join her father, and he made an effort to concentrate. "Can he be moved?"

Benjy hesitated, then shrugged.

Hugh reached a decision. "We can't leave him behind. With Katie's help, you and Dick should be able to take him down to the carriage. Don't bother to pack anything else. I'll meet you in the courtyard immediately."

Benjy disappeared, and Hugh finished throwing the wet uniforms into the box. Too late he realized that Katie had forgotten to change into more respectable clothing, so he took the gown, petticoat, shoes and stockings she had planned to wear and placed them on top of the pile. There was no time for him to shave, and, regretfully rubbing the stubble of beard on his jaw, he took his razor, soap container, and shaving brush from the top of the cupboard, and, after throwing them into a corner of the box, closed it.

Jordy, her eyes open, was staring at him malevolently.

"You made an unfortunate error," he told her. "Ladies become annoyed when they're called unpleasant names." He hoisted the leather box onto his shoulder, took a ring of keys that hung on a chain around the neck of the hapless innkeeper, and, after leaving the room, carefully locked the door behind him. An open chest of drawers containing bed linens, towels, and other items used by the chambermaids stood near the head of the stairs, so he shoved the key chain to the rear of the bottom shelf and, balancing the box as best he could, went down to the courtyard.

Toby and Katie's mare had been saddled, boxes had been tied to the broad back of the pack horse, and the Simpsons were sitting on the carriage box. Katie was inside, ministering to her father, and Benjy was pacing up and down nervously, which accomplished nothing but succeeded in frightening the horses. Hugh hurried to the carriage and, depositing the box on the floor, asked tersely, "How is he?"

August, who was slumped in one corner, opened his eyes and tried to speak cheerfully. "Ah, there you are, my dear lad. I've been struggling to keep awake until I saw you. I've caused you great inconvenience, I fear."

"Don't talk, Pa. Save your strength." Katie wiped his forehead with an embroidered silk handkerchief she had taken from his cuff.

"You can travel far more rapidly without me," August said weakly. "All I ask is that you take good care of Katie."

"I refuse to abandon you," Hugh replied firmly. "Katie, you'll ride with him in the carriage. Benjy, take her mare." He slammed the carriage door, mounted Toby, and, signaling to the Simpsons, led the way out of the courtyard.

The city was just beginning to stir. Here and there a shop owner was opening his shutters, the servants of wealthy Tories were carrying milk pails and empty breadbaskets to the markets on Wall Street, and a few merchants riding sedate geldings were going to their offices. Hugh's mind raced as he tried to cope with a new situation, and he didn't hear Katie call to him until she repeated his name. Turning, he saw her leaning out of a window, beckoning, so he slowed his pace until the carriage drew up to him.

"Pa is unconscious again," she said. "His breathing is shallow, and—well, I think he's right. It will be easier for you to escape if you'll leave us at some little inn."

"I'll offer you the same advice that you gave August. Don't waste your breath." In spite of her tension and sleepless night, he thought her face still looked beautiful beneath the coating of overly lavish strumpet's cosmetics. But her daringly low-cut dress would arouse the attention of every redcoat who saw her, and he frowned. "Why aren't you wearing that shawl you carried last night? You're half nude."

"That female tore it." Katie showed a sudden flash of anger. "She was your mistress, wasn't she?"

"In a manner of speaking." There were far more important matters to discuss than his affair with Jordy Fleming.

"I knew it! That's why she was so nasty. I don't think much of your taste."

"We'll talk about it some other time. When we reach the outposts, put August's hat over his forehead to shield his face. And let me handle the situation."

"What are you—"

"There's no time to explain, and you present a special problem. Where is the wedding ring we bought in Connecticut?"

Katie looked stricken. "Oh dear. I couldn't wear it last night, and I left it at the Duke of Albany Inn."

"It doesn't matter. No one would believe that a girl who looks as you do now could be anyone's wife, so don't worry about it. There wasn't time for you to change, so we'll have to do the best we can." Raising his head, he called to Benjy and Dave Simpson. "Turn onto Cortlandt Street, and go west to the Hudson River. We're taking the ferry to New Jersey."

He started to ride forward again, but Katie detained him. "Which ferry, south or north?"

Hugh was annoyed, but made allowances because she was so concerned about her father. "South. I want to reach the place where we spent the night on our way here as soon as possible, and by the most direct route. We won't be safe until we can hide there and give August the attention he needs."

Katie shook her head. "Not the south ferry. Captain Jaspar is in command of the road block, and he's a martinet."

"How do you know that?"

She tried to smile and speak lightly. "Perhaps some of those afternoons when I sat in the taproom encouraging British officers to gossip weren't completely wasted. From what I've heard, Captain Jaspar is very strict. Even though it might be a longer route, take the north ferry and then double back on the Morristown road. The block there is commanded by Lieutenant Carruthers, the younger son of Lord Bournemouth, and he's a fool."

Although the situation was desperate, Hugh felt a stab of jealousy. "Would Lieutenant Carruthers recognize you?"

"I've never seen him," Katie said with a flash of spirit. "I'm merely reporting what I've heard."

He rode in silence for a moment. "You understand, I'm sure, that every delay might be harmful—even fatal—to your father."

Tears appeared in her eyes, but she blinked them away. "We have no choice," she replied, and withdrew into the carriage.

A surprising number of Tories, most of them traveling to Philadelphia, crowded onto the ferry, and when Hugh and his comrades reached the New Jersey shore they saw scores of others, the majority of them crown sympathizers who had fled from Pennsylvania and were now hurrying back to their homes. The road block was the last major obstacle that had to be overcome, and Hugh, profiting from previous experience, decided that a bold front offered the best hope. It was unlikely that sentries stationed in New Jersey had heard about the raid on the *Phoenix* as yet, so there would be no need for him to change his identity or try to disguise the members of his band. He took the Morristown road, as Katie had suggested, then turned south, and, although the sun was almost directly overhead now, he didn't dare pause at one of the inns in the area for a meal.

"Benjy," he said to his friend, who was riding beside him, "you'll pose as my secretary. Go back to the carriage and tell the Simpsons they're to pretend they're in my employ now."

"All right. But what about August? And Katie?"

"I'll take responsibility for August. As for Katie, instruct her to say nothing."

Benjy dropped back, and after a short time the group saw a collection of sentry huts at the crest of a hill. Red-coated soldiers stood on both sides of the road, but when Hugh could see their faces he noted that the troops appeared to be relaxed. Howe's capture of Philadelphia was still influencing British thinking, and Hugh intended to take full advantage of the enemy's joviality.

A sergeant major stepped into the center of the road, and when he held up his hand, Hugh halted obligingly. "This is Lieutenant Carruthers' station, I believe?"

"Yes, sir." The soldier didn't move.

"Is he on duty? I'd like to speak to him."

"The lieutenant is busy right now. I'll conduct the investigation, as I've been authorized to do."

"I don't doubt your authority," Hugh said politely, "but I'm carrying a personal message for the lieutenant."

The sergeant major's attitude changed at once. "I'll fetch him, sir."

Lieutenant Carruthers, a petulantly handsome young man with a blond mustache, came out of the largest of the huts, buttoning his tunic, and it was obvious that, although it was only midday, he had been drinking.

Hugh went to him quickly and introduced himself. "I dined with your father a few nights before sailing back to the colonies," he said glibly, "and I promised him I'd give you his love."

The young officer blinked in surprise. "Then he's forgiven me for running up those gambling debts?"

"Lord Bournemouth isn't one to carry a grudge," Hugh replied, improvising suavely.

Carruthers laughed savagely. "You don't know him. He expects perfection from his sons. Cedric will inherit the title, so I suppose it's fair enough for him to toe the mark, but I don't see why the rest of us must behave like angels."

"His Lordship is very fond of you, Lieutenant. That's all I know."

The odor of brandywine was strong on Carruthers' breath as he leaned closer to Hugh and murmured, "If that's true, then perhaps I'll be relieved of duty at this dismal outpost. He was responsible for my transfer here after I'd had a particularly bad streak of luck at the gaming tables, and I've been afraid he was using his influence to keep me here until the end of the war. You're quite sure he sounded friendly, Mr. Spencer?"

"So sure that I've traveled out of my way to give you his message." Hugh's smile was reassuring, and he refrained from saying that, if a superior saw the lieutenant in an intoxicated state while he was on duty, he would be brought before a court-martial board and would be dismissed from the army. Eventually Carruthers would be caught, so Hugh added

truthfully, "I think you can count on spending the winter in
Philadelphia or New York."

"That's the best news I've heard in months. We'll celebrate
it together. I can't offer you much in the way of hospitality,
Mr. Spencer, but I hope you'll share a cup with me."

"I wish I could afford the time," Hugh said. "But I'm anxious to reach Philadelphia. I own considerable property
there, and I want to see how much the rebels damaged and
stole."

"I insist you join me in a toast to my reprieve from this
life of boredom." Carruthers sounded like a fretful child.

A firm refusal would anger the officer and create a situation
that Hugh was trying to avoid, so he concealed his impatience and smiled. "You're very generous."

They walked together to the hut, where the lieutenant
drew an earthenware jug from beneath his cot, removed the
cork, and, after pouring a large quantity of liquor into a pewter cup for Hugh, greedily raised the jug to his own lips.

Hugh sipped a small quantity of the raw brandywine.

"I've drunk better, but I've grown accustomed to the taste
of this cheap wine." Carruthers tilted the jug again.

Hugh took advantage of his preoccupation to spill the better part of his drink on the ground. "Delicious," he said, and
pretended to drain the cup.

"Have another." Carruthers' eyes were watery.

"I wish I could spare the time, but it's imperative that I
arrive in Philadelphia as soon as I can get there."

The lieutenant sighed.

"As soon as I've put my affairs in order," Hugh declared,
"I intend to write Lord Bournemouth and tell him I've enjoyed the pleasure of seeing you."

Carruthers tapped the jug with a fingertip. "You won't
mention this, I trust?"

"You may rely on my discretion." Hugh placed the cup on
a small table and moved toward the door. "Perhaps you'll l

good enough to conduct the inspection yourself so my party and I can resume our journey."

"It's the least I can do for a friend." The lieutenant stumbled as they left the hut.

Hugh took his arm and they walked slowly toward the carriage. The Simpsons and Benjy looked relieved, and Hugh could see Katie peering apprehensively out of the carriage window.

"You have the necessary travel passes, of course." Carruthers voice was thick.

Hugh forced a laugh. "My dear fellow, they aren't necessary any longer. Now that we occupy both New York and Philadelphia, travel between the cities is unrestricted."

"I haven't received any orders telling me of a change in regulations." The lieutenant frowned, then shrugged. "Headquarters never sends me orders promptly. Sometimes I think they've forgotten I exist."

"You'll enjoy a change of scenery soon," Hugh said with conviction. "That's my secretary, Flaherty, and those men on the box are my servants, of course."

Carruthers ignored the trio and let Hugh guide him to the carriage.

"My father," Hugh said, as he opened the door on August's side of the coach and gestured toward the unconscious man, "celebrated Sir William's capture of Philadelphia a trifle too enthusiastically last night."

"I envy you. I wish I had that sort of father." Carruthers caught sight of Katie and his interest quickened. "Who have we here?"

Hugh winked at him.

"I've been alone for months," Carruthers said unhappily.

"Come out, sweetheart, and let the lieutenant see you." Hugh simulated the callousness that members of the gentry habitually displayed in their dealings with courtesans.

Katie didn't know what was in his mind, but realized she was required to play a part, so she climbed down to the ground and walked around the carriage to the two men, her hips swaying.

Hugh put an arm around her waist and drew her to him roughly. "She makes it easier for me to tolerate the barbarian colonial life, don't you, sweetheart?"

Katie's coarse giggle was so completely in keeping with her role that it startled him.

Carruthers moistened his lips. "Will she stay in Philadelphia with you, Mr. Spencer?"

It was impossible to ignore the officer's broad hint, and Hugh decided not to take any chances. "For the present," he said, "we have a satisfactory arrangement." Deliberately raising his arm, he cupped Katie's left breast in his hand.

She was shocked, and stiffened for an instant, but knew her behavior was out of character and leaned indolently against Hugh, permitting him to fondle her as he pleased.

Carruthers' bleary eyes gleamed.

"If you don't mind," Hugh said casually, "I'll be grateful if you'll inspect my luggage."

The lieutenant turned away from Katie reluctantly and looked into the carriage. "A token will suffice. Do you have the key to this box, Mr. Spencer?"

Hugh realized he had made a grave tactical error, and as he reached into his pocket for the key, he whispered to Katie, "The naval uniforms are in there, under your traveling costume."

Carruthers fumbled with the key, but finally unlocked the box and opened it.

Katie had followed Hugh's instructions and said nothing, but she knew how to handle the lieutenant now, and, leaping forward, she clutched his arm and pulled him out of the carriage. "Don't you 'aul me finery about wiv your great paws!" she cried indignantly in the accent of London's lowest class. Snatching the petticoat from the top of the case, she waved it before the flustered officer's face.

Carruthers retreated a few paces.

"You men are all alike," Katie declared vehemently, climbing into the carriage, throwing the petticoat into the box, and
closing the lid. "You're so 'igh and mighty you think you can
do wot you please wiv a girl's property!" Locking the case,
she dropped the key into her dress.

"I say, Mr. Spencer, you've found yourself a spirited
wench." The lieutenant was still startled.

Hugh's admiring chuckle was genuine. "She has more than
enough fire."

Carruthers took his arm and led him off to the side of the
road. "You aren't planning to take her to any of Sir William's
receptions or victory balls, I hope?"

"I really hadn't thought about it," Hugh replied cautiously. "But she's a handsome baggage, and I've never seen
a Philadelphia belle who is prettier."

"I'll grant you that she's handsome." The lieutenant
glanced at Katie, who had resumed her seat in the carriage
and was glaring at him. "But I'd like to return your kindness
with a word of warning. Sir William is very fond of the
ladies, but he insists that they must be ladies. Your doxy will
cause you considerable embarrassment, and if I know General Howe, he won't forgive your indiscretion."

"Thank you. I'll remember your advice." Hugh was growing
increasingly restless.

"I can solve your problem for you." Carruthers smiled las-
civiously. "I'll gladly take the wench off your hands."

Hugh controlled himself with an effort. "You've given me
an idea," he said quietly. "I promised to take her to Philadelphia, and frankly, I'm afraid to face her anger if I don't
live up to my word. But I'll be even more candid and admit
that I've wondered how to get rid of her."

Carruthers' smile became broader.

"I'm sure you'll be transferred in another week or two at
the most, so I can send her here to console you during your
last days in this lonely wilderness. But she's expensive."

"When I'm free to return to New York, I can win enough at the gaming tables to keep her in style for a year."

"Then we've struck a bargain. I'll send her back to you in two days, three at the most." Hugh held out his hand.

The lieutenant grasped it enthusiastically, then turned to the men who were guarding the gate that blocked the road. "Remove the barrier for my friend," he shouted.

Hugh tipped his hat as he rode past the sentries, and Carruthers, weaving unsteadily on his feet, tried to catch a last glimpse of the girl in the coach. The road ahead was clear, and Hugh increased his speed, hoping to make up for lost time. Dave Simpson handled his team expertly, and for a long period the horses maintained a steady, rapid pace; only Benjy, who neither understood nor liked horses, was unhappy as he bounced up and down incessantly in his saddle. In mid-afternoon Hugh turned off onto a side road barely wide enough to accommodate the carriage, and, although he was forced to ride more slowly, he continued to press ahead.

He was satisfied with the results of the incident at the road block and felt confident that, with Katie's help, he had succeeded in confusing the brandywine-befuddled Carruthers. It was possible, even probable, that when the sentry outposts received a warning to keep watch for the fugitives who had raided the *Phoenix,* the lieutenant, dreaming about the bawd who would join him in a few days, would not recognize the description of the desperate men. However, Hugh could afford to take no chances and didn't pause until he saw that the horses, particularly the pair pulling the coach, needed a rest.

When he reached the comparative shelter of a small patch of woods he called a halt, and, dismounting, threw Toby's reins over a tree branch. Stretching his legs, he walked back to the carriage, and Katie opened her window. "How is August?" he asked.

"I don't know. He's still unconscious, and every now and then he moans. The ride is shaking him, I'm afraid."

"I'd ride more slowly if I dared," Hugh said apologetically, "but there are too many enemy patrols in the area, and I want to reach the farm by sundown. Is he bleeding again?"

"No, but I've looked at his wound, and it's a nasty gash." Katie bit her lower lip. "Is there a physician at the farm who can treat him?"

Hugh refused to lie to her. "A number of patriotic physicians have taken shelter there at one time or another, but I don't know if any will be there now."

She caught her breath. "Poor Pa is so weak. And at his age I don't know whether he can stand the strain."

He wanted to console her, but was afraid she would weep if he sympathized with her, so he became brusque. "Are you carrying any rouge and black eye-grease?"

Katie smiled faintly at his description of antimony. "There are both in the pouch I was carrying."

"Use them. The gloss has worn off, and we don't know when you may have to play the part of a strumpet again."

She obeyed reluctantly. "I hope," she said, "that I've acted that role for the last time."

"Your last performance was brilliant. And your information about young Carruthers was accurate. He's a fool, and your rage frightened him."

"I was really angry, but not at him." Katie finished applying rouge to her lips and looked coldly at Hugh. "Was it necessary to maul me as you did in front of all those soldiers?"

He was pleased that, in spite of her worry over her father, she was showing spirit. "They would have thought it odd if I had treated a bawd in any other way," he said deliberately, and grinned. She was accomplishing nothing constructive by brooding over August, and he wanted to give her something else to occupy her mind.

"You enjoyed humiliating me." Her eyes flashed. "You were reminding me that I'm still your prisoner."

"You could have escaped a thousand or more times while

we were still in New York, and nothing prevented you from handing me over to the British."

His bantering tone infuriated her. "I suspect that you've wanted from the start to degrade me. You tricked me into living with you, and you've forced me to act like a strumpet."

It was difficult for Hugh to dissemble, but he didn't want her to become fearful and lethargic again. "I owe you no explanations of my conduct. I suggest that you draw your own conclusions about me." He turned away, and, as he started back toward his stallion, saw out of the corner of his eye that Katie was thoroughly aroused. Later, when they reached their destination, he would apologize; in the meantime, she was so indignant that her sense of despair had vanished, so he had accomplished his immediate purpose.

They resumed their journey, and saw no one on the road. Occasionally they passed a house and caught a glimpse of a farmer, usually a middle-aged man, working in the distance, but the residents of the area pretended to be unaware of travelers. The district had suffered twice in two years as the opposing armies had swept through New Jersey, and now that the whole region was in enemy hands again, patriots carefully minded their own business, tried to avoid disputes with the occupying forces, and resolutely ignored Tory sympathizers, whom they hated.

Shortly before sundown, when Hugh and his companions were no more than a few miles from their refuge, there was every reason to believe that the flight would end successfully. Benjy was tired and was lagging, so Hugh rode alone in the lead, and when he reached the crest of a small hill, he saw the silhouette of the farmhouse that served as an American espionage center, and he felt infinite relief. Smiling to himself, he started down the hill, then halted abruptly when he saw three British Dragoons in a small valley directly ahead. A corporal, who was in command of the patrol, was alternately staring at the party at the summit and studying a paper he held in his hand. Obviously the redcoats had been notified of the raid on the *Phoenix,* and searching parties were hunting for the refugees.

The corporal, satisfied that he had found the quarry, shoved the paper into the belt of his crimson tunic, and, drawing a pistol, said something to his subordinates, who ranged themselves on either side of him. "Halt in the name of King George!" he shouted.

Hugh reacted instinctively and dug his heels into Toby's sides. The huge stallion raced down the slope, and Hugh drew his sword, flourished it over his head, and headed straight for the trio of enemy riders. Royal cavalry had been employing similar tactics ever since the Great Rebellion in the seventeenth century, when commanders on both sides had adopted the techniques developed by King Gustavus Adolphus of Sweden, who had believed that mounted units should be used exclusively as instruments of attack. Presumably the redcoats at the base of the hill were familiar with Hugh's maneuver and had practiced it themselves many times, but they were startled to see a lone man bearing down on them at great speed, waving his blade as though he held a Turkish scimitar.

The corporal, who had the greatest presence of mind, raised his pistol and fired, but Toby was galloping so rapidly that the soldier's aim was poor. The bullet sang past horse and rider, infuriating both, and Toby raced down the hill even faster. A wild sense of elation filled Hugh as he charged, and he realized that he was not fighting in secret now, but was meeting the foe in the open. He was a soldier, not a spy, and, half standing in his saddle, he sent Toby hurtling at the corporal's mount. It did not cross his mind that he was badly outnumbered, and he was completely indifferent to his own safety, even when he saw the corporal snatch a pistol from one of the other men.

Before the redcoat could fire again, however, Toby thundered toward him, and Hugh, wielding his sword like a heavy saber, slashed at the corporal with it. The cavalryman's horse shied as Toby, his teeth bared, bore down on him, and the animal's panic saved his master's life. Hugh inflicted a deep cut in the corporal's shoulder, knocking him from his saddle, but he was still alive and tried to crawl into the ditch.

Suddenly a pistol shot echoed across the countryside, and a second redcoat slumped forward in his saddle. The third soldier lost all interest in the fight and, crouching low in his saddle, galloped off across the valley toward the east.

Hugh, afraid the man would raise an alarm, quickly sheathed his sword and fired both of his pistols, but Toby was rearing and bucking, so he missed his target.

The corporal reached a field of clover beside the road, where he collapsed, and the other man slid from his saddle to the ground, where he lay still, his eyes glazed and vacant. Benjy joined Hugh, and when he proudly waved a large pistol, the mystery of the shot was explained. "I took this from one of them sailors last night," he said. "I guess that maybe I've got a sharper eye than I figured." Grinning, he reached for the reins of one of the riderless horses.

"Don't take either of those animals," Hugh told him sharply. "Dragoons will be searching this whole area, and they'll recognize their own mounts."

Benjy sighed, but obeyed and sat upright in his saddle. "Life was easier when I was a criminal," he muttered.

The carriage was moving down the hill, and Hugh beckoned to the Simpsons. "Hurry!" he called. "Don't spare your team!" Not waiting for a reply, he gripped Toby's reins firmly and started across the narrow little valley toward the next hill.

The final portion of the long day's ride was tense, and Hugh expected to see a troop of crimson-uniformed Dragoons appear at any moment, but he reached the farmhouse without further incident, Benjy and the carriage close behind him.

A farmer was raking leaves in the front yard and looked out across the fence reproachfully. "I saw your battle through my spyglass. You can't come here, Captain Spencer. If the

British find you, the value of this place will be lost to the United States."

Hugh's voice was firm as he replied to one of Major Tallmadge's principal deputies. "I'm sorry, Major Edwards, but I have no choice. I completed my mission by raiding an enemy warship, and I'm carrying the counterfeit plates in my pocket."

The surprised "farmer" laughed.

"What's more," Hugh continued forcefully, "a civilian member of my unit has been hurt. Even if I could stay on the road and elude the enemy, he'll die unless he receives proper care."

"Why didn't you say so in the first place?" Edwards unlatched the gate, turned toward the house, and waved.

Seven or eight men hurried across the yard, and, as soon as the carriage drew to a halt, August was carried into the house. Two of the men stared at Katie for a moment as she accompanied her father's bearers, but the group was too busy to study her at length. Dragoon patrols would spend the night scouring the area, and Major Edwards was preparing for the inevitable inspection of the house and grounds with the thoroughness of a commander leading his troops into battle.

"Hitch that team to a plow in the south forty," he said. "Take the carriage to the old barn and shove it into a corner behind some farm equipment. Scrape off as much paint as you can, remove the left rear wheel, and smash one of the windows. You might smear some dirt on it, too."

His subordinates obeyed without question, and the Simpsons would have joined them, but Edwards halted them. "Anyone would know that you're brothers, so you'll have to go into hiding. Abel, take them to the dormitory. You can go with them," he added to Benjy.

"I'm worried about the old man," Hugh said when they were alone.

"They're taking him to the secret room in the attic, Captain. There's some risk, of course, but the British have searched the house from top to bottom scores of times and haven't found it yet, so he should be reasonably safe there, and we'll give him every attention."

"Thank you, Major."

"I'm afraid you'll have to go to the dormitory too, whenever searching parties come here."

Hugh didn't relish the prospect of being banished to an airless underground chamber that had been dug beneath the cellar, but he knew there was no choice. "The enemy might recognize my stallion, too," he said.

Edwards was lost in thought for a moment, then he beckoned to a man who was pruning bushes at one side of the house. "Nate, give Captain Spencer's horse a henna bath. Change him into a roan, and paint a white diamond patch between his eyes."

"Be careful," Hugh added. "He doesn't trust strangers."

The man grinned and led Toby toward the stables at the rear, speaking softly to the beast and trying to establish a rapport with him.

"That leaves only the girl," Edwards said. "She's the same one who stopped off here with you when you went into New York, of course. I recognized her hair—and so will the British. She'll have to change her appearance drastically."

"The old man is her father. I doubt if she'll leave him."

"She'll do what she's told, or all of us will hang," Edwards said curtly, and started toward the house.

"Let me handle her, then. She's even more temperamental than my stallion, if that's possible. Tell me what you want done, and I'll persuade her to follow instructions."

They climbed the stairs to the attic, and Edwards pushed a wall panel. Beyond it was a small chamber without windows or a hearth. Several candles were burning, and the newcomers saw a man bending over August, who was stretched out on a narrow cot. Katie was kneeling beside her father, dipping rags in a basin of water, wringing them out, and applying them gently to his forehead.

"Burnham was a pharmacist before the war," Major Edwards said.

The man was cleaning August's wound with swabs, and didn't look up. "This cut is deep, but I think I can get rid of the poisons so gangrene don't set in, Major. I reckon I'll have to keep watch over him all night."

Hugh saw that Katie was weeping and that the cosmetics she had been wearing streaked her face. She resisted when he lifted her to her feet, but he forced her to accompany him to the outer attic. "Katie, listen to me."

"Pa needs me." She tried to push him aside.

"You'll have to let others look after him tonight."

"No."

He caught hold of her shoulders and shook her. "All of us, your father included, may hang unless you follow orders. Major Edwards says that you're the most easily recognizable member of our party, and he's right. The British will be searching for a red-haired wench who looks like a trollop, so he plans to use you as a decoy."

Katie made an effort to pay attention to what he was saying.

"The woman you met the first time we were here will give you some logwood dye that will turn your hair black. You can cut it or change the style drastically. We'll leave that detail to you. You'll scrub your face until it shines, you'll burn that harlot's dress, and you'll wear old linsey-woolsey clothes that will hide your figure."

She shook her head. "I won't leave Pa."

"Don't you understand that Dragoon patrols are probably hunting for us right at this very moment? When they come here, the major wants you to be sitting in the parlor, knitting. If the enemy should find August, you'll have to trust Edwards to protect him. You're being called on to play still another part, and you've got to remember that the future of the United States is more important than any one of us."

"If Pa dies because he doesn't get enough care—"

Hugh cut her short by taking the counterfeit engraving plates from his inner pocket and holding them before her dazed eyes. "If the British regain possession of these, your father's suffering will have been in vain."

"You're making me pay for my sins, aren't you?" she asked tremulously, looked past him, and stared silently at the unconscious August for a moment. "He'd want me to do my duty," she said, and raised her head.

Major Edwards joined them. "Well?" he demanded impatiently.

"She agrees," Hugh replied.

"Not completely," Katie declared angrily. "Even if the redcoats catch me and hang me, I refuse to cut my hair!"

Hugh concealed his smile of relief. Her display of temper convinced him that she would overcome her fatigue and her deep concern for her father. She would give another magnificent performance.

XIX / *October 1777*

THE days passed slowly, British patrols visited the farmhouse frequently, but the precautions Major Edwards had taken proved effective, even though the enemy searched the property systematically. August's hiding place was not discovered, Hugh and the other men concealed themselves in the underground vault beneath the cellar with several members of Edwards' unit, and Katie fitted smoothly into her new role. Her spirits revived when her father's condition began to improve, and she threw herself into her new part with such zest that even Hugh scarcely recognized her when he was allowed to come into the open.

It was significant that the men who had observed her with such interest when she had arrived at the farm paid no attention to her now, and Hugh told her that her new transformation was the most remarkable she had made. Her hair, dyed a dull black, was scraped back from her forehead and hung listlessly in two long pigtails; a shapeless dress of coarse linsey-woolsey gave her figure a lumpy appearance, and she experimented with several vegetable oils until she found a mixture that gave her skin an unappetizing sheen.

August failed to recognize her the first time he saw her after he regained consciousness, and he was so pleased by her ingenuity that his own will to live became stronger. Katie spent several hours with him each day, but hurriedly returned to the living quarters whenever a lookout beat on a small gong, a signal that an enemy patrol was approaching the place. Hugh saw August frequently, too, and sought Katie's company when she wasn't busy, but she seemed ill at ease in his presence, and often reminded him that she was still his prisoner.

Major Edwards reported that the British were still searching for the bold raiders who had boarded the *Phoenix,* but a spy arrived from New York with the encouraging word that the enemy high command was beginning to believe that the group had escaped through the lines successfully. Then, in mid-October, the British had something far more urgent to occupy their energies and attention.

A messenger arrived at the farm late one night with news so breath-taking that Edwards and Hugh found it hard to believe. General John Burgoyne, one of England's most competent senior commanders, had led an army into New York from Canada, and General Howe had promised to send him support. But Howe was enjoying life in Philadelphia, and Colonel Barry St. Leger, who was leading a column of Tory regiments and Iroquois Indians, was defeated by Mohawk Valley settlers defending their homes. The Indians vanished into the forests, St. Leger's troops were scattered, and Lord Burgoyne's divisions faced the Yankees alone. An American army of Continentals and militiamen commanded by General Horatio Gates fought valiantly, then faltered, and for a time it appeared as though a dreary, familiar story would be repeated. But General Benedict Arnold of Connecticut rallied the Americans, who recovered and defeated the redcoats so decisively that Burgoyne was forced to surrender.

The Battle of Saratoga was the greatest victory the United States had won, and Hugh sat up until dawn with Major Edwards, discussing the triumph. Both men wondered whether the British would be forced to withdraw from Philadelphia and whether the War Office in London would replace Sir William Howe with another field commander, but neither knew enough about the enemy's situation to indulge in anything other than speculation. They agreed, however, that the effect on the people of the United States would be great, and that new recruits would swell the ranks of Washington's Continentals. Hugh, bored after weeks of inactivity, wanted to leave at once to submit a report in person to Major Tallmadge and obtain a new command.

But Edwards was cautious and insisted that he wait until they obtained more information on the British reaction to Saratoga. In less than a week they learned all they needed to know: Howe was drawing in his outposts and maintaining only a single, direct line of communication between New York and Philadelphia. General Washington was maneuvering near Philadelphia, men from every state were joining him daily, and the risk of capture by a British patrol was reduced to a minimum.

August had regained enough strength to travel, so the entire Scoundrels' Brigade left the farmhouse early one morning for Pennsylvania. However, Hugh preferred to take no unnecessary chances, and the carriage remained in Edwards' barn. The whole group rode on horses, all wore civilian clothes, and Katie was still disguised as a plain, black-haired country girl. August tired easily, so the journey was made in easy stages, and Hugh called a halt each night at small country inns that Major Edwards had marked on a map. The owners of these establishments were confirmed patriots, so the party encountered no troubles anywhere.

But Katie continued to avoid Hugh, and finally August told the younger man in confidence that she was morose because the mission had ended, there was no useful function she could perform, and, having learned the significance of true personal integrity, she dreaded the prospect of being returned to Providence and standing trial as a common criminal. Hugh listened carefully but kept his views to himself, although it was obvious that August was disturbed about his own future.

Farmers directed the party on the last stage of the journey, and early one afternoon in late October, Hugh rode into the American bivouac at the head of his motley command. A young officer led the group to the commander-in-chief's headquarters, and soon Hugh was sitting in Major Tallmadge's tent with his superior. Tallmadge listened quietly to Hugh's report, examined the counterfeit plates carefully, and finally extended his hand. "General Washington will want to see you and offer you his congratulations, Hugh. In the meantime, accept mine."

"Thank you, Ben." Hugh leaned forward on the empty barrel that served as a stool. "This is a good time to remind you of your promise before I took this assignment. I hope I'll be returned to duty with a combat unit."

Tallmadge stretched his long legs beneath the board, supported by two kegs, that he was using as a desk. "The Battle of Saratoga," he said, "is going to make an enormous difference in the conduct of the war, although we don't expect specific results before next April, at the earliest. General Washington is confident that our envoys in Paris will be able to persuade the French government to sign a treaty of alliance with us now. But we face several problems in the coming months."

Hugh watched him suspiciously.

"Our chief military concern is keeping the army together as a fighting unit. The engineers are looking for a winter campsite, and I hear that some of them favor an area nearby called Valley Forge, where the brigades can keep watch on Howe's movements between New York and Philadelphia. Strictly between us, it won't be possible to recapture Philadelphia before spring. We aren't strong enough."

"There's a place waiting for me in my old regiment," Hugh said firmly.

Tallmadge didn't reply directly. "The brigade commanders must solve the problem of keeping their units intact. I have other worries. Look at these." Reaching under a pile of papers on the board, he drew out several Massachusetts two-pound notes and handed them to Hugh.

"Counterfeit?"

"Yes, and clever ones at that." Tallmadge paused for an instant. "I've recruited several more men for you during the months you've been in New York. Naturally, you'll want to interview them yourself, and you're under no obligation to accept any you don't want."

Hugh threw the money on the makeshift desk. "I'm a combat soldier!"

Tallmadge looked at him gravely. "You're one of the finest intelligence officers in the army, and the only man qualified to command a unit that will rid the country of counterfeiters."

"Are you rescinding your promise?"

"I have no choice, Hugh. Massachusetts is being flooded with false money, there are complaints from Georgia and South Carolina, and counterfeit notes are beginning to appear in Baltimore. I'd release you if I could, but I need you."

Hugh picked up the Massachusetts bills again, studied them briefly, and tucked them into his pocket. "I'll want all the additional information you can give me," he said curtly.

"I'll be at your disposal all day tomorrow. You'll probably want to leave for Boston as soon as you've interviewed your recruits, and you may want to send a squad to do some preliminary work in Baltimore and the south." Tallmadge smiled, and his tone changed. "I'm grateful to you, Hugh."

"War isn't logical. I've learned that much. We need combat officers, and I'm an experienced cavalryman, so I'm spending the war hunting down counterfeiters." Hugh shrugged and grinned wryly. "At least the issue isn't in doubt any longer. Saratoga has proved that we're going to win." Hugh put his regrets out of his mind and concentrated on practical matters. "If you're giving me an expanded command, I'll need a junior officer to help me. I recommend that Sergeant Flaherty be granted a commission as an ensign."

Tallmadge made a note on a scrap of paper. "If he can find a tailor, he can order his uniform today."

"And I think the Simpsons have earned their right to wear sergeants' sashes. They can instill discipline in the new rogues you're assigning me, Ben." Hugh laughed. "I feel sorry for any recruit who disobeys an order. Dave Simpson isn't the sort of man who'll tolerate insubordination."

"You're in charge of your unit, so you're entitled to name your own sergeants." Tallmadge picked up a sheaf of papers and glanced through them. "According to the report you wrote to me from Edwards' farm, Dale and his daughter took great risks for our cause. What do you think we ought to do about them?"

"They're waiting outside," Hugh replied. "If you don't mind, Ben, I'd like them to hear what I have to say."

The major nodded to an orderly who stood at the entrance, and Katie was ushered into the tent. She held her head high as she curtsied to the major, but avoided looking at Hugh. August, who followed her slowly, was unable to hide his fears, and his thin, pale face was grave. He smiled when Tallmadge shook hands with him and bowed to Katie, but remained apprehensive and alert.

"I sent for you," Hugh said, "because we're going to discuss your future, and I want you to hear what we say. I intend to make certain recommendations, and if the major approves, I'll submit them to the commander-in-chief."

"I have full confidence in you, Captain Spencer," Tallmadge replied formally, "and so does General Washington. I know from my last discussion with him on the subject that he's prepared to accept any reasonable suggestion you care to make."

"Do you think," Hugh asked, "that the state of Rhode Island will feel the same way?"

"General Greene has been in correspondence with some of his friends there, at my request. And he's been assured that the state will agree to any disposition of the Dale case that

General Washington cares to make. A formal court confirma-
tion will be required, of course, but that's a technicality."

Hugh looked at Katie, whose face was expressionless, then
turned to August, who grinned feebly. "Sir, I recommend a
complete pardon for Mr. August Dale. He performed heroic
services for the United States, he risked his life for our country, and he sustained a wound in battle as grievous as any
suffered by a soldier in combat. In my opinion, sir, he has
earned his freedom."

August brightened, and, for the first time since the fight
on board the *Phoenix*, he showed a trace of his customary
jaunty composure. "I knew I could rely on you, my dear lad,"
he said.

"You might change your mind when you hear the rest of
my proposal." Hugh addressed himself to Tallmadge again.
"Rhode Island suffered financial losses because of the counterfeit money that was made at Black Ox farm, and I know
the governor and state treasurer would like to receive com-
pensation."

The major nodded thoughtfully.

"So I recommend, sir, that Mr. Dale be permitted to live at
the farm until the end of the war, but that he be required to
give the property to the state after we've won our final victory. The sale of the house and land should balance the books,
justice will be served, and the state treasurer should be
satisfied."

"Very fair," Tallmadge said.

August wanted to protest, but was afraid to express himself too forcibly. "A drastic recommendation," he muttered.

Katie felt under no obligation to remain silent. "If you take
Pa's property away from him, he'll starve in his old age," she
cried furiously.

"I haven't finished," Hugh told her, braced himself, and
said, "Major, in my considered judgment, it would be a serious mistake to grant a pardon to Katie Dale."

Katie stared at him, and August blinked incredulously. The

major looked surprised but said nothing and waited for Hugh to continue.

"She has a violent temper, sir, and a dangerous tendency to act independently. For example," he added grimly, "she decided on her own initiative to engage in espionage work in New York, and without telling me what she was doing, she induced various British officers to talk to her freely."

"We benefited from the information they gave me, and you know it!" Katie realized she was shouting, but didn't care.

Hugh paid no attention to the outburst. "Therefore, sir, I'm opposed to giving her freedom that she'll abuse. If she's placed at liberty, she'll cause trouble."

Tallmadge and August heard an undertone that made them smile, but Katie was too angry to listen.

"In view of her services," the major declared, "it would be a miscarriage of justice to send her to prison."

"It would, sir. So I recommend that the present court order be extended indefinitely, and that she be placed in my custody permanently."

Katie stamped her foot so hard that she dislodged a small stone in the ground, and for an instant Hugh thought she would pick it up and throw it at him. "You think you're clever!" she said. "But you're not!"

"I've given the matter great thought during the weeks I was forced to remain idle in New Jersey, and there's no other satisfactory solution, sir." Hugh took a folded sheet of parchment from his inner coat pocket. "I've prepared my recommendations in written form for submission to the commander-in-chief."

Tallmadge took the paper and dipped a quill into a jar of ink. "This will need my signature, too," he murmured.

Hugh turned to August and grinned. "You may not realize it, but you've retired. After the war, when Katie and I move to the Ohio Valley, you'll come with us."

"A splendid idea." August beamed and patted his hair. "I have no doubt that I can offer you valuable advice in selecting a suitable property, building a comfortable home, and settling down."

"Pa!" Katie looked stricken. "You aren't deserting me?"

"My dear child, I've been hoping for some time that I can enjoy my declining years surrounded by doting grandchildren."

Tallmadge, still holding the sheet of parchment, took the old man's arm with his free hand. "We'll leave this document at the adjutant general's tent on the way to my private quarters, Mr. Dale. Our supplies are limited, but we captured a British wagon train two days ago, and the rum is tolerable." Pausing at the entrance, he glanced back at Hugh. "I believe in allowing my subordinate commanders to settle their own disciplinary problems," he said.

There was a brief silence when Hugh and Katie were alone, and when he took a step toward her, she retreated to the far side of the tent. "Don't come near me!"

He looked at her reproachfully. "As we were riding into camp I asked Benjy to find a chaplain. We'll be married this evening, after I've reported to General Washington."

"I won't marry you, as I've told you for weeks. And you don't really want to marry me. You prefer women like that horrid brunette in New York."

"At the moment you're a brunette yourself," he reminded her.

"That's because I haven't had a chance to wash the dye out of my hair, so don't mock me!"

Hugh's smile faded. "Why are you so opposed to marrying me, Katie?"

"There are many reasons," she replied stubbornly, lifting her chin.

"Name them."

"If it weren't for me, you'd be living on your estate in England. That will always be a barrier between us."

"If it weren't for you," he said quietly, "I wouldn't have learned the meaning of liberty. You're responsible for the most important change in my life. I've become an American, and I'll always be grateful to you."

Katie wilted, and tears filled her eyes. "How can you respect me? I've let you make love to me, and I've lived with you like—like a strumpet."

"No, like a wife." He moved toward her purposefully, and she couldn't escape. "My next assignment is in Boston, so I'll escort you and your father to the farm in Rhode Island. You'll stay there until the end of the war, and I'll visit you whenever I'm granted a leave." He put his hands on her shoulders.

She made no attempt to draw away from him, but shook her head.

"Katie, look at me." He waited patiently until she raised her eyes. "Do you remember telling me that you'd never lie to me?"

"Of course!" she replied indignantly. "And I've told you the truth ever since I made my promise!"

Hugh tried not to smile. "Are you sure?"

"Positive!"

"When I left you in that room on the Queen's Walk in New York to lead the raid on the *Phoenix*, you said you loved me."

Color rose in her face.

"It should be obvious that I feel the same way about you. If it isn't, let me offer you proof." He took her in his arms, and her surrender was complete.

Postscript

THE facts of the secret struggle between official British counterfeiters and American counterespionage agents during the
War of Independence have come to light only recently, although it has long been known that England, in an attempt
to ruin public confidence in the money of the new nation,
printed vast quantities of counterfeit Continental dollars.

Initially that policy was so successful that the phrase "not
worth a Continental" has survived to the present day. And
virtually every major nation has imitated the British in subse-
quent wars. In brief, government-sponsored counterfeiting of
an enemy's money has become a "legitimate" weapon in time
of war.

With the exception of obvious historical persons, the char-
acters in *Scoundrels' Brigade* are the product of the author's
imagination and bear no resemblance to any real persons, living or dead. However, the operation in which Hugh Spencer
and his companions engaged actually took place, and history
has substantiated the following:

American officials first learned that counterfeit dollars were
being sent from British-occupied New York when several
wagons in which the false notes had been concealed were inspected.

Major Benjamin Tallmadge, General Washington's director of intelligence, assigned several former counterfeiters to go to New York in disguise, find the plates and equipment, and destroy them.

The group made little progress until Yankee privateers captured two British ships, the *Blacksnake* and the *Morning Star*, which were carrying large quantities of counterfeit dollars.

The master of one of these vessels, hoping to win the favor of his captors, revealed that the money was being made on board the H.M.S. *Phoenix*, a frigate anchored in the East River.

Major Tallmadge relayed this information to his men in New York, who raided the warship and escaped from the city. Unfortunately, the records tell us no details of the operation, but merely state that the unit continued to function until the end of the war. In a sense, then, it was a left-handed parent of the United States Treasury Department's Secret Service.

The counterfeiting techniques described in this book were commonly used in the eighteenth century, when the minting of coins was crude and the printing of paper money clumsy. The device ascribed to August Dale, that of transferring a print to muslin and then to a blank sheet of paper with a hot iron, was developed by one of the most successful counterfeiters of the age, who had realized that the ink on most American bills was too thick. He operated successfully for years, and although the authorities suspected him and raided his house frequently, they could find no plates, no presses, and no engraving tools.

The man was hauled into court on several occasions, but the charges against him were dismissed because of a lack of evidence. It was difficult to convict a suspect because he owned a jar of Frankfort black ink and several crow quills. This clever criminal became one of the wealthiest men in Rhode Island, retired from "business," and was respected by his neighbors. His ingenious system was revealed after his death by a nephew and niece whom he had excluded from his will; fittingly, they were prosecuted for their failure to speak earlier, and both received prison sentences.

I have used the clever uncle as the model for August Dale, of course.

A final word: counterfeiting was a plague in every civilized nation during the eighteenth century. It has been estimated that approximately 40 per cent of the copper coins circulating in France were false, the Spanish government was forced to stop minting pieces of eight for almost twenty years, and England was deluged with counterfeit paper, pewter-filled silver, and copper mixed with base alloys. Desperate officials, trying to stem the tide, passed severe laws, and, particularly in England, the pressure of outraged public opinion was so great that many innocent men were transported to the North American colonies. Hugh Spencer himself is a fictitious character, but there were many real Hugh Spencers.

—C. A. V.